BEBOVE

J.B. Rehnstrom

Irish Writers' Exchange

Bebove
Copyright © 2013 J.B. Rehnstrom

The moral right of the author has been asserted.

Published by the Irish Writers' Exchange
13 Bissett's Loft
Malahide
Co. Dublin
Ireland
http://www.irishwritersexchange.com

Cover photo and intro page photo © J.B. Rehnstrom 2013

ISBN 978-0-9567167-2-9
First Edition September 2013
Printed in Ireland

Be bov. Be, att allt det du stulit är ditt nu.

"*Kafka is saying that meaning (the truth, the law, the single sense) is like a brief radiance glimpsed on the far side of a door that one cannot go through. The things we try to understand nowadays have 'intermittent radiances' only, and these are 'uninterpretable'. Note that it isn't necessarily the case that there is no truth, nor that we never have intimations of it, only that we can't in any sense finally arrive at it. We can orient ourselves, but we cannot arrive.*"

Lewis Hyde, Trickster Makes This World, p 288 -289, 2008.

These long days are so bright they hurt my sense of direction. Indeed I feel like I could lose myself in my silly sized space. The corners sort of melt away as if they were made of water, but then not really, the effect being that I hurt myself quite substantially and often. Bruises dark amass across my body trying to blot out the brightness somehow, trying to make me a shadow, trying to draw a line between me and life. The net-curtains of dust particles, like bubbles, never release a perfect clarity into my den, catching my feet and my body in wait for that splendid volume of the sun, its fifty thousand and eighty eyes trained on its quarry, eight legs carefully moving forth, like a luminous momentous insect warrior god. Spools of sunlight unravel across the floors and walls, trapping me in summer. I think of how hard it would be to say anything about my predicament, am not really supposed to complain about warmth and heat and brightness, am just to adore and suffer it silently, or incur the wrath of the worshippers that overwhelmingly impose their majority on fuckers like my very own self. I swear my eyesight is going as well, so perhaps I should just get it over with, stare into the golden globe fearlessly and welcome the permafrost and dark into my soul, as if it is not there already. Funny that, the fact that too much of a bright thing will lead you right into that mammoth darkness, that womb. That's why life never is perfect, nevertheless I believe in that which I feel, yet do not always feel that which I believe.

We could not survive a perfect life. No, life would not even be perfect as perfect, because it would lack its resistance to that which makes it what it is. Binaries, doubles, twins, poles apart, opposites attract, and all that. Perhaps this is how Fidel and I came about, impossibles drawn to each other like magnets, impossible to keep apart, hurdling randomly but destined into that chaos that was to ensue. My girlfriend at the time, Miranda, had been indulging herself in kinesiology, being pushed and pulled with a mesmeric frenzy, realizing her capacities and her weaknesses, coming home raving about them, finding her body in herself and so on. I listened half-heartedly but apparently with a look of concern and interest, as she babbled on and on freely. Her intestines not liking coffee in particular, yet still well able for it, thus not entirely deterred by the residue of the brown granules that slipped up the water in the espresso maker. I came up behind her, raised her skirt and cupped her cheeks, pressed myself against her. Who cared what the hell she was on about, we could get in on, and then we would not have to talk anymore and even I would get something out of this evening. She pushed me aside abruptly and accused me of not listening. That was not going to get me anywhere. My impulses were moronic and unfair. I could not understand why she had gone so cold. I mean she used to be up for a bit of impromptu fucking, even on her lunch hour, but now nothing, just a push and an accusation. She went to her sister's and the evening was all of a sudden unplanned and unadjusted to the future. I sat down in front of the TV for a moment, but my legs were itching, and my dick was still up and ready, pushing and pounding. I got into my training gear after having wanked the worst out of my boner, but my brain was still on a lonely one-way track. At least running might clear my head. The park lay spotted by lamplight, the night moving around these glaring circles with its predatory eyes on the prize. After half an hour's run in the shadows, sweating like a pig, my legs felt like broken springs

2

when I stopped in one of the pools of light. I leaned over my feet, hands on knees and huffed and puffed. A short whistle pierced the evening and a man's voice encouraged me to "come look". Innocence and I stood dumbly up, looking into the messy dark, then not wondering at all but just a bit bovine-like moved towards what sounded like an invitation to something worth discovering. Between the branches, eyes adjusting gradually, there he was, Fidel, just leaning on a trunk. That was all there was to see. I stared back at his hooded watch, and all of a sudden, to my great surprise, felt a flurry of horniness return unhindered by meaning. Fidel was dressed in a pinstriped suit. His shirt was open and he was holding his tie in his hands, stretching, pulling and snapping it. He was thoroughly uninterested in talking. His hair was cut short and respectable, his chest muscular and well defined. Incredibly handsome, and not repenting it in the least. His hand moved down to his zipper and he released a fine-looking cock. And although I had never really thought of guys in that way I moved up to him as if in trance, kneeled down and gave him a blowjob. He demanded this, and I had to oblige. That was that. When I was done and he had come all over my gear I stood up ready to go but he grabbed a hold of my t-shirt and brought me back. With his hand on my dick, that got harder by the second, he showed me where to go, soon I was riding him hard, the forest going darker and darker until it splintered around and in me. A cough brought me back. I pulled up my trousers and he pulled up his. We parted ways, never to meet again, fulfilled as fulfilled could be.

Afterwards I thought of the incident with a sense of shame. Never had I done, or even really thought, of a thing like that. Usually my fantasies concerned big-chested women that competed for my hardness by pleasuring themselves, or each other, then gave me come-hither-looks that eventually forced me to go over to give them what they needed. And there I had been on my knees in the dark and dirt with a businessman's cock spilling itself into my throat and all over my face. The odd thing was that I got hard thinking about the incident as well. It was Fidel himself that brought that weirdness out of me. Of course, I did not know his name at the time. The only thing that I could figure out about him then was that he must be well off, and gay. Jesus, the diseases that I could have contracted! I froze in a panic. I had not thought of this at all until this moment. I sat in my armchair for a good hour before I was able to move. Then I organized a clinic appointment, had three months of despair mixed in with hopeful dreams of a life less complicated. Meanwhile Miranda and I had split up, which in itself was unimportant but considering the consequences, pivotal to the rest of the story. We had had our final argument, we both were aware of it, and like two animals after a life-or-death fight we pulled back, licked our wounds and gathered our belongings as if they had never really been shared. We bickered a little about items that might be coloured by either side of the divide, but generally we just let go, wanting the slight pain to go away. I fell back into my old self, experienced an enormous sense of relief and ordered my things in my new flat my way. I lived as I was meant to live, free and undisputed, coffee cups left to themselves for weeks, until gathering a dust ring, until growing new life, just for the symbolic sense of it. I loved it. None of the previously organized life was left in me, and the free will of objects, colors and smells could reign supreme, owning their own, claiming their own. I was ok with it all. I do not even think that people at work realized that Miranda had disappeared, as I just seemed more and more content. Some of my colleagues whispered about the possibility of that I soon was to become a father and thus on the way to really settle into a life of paternity and marital bliss. Little did they know. Even my buddy Raj at work seemed oblivious to the eruptions in my life. Not that we talked abut anything like that, only you would think that people

4

that find themselves in such regular close proximity to you would somehow be able to sense changes, but no, nothing. Raj just plodded along his usual route, begging me to come out for a beer on Fridays, putting inappropriate images up on my computer, that, and all that which Raj did. I let them all remain unaware to save myself any pity or blind dates. I wanted to remain like this forever, for now. My days floated on by with such calm that I was able to believe that I had found some type of happiness or contentment in life. But I guess life could not continue like that.

I pulled the hand-break, set the gearbox to neutral and shut off the engine. The music kept on pounding until I pulled the key out of the ignition, then it all went very quiet, eerily so. I removed my shades. As I looked over to my door to open it I suddenly spotted Fidel on the other side of the street where I had parked up. He was just walking down the street; striding perhaps I should say, confidently. He was wearing a very similar suit to the one he had been wearing when we "met", but his hair seemed shorter. I froze, took my hand quickly off the door handle as if I had burnt myself and hit the steering wheel with a big thump, and then slammed my injured hand over my mouth to suppress a groan of agony. Ridiculous I know, as if he could have heard me. I slumped down a little and as I did I realized that I was getting hard, I looked down at my groin in a bit of amazement. How the hell did this work! I looked up again only to see Fidel turn around the corner. All of a sudden my thoughts returned to me. I started breathing again. My next impulse was to quickly get out of the car and run after him, but as I let the thought run through my head I realized that I would have very little to say to him. Fuck, he probably did not even remember me at all. He probably did things like that all the time. Cottaging it was called, like George Michael. And what would I say: hey remember me, from the bushes some months ago or more? I don't think so. I know I am bit stupid

5

sometimes, but, really, not that stupid. Then my phone rang. I picked it up out of habit, and when I had finished my stunted call it was too late for any action other than to drive in Fidel's direction. Why? I'm not sure. I let the car dash out, made it over to the right lane, tried to take the turn but pushed the car a little too hard so that it skidded. Shit, that would be a way to make a re-connection. Run him over. I slowed down, and scanned the sidewalks, but no Fidel. I went up, turned around, and returned on the other side of the street. No Fidel. I do not know what I would have done anyway as I was not even aware that I would have liked to have met him again. Nevertheless, I was still hard, and I knew that the only way that I could stop thinking about him would be to jerk off. I turned up into a park, and rid myself of the panic. Sitting there in the car with my dick in my hand thoughts came creeping up about how perhaps he was in the park. I tucked myself away and got out of the car. Walked down a lonely path which then branched into another which then branched into another and so on. In an opening I stopped a little as I heard a noise, rustling bushes. I stood stock still, holding my breath, maybe hoping. Instead, out of the bushes came a three or four-year-old girl, seemingly intent on her mission. She said "hi" but did not smile at all. She looked up at me briefly and I could see that her right iris was strangely shaped like a keyhole. Stunned I stared, and thought selfish thoughts. Perhaps her eye was a sign for my chase? She disappeared at the other side of the opening. I could hear rustling. She walked on. She had been there but soon there was not a trace. I thought to myself that I had been visited by an omen, that there was some meaning to my vision. I did not know what, and Fidel was nowhere to be seen. However, I still needed a further wank, so I stopped in a secluded bunch of bushes and went to work. Better than dirtying the car again. A little later after some random forays in the wrong direction I worked my way back to the car. Got in, disappointed. Drove off home. In a big city like this I was most likely not going to run into him again. I kept thinking about destiny and meaning, arguing with myself as to the reasons for me reacting as I had done. I came to no conclusions. I was as confused as before.

Another couple of months went by and my Fidel obsession had abated ever so little. I had deep-seated memories of him, as if we had had a relationship for years on end. The smallest things would bring him into my head. Nevertheless, it seemed I could at least concentrate on my work but I was not the same as I had been up until quite recently. I had even made a pact with myself that as the whole thing was so unlikely in every way I was from now on to really work on forgetting rather than taking my pleasures reveling in its dead remnants. Then, I was at a party at a friend of a friend's feeling rather self-assured and good-looking. I noticed that the women were paying me attention, and that when they spoke to me they looked at me with purpose. I was ready to move on. Even if a whiff of thoughts of Fidel made itself known somehow here, I swore, I would squash it with as much force as necessary. I was back, busy with life. This shorthaired blond was particularly interested, touching me and smiling at me in such measures that I started imagining that we could get in on, in an alley somewhere perhaps, or in a back room here even. My body was reacting as it should to her advances. I felt relief. The blond, Ciara, had my full awareness. She turned out to be impressively educated and seemed to have been concentrating on her way through education as well, rather than slip sliding to a pass. She made me laugh. She was not the pushover that I initially had expected. We made a date for later in the week, instead of ravaging each other then and there. This was better than I had expected. I imagined that I would send my Fidel obsession packing, at least the worst of it, and then I hoped to come out relatively unscathed on the other side of it. Life was good. I went to work with a spring in my step. I did not give myself much time to think out the finer details of anything that I did. I simply went were it felt good. Ciara and I started dating on a regular basis, and things got on swimmingly. She was so much more than what I had set out for her to be. In comparison to Miranda she seemed so together and whilst independent still definitely here with me. I was happy with the way that it was. We'd meet up three, four times a week, for the main part we would end up at her place rather than mine. There was no particular reason for this other than that hers was a little easier to get to at the end of the evening. She did not contact me during the day at all, but rather we would make up dates as we met for the week to come. We had not introduced each other to parents or family yet, and neither of us seemed to be leaning in that direction. There was no hurry. We enjoyed similar types of events and kept a nice equilibrium as to who booked them and how we attended them. She never got jealous and neither did I, we were too comfortable in our skin and the relationship to bother, or get bothered, by such infantile exercises. I thanked the universe for altering the course for me. In all this Fidel had a miniscule place. He would force his taste onto my lips only once in a blue blue moon, as the weather predicted rather than my emotions and fantasies. As well, my fantasies, at that, were stalwart in their direction, healthily so. Yes, I nodded to myself in the mirror: things were just fine.

Ciara had asked me to come around to hers. She wanted me to meet her sister. I had hesitated, and after six months of going out together, Ciara did not take this as a good sign. She had hung up on me without another word. We had never discussed our relationship, there hadn't been a need, it was going fine. We were fine. It was fine. I could not understand how or why she would all of a sudden change her tack. I did not bother calling her back. A couple of days went by, and then, thinking that it was now safe to continue as normal, I called her to meet up. I immediately noticed that she still was very sore. Her sentences were clipped. Her imagination obviously tampered with by some busy commitment devil whispering loudly in her ear. Thinking that this was a temporary glitch in our fine dealings I suggested that we'd meet up to discuss what had gone wrong. She reluctantly agreed. We met in neutral territory: a bar in town. As I walked in I could sense her anger and frustration. Nevertheless, she was happy to see me. I was too. She warmed up with a couple of glasses of red wine and a laugh or two. Turns out, her sister was the guilty party in this ridiculous mess. She'd been there, telling Ciara how to run her life. Everything that we had together, had to lead somewhere soon, as life and fertility did not go on forever. Was I or was I not the one to settle down with? Was I husband and father material? What did I want from life? What did I want from Ciara? Was I just toying with her? I sat through the rant in amazement at the profound absurdity of the thought process. Surely life was more than this? Surely relationships had more angles and reasons to them than being there simply for procreation and stagnation? I was thinking all this to myself whilst agreeing with Ciara that I might have been a bit limited in my understanding of her way of reasoning. I even agreed with her that we would start again, that we needed to have a serious discussion on the future of us. We went home to hers and I slid into her a bit starved and more than ready. Her moans sped their way around the room. Hazily, I rammed that last movement into her and collapsed. There. What more could she want? I thought that I might start using condoms, cause who knew where this could lead, the desperation of women that want to start a family knew no bounds, or so I had been told. However, there was no way that I could introduce this new element whilst she was on the pill without mortally offending her. It was just a stupid idea. Simultaneously, a woman at my work had made advances towards me. Touching my stomach, running her finger down towards my crotch whilst having a work-related discussion. I thought what the fuck, and then I did. This woman: nameless, easy, and temporary. We grabbed our opportunities without ever reverting to using our homes. We fucked away into the soon approaching sunset. Ciara and I discussed our possible future together and I agreed to meet her sister as a peace offering and emblem of what was to come. I had no idea how and why I had agreed to this in the end. I should have ended the relationship then and there. This was not what I wanted. Yet, I continued on. I felt there were no alternatives.

Ciara's sister, Siobhan, was; in contrast to Ciara's lithe, small-breasted, slim-hipped, early thirty-something casual presentation, a buxom, big boned, late thirty-something brunette with a strange amalgamation of yuppie/hippy fashion sense. She eyed me suspiciously and every question was so loaded that it was difficult for her to let it out over her lips. Ciara was the youngest. Siobhan wanted everything to be good for her. She loved her. I watched her lips babble on and imagined them around my dick. What would she be like in bed? She was not bad looking at all, but a bit too severe for my liking. I nodded and persevered with a sense of dignity whilst calming her fears. Yes, I thought about the future. Yes, I was planning on making a decent woman of Ciara in the not-too -distant future. Yes, we had spoken of kids. Yes, I understood that a woman was not able to have kids after a certain age. She licked her lips and I twitched. Bet she was feisty and bossy. Could be interesting. Then as if she had read my thoughts she moved in her seat revealing her cleavage a little more by bending towards me. I stopped breathing for a moment. Caught myself, and answered her question slowly so as not to slip on all the obstacles that she had put in the way. She was probably provoking like that to prove herself right. Don't stumble into her trap, I thought to myself. I was well behaved in every conceivable way. She was not going to get me. But in my mind I could do whatever I wanted, and I did, mostly out of spite. I did not like being put into this position at all. The audience finally ended, but even after I got home to mine it took a few hours for the sparks of irritation, it had caused within me, to die down. Ciara was staying on with her sister, I assumed, to consolidate the information that had been gathered. I had been so annoyed and frustrated by the whole thing that I even considered eloping with Ciara and marrying her just to shut her bloody sister up. When Ciara returned we said nothing more about the interrogation, and went on with life pretty much as before. Only now there was a certain smell of the need to move-in together, to buy property, in the air. I was feeling resistant to the apparent juggernaut that had been set in motion by that cow of a sister. However, I took each day as gently as I could. I continued on with my life trying to pretend that it was not slowly being torn into tatters. I guess there was nothing much that I could think of as alternatives. Ciara and I were good together, in most ways. I had not had it that good ever. Could I overlook the influence and clout of Siobhan for my own sake, for our sake? I thought I could. I decided I would.

From then on Ciara and I spent most of our time searching for a suitable property to set up our joint home. We looked far and wide but then narrowed the search down to the city as we both decided to stay on in our jobs. It was a necessity, which relieved me considerably because I had feared an abrupt end to all that a city could offer would perhaps send me off the deep end. It was one thing moving in together and then most likely marrying, but a swift blow to the opportunities of anonymity and secrecy I would not have managed. Finally, after finding a few houses that seemed suitable but which slipped through our hands by outbidding, we put an offer on a house in a decent neighborhood, which stuck. The real estate guy called us back with the happy news and we began to pack up our two separate flats, no doubt both of us in trepidation of what was to come. Siobhan kept her claws in just as before, staying around like a bad odor or premonition. She gave me the creeps now. All she

11

seemed to want was to cause consternation, if not outright ill will. Even when she called and I answered I dropped the receiver as quickly as possible to hand it on to Ciara. I do not know why Ciara overlooked the way that her sister made me feel. Perhaps she was feeling in some way similar to me about Siobhan, although she could never admit to it, thick viral family blood ticking through her. Whereas Ciara went all the way and sold her flat, I held onto mine. I explained that it was an investment that I did not want to lose, and so rented it out to a clean and tidy looking young career woman. Really, I wanted to keep it as an escape clause, and nowadays (I was strategically thinking to myself) if we did marry I most likely would be the homeless one at the end of a divorce, should it come to that. I was thinking ahead. Ciara resented me for it. She saw it as a way out of a full commitment. I ignored her, and kept all the paperwork in regards to the flat at my office so that she would forget about it at some point. She could not hold on to the idea if she never was confronted by it.

We moved into the new house almost half a year after we had made the decision to put the bid on it. During those six months we were primarily in preparation for the immensity of the act. We still were happy with our decision although we avoided discussing it at any great length as that might have affected the outcome. Ciara moved into Siobhan's for a few months as her flat was being sold, and I lived in a perpetual state of moving where only the necessities had been left out of the wall of boxes that cramped my living space. I was ready. Ready for anything. I never thought of Fidel. The house became ours in more than name and we shifted two single people's paraphernalia into its gut. Box by box the contents of our lives spilt onto the floors and walls, mingling and getting increasingly entangled. It was a mirage, a goddamn mess, a beginning. Life was beginning to seem like it was supposed to seem, according to the standards of most around us. We woke, showered, had breakfast, listened

12

to the news, went to work, came home, had dinner in front of the television, went to bed, woke, showered, breakfasted, worked, ate, watched television, went to bed, and then every now and again, fucked and went out. Someone was playing Sims with us. I was running out of energy and was getting more and more tired. I could sleep away whole days, and often did with pathetic excuses of illness to the office, but never to the extent where my future was at stake. No, that was set in stone, set in the mortar of our safe and settled home.

One early morning we woke to a cacophony of loud scraping scratching noises coming from the attic. We froze, both insanely afraid of rats and mice. Ciara looked as if she was trying to disappear into a place where closed eyelids removed the rest of the world. Then wild chirping began, but this did not make anything any better. Both as freaked out by Hitchcock's The Birds, this was not a preferred scenario at all. Ciara said that rats and birds were really the same thing, only one of them had wings and could follow you anywhere. Poe's rats were the ones I really truly feared, so her likeness of birds to rats increased my already fervent phobias tenfold. Ciara asked me to go up and have a look. I thought she had gone crazy, but she elaborated that she needed to tell the pest control people exactly what they would face when they turned up. With serious trepidation I rigged the ladder and lifted the hatch. It all went eerily quiet. I brought up the torch and it made a snapping sound as it illuminated the recesses. I did not know what to expect. I almost ducked at the sight of my own shadow. Fuck, my hands held on to the torch by a miracle. It had sounded like small birds alright, yet I had not been prepared to lay eyes on a sparrow as large as a man. At first there was nothing at all to note other than the sounds coming from gaping tiny beaks that hysterically gulped and groped at the stagnant attic air somewhere in a corner. Then, suddenly, the fear I had foretold appeared. I dropped the torch. It went black. Just prior I had seen the attitude on his face, his killer instincts, and the rise of the shadow that was to descend as quick as the light. His beak had curled over a sinister bird smile, he had been intending to scatter me across the dusty floor. A former fearful human. Morsels for the babies to feed upon to gain strength for the first freedom flight away from this house. My head, popping up like that, must have looked ridiculously small for all the noise and light it brought with it, and given that the sparrow could not see the rest of my body, I must have seemed a possible opponent for him. But as I slammed and locked the hatch I heard him screech at the top of his voice scratching at the hatch, just centimeters away from my eyeballs, I felt a very tiny little victory flicker through my panicked brain. It did not last long. There were almost sparrow-sized holes in the hatch; I assume for airing the attic, and his head was popping through, leaking sparrow vitriol onto my silly victory, which instantly deflated. I raced off down the ladder, closed all the doors and ran for cover. I was still hearing him rule the house hours after my retreat. Ciara was laughing at me but it was a strained merriment, and she did not go anywhere near the hallway that day. Indeed until the arrival of the pest control people we sat lulled in a world where the television was blaring and we never needed to use the hallway again.

The next day Siobhan called to arrange for us to come to hers for dinner. By this time she had somehow become nearly civil with me. Guess that she felt that all the boxes had been ticked and I was now to be tolerated, even if it was a struggle for her. Siobhan had been dating someone for a few weeks and she wanted Ciara's opinion of the poor sucker. I was to be the cover, the chaperone. I was not looking forward to it. I was trying to get out of it right until the last minute, but Ciara would have nothing of it. I was going and that was that. It was my duty, she joked. I reminded her that we were not married yet, and I was treated to a tearful look, which made me kiss her

14

to make it better. I had been cruel. It was nothing to joke about. She gathered herself and ten minutes later she was applying make-up in the bathroom mirror, as if it had never happened. The tap was running as I brushed my teeth next to her. I was looking at her in the mirror trying to understand the urge towards coupledom. She was avoiding my eyes that traveled far into the glass to find hers, as if she was trying to keep it simple, trying not to get snared by the cavernous evil that lurked in the depths of the darkened glass. I pulled the tie around my neck on and she tied it for me. Two silhouettes of the straight and narrow. Were we happy? I could not say. It was nice and easy. Making compromises did not hurt me as bad as I had imagined. I guess my laissez faire attitude probably helped, as I really had no other reason to find it possible. Ciara made compromises very easy. She was a sibling after all. I had never had to really share. Had always been my own boss, even in previous relationships. The other people had never really had a chance to a view of their own, as it did not count, for me. The taxi beeped outside the house and we grabbed keys and wallets making a hasty dash towards the car trying to avoid the rain that had just decided to fall.

Siobhan's flat was up on the fifth floor but first we had to politely wait by the buzzer for her to grace us with a crackly voice that mockingly wondered who we were. Ciara jokingly put on a man's voice and half whispered "Beelzebub". Siobhan giggled in response and the lock clicked open. The hallway smelt damp in its greyness. The elevator had long since stopped working and so we wound our way up to the fifth floor through the sharp echoes of our shoes against the tiles. I was a bit out of breath as we stood in front of the door. Ciara smiled, mentioned the benefits of the gym with a sly grin and kissed my cheek. I grumbled. Ciara's hand put weight on the door handle and we stepped across the threshold. Siobhan came gloating out of the living room, slobbered over us and told us that Denis

was just in the little boy's room, would we like something to drink, god is the weather not just dreary for this time of the year, had Ciara heard from their mother yet? Siobhan was obviously drunk. I wondered how Denis would fare in those stormy alcoholic seas, and then thought that I really could not care less. I heard the toilet flush and the sink tap being turned on. At least he washed his hands. Mind you, he could also have just turned on the tap so as to seem cleanliness himself but in reality only wanting to make it seem like he cared about not spreading his piss germs all over the flat, all over us, standing there by the sink staring at himself in the mirror trying on a smile or a sultry look, puffing his chest up, arranging his balls with a flicker of the movie that he was expecting to unroll tonight playing on his mind: Siobhan on top of him, working him hard. Perhaps he then turned off the tap. Stood a while longer, as long as it takes to dry your hands and arrange your hair, biding his time. A deep breathe. Unlocked the door. Rubbed his hands over his jeans as even the turning on and off of the tap had left a few drops of water on his hands. I heard his steps nearing and was staring at the doorway through which he would materialize as Ciara called out for me and I turned in the direction of the windows where she sat on the sofa.
"Yes?"
Across the darkened windows his brightly colored shadow spread just as I answered an inane question on autopilot. My heart stood still, spinning insanely in one spot, making grooves in my ribs. God. I turned around as slowly as possible, not breathing. However, as I fully faced the man my anticipation collapsed into my lap. What had I been expecting? Here was Denis, a smart looking man that today wore jeans and a grey t-shirt. His brown skin a little reddened by recent exposure to the sun, so he must have been traveling. His hands were well manicured and as I shook one of them I could safely say that he was solid, and not a bit like anyone else that I might have known. I relaxed into the monotony of interactions, not even

16

pondering the fact that I had been expecting for life to lift itself out of its rut, as it does every now and again, every so often. We ended up having a really pleasant evening and us men were frequently left to talk amongst ourselves, as Ciara helped and gossiped with Siobhan whilst helping her with the food and cleaning up. Denis was talking amicably about golfing in Ireland and I politely listened although my interest in golf was extremely limited. However, Denis had a way of making the most mundane subjects manageable, partly because of his handsomeness, partly because of his hearty laugh, which was quick and deep. I felt an odd kinship with Denis. Perhaps I had feelings of brotherhood-in-pity in that we were both now entangled in the web that Siobhan was spinning. As Ciara and I left we were well fed and tipsy. We spoke of Denis in the car and we both agreed that Siobhan should hold on if she could. I thought to myself that this was unlikely to happen as Siobhan soon would show her true colors and that would surely scare poor Denis off in the right direction: away from her. However, I would have liked for him to stay around as he gave me a sense of comradeship, which definitely had been missing in my relationship with the two sisters.

That night I had an apocalyptic dream about our city being emptied of all people except for me, and Fidel. Fidel was wearing a blue overall, which barely contained his very hairy chest. I was wearing knickerbockers and a Tyrolean hat smoking a pipe whilst whispering codes to Fidel who would write them down in the sand in front of him with a metal pole. He told me that these vulnerable letters in the sand, were our legacy for the future, should it actually come. I laughed at Fidel's stupidness and explained to him that there was no future. There had never been any future, just tomorrow every day. Fidel laughed at me, but as he opened his mouth to let the laughter out, there came a long list of do's and don'ts imprinted on his unfolding tongue. The list was aimed at me: Don't sit still for too long. Do raise your head when you cry. Eat biscuits only on Sundays. Wait for life. Don't eat pork. Wear your skullcap at all times. Die quiet. I read the inscriptions as quickly as I could and then started to cry. Fidel sucked up the tongue like a lizard, made a pitying grimace with his mouth, and then kissed me whilst again unfurling his tongue. I felt it slither into my mouth and down the back of my throat. I tried to pull away but he had me in a grip, which was not possible to fight against. I felt like I was going to puke and resorted to the only means I had available: relaxing, to be able to survive the onslaught. Soon I felt Fidel's tongue inside of my toes pushing against my skin as if trying to make my toes longer. I started gurgling on a giggle and Fidel's eyes were so close to me that I just recognized a blurry field of skin. Fidel then, visually, could have been any man, but at the same time there was no doubt as to the very reality of just him and me alive in our city. I seemed at that point of the dream to let my thoughts wander over to Denis who appeared to have something to do with the way that the world had emptied, perhaps remembering Denis' job as a scientist. I woke up gurgling Ciara told me later. She said that I had been trying to talk but that nothing had been coming out, as if my mouth had been full.

"Strange," I said.

The dream had left me with a terrible sense of foreboding. What kind of dream were that, and how come that silly man that I had once, only once, transgressed with, was there? Was I being prepared for something? Why was I reading too much into something that most likely was meaningless? Over our morning coffee Ciara asked me if I thought that it might be time to try to start planning loosely for the wedding so that we would not have too much to do in one go once we had picked a time. I agreed with her but was in no hurry to actually do the work. I was not even sure that I would like to marry Ciara after all. She was good, better than most. But getting married was a commitment, which one should hardly take unless one was absolutely sure and that I was not. I was not sure I would ever be. Not with her, not with any woman. On the other hand it was not a big deal and one could marry anyone, anyone at all, as it all leads the same way: to over-familiarity, to boredom, to de-sexualisation, to the end. Two bodies rotting their way towards a hole in the ground, or in my case towards a funeral pyre. Then to be scattered, millions of tiny particles that once were a person now blowing through the dust, free and formless. I felt bile rise in the back of my throat. God I was morbid. I should be more religious. I should be like Raj who exercised his religious muscle in a weekly ritual much the same as he exercised his body at the gym every Tuesday and Saturday morning. Raj said that it was a question of different parts of the body that needed to be kept in good shape to function well. He was right, but I found it hard to even set up a schedule to which I could keep, other than coming and going into work. Even work was just a chore. It had nothing to do with reality, that reality in which contradiction did not really exist. I laughed at myself. I got dressed and went to work, like any day, like this today.

My desk at work lay covered in files even though I had left it pristine and clean. As usual I had to start again. Case after case was reviewed and evaluated. By lunchtime my desk had a semblance of organization. I stood up to go nodding at Raj who was similarly in the process of putting his jacket on for the daily rut to be punctuated by a soggy sandwich and a coffee. Just then, out of the blue, the day was made jagged with difference, as the phone rang and against my better judgment I picked it up. It was Denis.
"Denis?"
"Siobhan's boyfriend."
"Of course, I know, just felt it a bit misplaced."
"Yes, sorry, I know that this is incredibly forward, to call you at

work like this, but I thought that perhaps you would not mind meeting up with me. I had a few questions for you. Things I wanted to clarify for myself."

"Well, huh, yeah. No problem...?"

"Tonight, at The Quag, you know the pub by Zimmer Park."

"Yeah, I know. How about at six, should be all done by then, I suppose."

"Great. Thanks. See you then."

The silence of Denis hanging up brought a slight sweat out of me. What the hell was that! I did not even know the guy, and here he was calling me as if we were best buddies. Well, true, he had sounded a bit hesitant and self-aware. Perhaps it was something important. Raj was looking at me funny as I was interrupting our routine with a strange unsolicited phone call. I did not explain myself to Raj, just shrugged my shoulders, even though he was quizzing me silently as to the surprise that still was readable on my face. He knew that the phone call had not come from Ciara, and as he got up next to me as we marched down the corridor he nudged me and smiled.

"You dirty bastard."

I stuck my hands in my pocket and stared at my feet as they took me down the hallway towards lunch. Perhaps Denis was having doubts about Siobhan? The Quag was a fairly non-descript place, did not give anything away as to why he would like to meet. How did he get my number? Siobhan must have given it to him... but under what pretext?

I came up to The Quag after a rather long walk, which I had planned in for more time to think. However, as I began my walk I was struck by the sheer stupidity of expending so much energy on something that soon would become clear to me anyway. Thus, I spent the hour dreaming of sundry pleasures instead, whilst my legs slid like clockwork underneath me. As I reached The Quag I was quite euphoric. I leaned on the door to get in and felt a spider run leg-by-hairy-leg across my spine, a chill followed in its tiny wake. I searched the dark bar squinting but could not spot Denis. I went through into the back room. There he was, his back to me bending over a paper with a coffee cup steaming in the tiny shafts of light that staved the ceiling. As I slunk into the seat opposite he looked up with a drowsy smile, and I nodded at him.

"Thanks for coming."

"No problem. What can I do for you?"

"Yes, of course, let's get right to the point."

He pulled a hand through his hair.

"This is going to be a bit difficult.."

I think he was aware of the surprise and slight trepidation that I felt by the way that he was looking at me. This all sounded a lot worse than I had imagined, but I could not for the life of me figure out what it could concern. The possibility of that he might have had an affair with Ciara flashed through my head. On the television screen behind his head a picture of a burning jeep stayed on the screen for quite sometime. Next a burning man was sprayed by firemen, skin peeling like onion layers by the pressures of the water hitting him. His hair was patchy and a horrendous grin burnt into his charred face. A hole. He was being dragged along the ground, no doubt leaving a trail of skin and flesh in the grooves of the asphalt. Momentarily I was focused away from this looming disaster that Denis seemed to be the harbinger of, by the real disasters of the world. However, Denis' news was waiting inside his mouth. He leaned closer to me and as he spoke I sat rigid in my seat, I did not even lean in to make sure that I wasn't getting the wrong end of the stick.

"I was asked to come and talk to you."

It was Siobhan. What the hell was Siobhan doing sending her new man to come tell me her shit. I was getting pissed off and ready to explode.

"I have a message."

This was outrageous indeed. I was barely able to stay seated. Any moment now and I would storm off. However, something was holding me there. I had no idea, but something seemed to suggest to me that all was not as it presented itself. Then, Denis' voice lowered considerably and just audibly he whispered to me.

"Fidel has something to tell you."

My world was turned on its head ten times over. I had no idea who Fidel was at that moment, yet it could only be that one person that would come upon me like that, without being there, with some message from a space in which things happen that do not happen otherwise, in the regular universe. This was something else, something utterly baffling. My body stiffened even more, eagerly waiting for Denis to continue. The light breeze that wafted through the place from some body entering through the front door hit my shins where the skin was exposed between the socks and the trousers, after the trousers had been pulled up to avoid knee moulds. My hands sought their way towards each other and lay quivering on my lap, hot and useless, panting and outstretched with palms to the ceiling, waiting like beggars.

"I was to explain that, in case you were unclear, Fidel is the man that you met in the park some time ago."

There it was. Fidel, how fitting. Fidel. The smell of the coffee rose up intensely and I think a caffeine buzz hit me like coke. My brain whistled through with theories and explanations that might have had something to do with my current inexplicable situation. Fidel had organized a private detective to follow me around and report every move to him. Fidel was himself a spy hired by Siobhan to ensure that Ciara and me never would fully commit to each other. Fidel was my conscious, not really existing, just like Denis here. Denis took a breath readying himself to speak again. I felt my hands squirm and then ball up into fists, slowly, very slowly. Denis pushed the words out:

"Fidel, wants you to know that he has not forgotten and that he is waiting for a suitable moment for you two to reconnect."

Denis took another long breath, then held it before speaking again.

"He wants you to know that there is nothing you can do in the meantime other than plan your wedding with Ciara. He wants you to become her husband. That is the means to the next meeting."

I must have looked ridiculous. My head hanging forward, my mouth slightly ajar, my trousers hiked up and my fists now curled up like helpless babies on my corduroy lap. I was not even looking at Denis and did not stop him from leaving. I could not even see him leave as I sat there stupefied, staring into space, breathing as if just returning from a brisk walk. My chest filling up and emptying, by turns increasing and decreasing my space occupying the world.

I returned home with cold shivers having turned into burning liquid, they were zinging down my back in rivulets. The front door felt heavy as I pushed it open. I was as quiet as possible and stood for a while listening to see if I could find where Ciara was, what she was doing, before I entered fully. I felt the shape of the threshold under the sole of my foot and the doorframe resolutely under my left hand. I did not want to reveal myself until I felt that I knew how to handle the situation, until I was calm. Somehow. I was relieved as well. It was as if this was that which I had been waiting for, even though I had not really been aware of this waiting, and it had now come to pass. I did not have to wait in the same manner anymore. This was a second phase of waiting. A more promising phase. I felt elated, and absolutely paranoid as well. Why had I not questioned Denis? Who was Denis? I entered the house quietly, and let the door close ever so slowly under the guidance of my hands. I slid off my shoes carefully. The tiles were clammy under my feet. I proceeded gently towards the kitchen and listened outside the door a little before I tiptoed in. Ciara wasn't there. I opened the fridge got some juice out and drank out of the carton. Then I heard footsteps on the stairs. Ciara was coming.

She was talking to someone on her mobile phone and so when she saw me she twitched and went a little pale for a split second before she smiled at me and winked. I was watching her as she went to the kitchen window and stared out of it as the conversation continued. I was watching her back and was trying to arrange words in my head, which would sound as normal as possible. What was normal? What was a normal day? The universe seemed to have twisted on its axle and I had a hard time remembering what would happen each and every normal day. What time was it anyway? Was I supposed to have been home tonight? Were there other plans made? What days of the week did I usually go to the gym? I panicked as to the day of the week it was, and was left hanging there in my head as I heard Ciara wind the conversation down. The wheels slowed, the closing words echoed loudly in the kitchen. Ciara now looked at me, preparing to turn her attention my way. She seemed puzzled by my being there. Where the hell was I supposed to be?

"Night."

Ciara continued her quizzical look as she pushed the button on the mobile and laid it down on the kitchen counter.

"Hi you."

I smiled at her. She moved towards me and stuck her arms in under mine whilst her face reached for mine until lips touched.

"What are you doing home so early? Not going to the gym tonight?"

I had planned to say that I had met up with Denis but just then realized that this sounded very odd, and would inevitably lead to questions as to the purpose of the meeting, and I had no idea what could be made up for that to sound somehow real and possible.

"Just wanted to come home. Long day."

"Oh, yes I know."

She let go of me and moved towards the fridge. She stood staring into it half-heartedly. "You hungry?"

"No, I'm ok. Feel a bit weird. My stomach."

"Did you have lunch?"

She was still staring into the fridge.

"Yeah, the usual. Raj demands habits to be kept and I am too lazy to bother to protest."

In my head I was by now planning to call Denis up at Siobhan's. I planned to ask him for a game of tennis, claiming that my regular partner had got ill. I thought this sounded plausible and not at all suspicious. Siobhan would most likely just pass on his number. I wanted to ask him why all this had happened. How he knew Fidel. Who Fidel was; even though it did strike me that Denis might get surprised by my lack of knowledge of Fidel, and how they knew each other. It was a gamble, but at least I could get a chance to make the whole thing a bit clearer.

"You talked to Siobhan yet?"

"Yeah, earlier."

"You calling her again?"

"Why?"

"Wanted to check if she could pass on Denis' number? Wanted to see if he would want to play a game of tennis this week. Brian's ill."

"Hmm, sorry babe, don't think that will be possible."

"Why?"

"They broke up this afternoon. Bloody idiot."

"Why? What happened? I thought they were just getting started, seemed really into each other?"

"I know it's mad. He called her up on the phone this afternoon and gave some really lame excuse about compatibility. Poor Siobhan is in shock."

I pulled out a chair and collapsed into it with as much decorum as I could muster. What the hell was this? Had Denis just been seeing Siobhan to pass on a message to me? There must have been easier ways to do so. This was complicated beyond belief.

"Oh my God you look all pale, love."

25

Ciara came up to me and felt my forehead.

"Maybe you've got a bout of food poisoning or something. Here have some water."

She filled up a glass and handed it to me. The glass looked so fragile, as if it was going to shatter, but my hand reached out anyway.

In bed later that night I tried to probe for more information on the Siobhan-Denis showdown, but Ciara really did not have much more. She told me that it had come out of the blue and that there had been so little in the way of explanations that Siobhan almost had thought she had dreamt the whole thing. Apparently Denis had uttered three, four sentences to which Siobhan had said nothing after which Denis had simply put the phone down. Siobhan had been ringing his mobile afterwards, but it was no longer in service. It was all as strange as it could be. Siobhan knew only what neighborhood Denis lived in, but she had never been to his place. For all she knew he might have lied about all that anyway. It was just absolutely mad. Imagine! I heard Ciara's breathing slow down as she slipped off into the land of nod. My head was spinning. All the elation that I had felt earlier was now gone. What the hell was this? It did not make any sense. Life was not some kind of play where actors slunk in, did their part, slunk out, and I was left standing here paralyzed by the hollowness of it all. My whole body was feeling itchy inside; it was uncomfortable to try to lie still, to breathe, to move. I was burning up, sweat pouring out of me, leaving the sheets all cold and clammy. I could not take it anymore and got up. Sat in the living room in an armchair under a blanket until the wee hours sent their tendrils in. I watched light-covered dust-arms creep towards my feet until sleep overcame my reluctance of it. All of a sudden, I was standing in a tobacco shop with my hands full of pouches of tobacco. I was really big and fat and seemed to take up most of the shop with my cargo and size. A little granny-looking woman stood behind the counter looking up at me as if I had ten heads.

"Can I help you?" she asked.

I poured my armful of tobacco onto the counter and grunted at it as if she just needed to get on with her job instead of talking so much. She continued to stare at me and as I looked at her more properly I realized that she looked very much like Ciara. She called out for someone to come help her and then Denis stepped out from behind the curtain. I stared at him and followed his every move as he picked each pouch up, smelt it and bagged it whilst giving Granny Ciara orders as to the cost of each. Granny Ciara licked her lips each time she put a number into the cash register. Denis smiled, looking quite evil as he continued with his task as on a factory line. When he was done he pursed his lips at me, stuck his hand into his trousers and held himself whilst continuing looking at me.

"Anything else?" he wondered.

Weeks went by and Denis was no more contactable than he had been immediately after our meeting. Siobhan was getting stuck back into work, and seemed to reconcile herself with the idea that the whole thing had had nothing to do with reality. Indeed it did seem wholly unreal. Denis' mobile was never put back into service, at least not while Siobhan kept trying. I never did speak to Siobhan directly about the incident but heard it all secondhand from Ciara. She figured that Siobhan had panicked the man somehow, and he had run for the hills. Hell, for all Ciara knew he might have left town, gone for a job somewhere at the other end of the country. I tried not to seem too concerned about it and agreed with the scenarios that Ciara painted. It did not really matter after all. If he was that weird then Siobhan should count herself lucky. She got out before she had had too much invested in it. She was lucky. I was not. Denis had left me in a bubble that was extremely uncomfortable; a bubble with spikes sticking out of the walls, and me, rolling about in there unable to avoid the spikes at any turn. A bloodletting, not letting me get on with things at all. But then, time heals, life gets in the way. The incident gathered more and more dust until gradually you could not see much of it at all. Only Denis' hand uncovered in the dead of night sometimes, poking me, taunting me, from a resistant corner of my psyche.

It was winter. The snow gathered its piles dutifully outside our windows. The sun poked at the drifts and then sought itself into the dirt underneath as if wanting to hide away. The house was almost finished the way that we wanted it. Ciara and I had decided that we would go ahead with the wedding plans. We had begun the process, hoping to have it all organized for the following summer. It was incredibly intricate. All the people one would have to hire and invite, all the arrangements that had to come together seamlessly. One day. One day like any other, like no other. A pinnacle. Sure, I did not have the same sort of dreams about all this as Ciara. For me it was simply a step in a chain of events, which always began with a screw but seldom led to this grand and expensive culmination. However, to let Ciara get to enjoy this fully, my total participation was necessary. I entertained her wishes and ushered in the event. Ciara wished and wished away. I said to myself, one should wish ever so carefully, yet also succumb to one's destiny, as wishes were never enough, and hardly ever were made for the right thing. I must have been removed and secretly reluctant, unbeknownst to myself, in wait for other events to come running down the road screaming at me to flee whilst there was still one second, one moment, between me and the unstoppable.

Every film depiction, every literary attempt, to describe the ceremony of a wedding seemed superfluous and ill fitting to me when it really came down to it. The supposed fear at the moment of realization that one has to sleep with one woman alone from now on, and all that other jazz, made me laugh. God, how serious can one take commitments? Yes, it would be God there would it not, a big fat finger wagging whilst ominous music boomed up from below. But if one had no God, there was nothing that one needed to answer to other than one's conscience and even that was relative and malleable. I had no intentions of holding onto one supreme reality, and no inclinations for that either. I would wait and see. This seemed the thing to do for now. It was what it was and nothing more than that. Life could change, I would make the best out of what I had been given, that was all that I could tell myself, and Ciara. She was happy with that, although she saw me as a bit too realistic and perhaps lacking in the romantic department. However, we were both in our mid-thirties now and the misconceptions about love and romance had long gone, to give way to truer understanding of needs and affection. Mine were perhaps a lot more cynical than hers, but she was still on the same track as me. I did wonder at times if Ciara believed in monogamy as firmly as her sister seemed to think, but let the thought go as soon as it bopped up as it would be thoroughly unhealthy to pursue it. Ciara walked up the aisle; propped on her proud father's stiff-arm, confidently and brightly. She was in full control of the event. She beamed at me as she got up close and I could not but help return her enthusiasm with a smile. We flittered through the do's and don'ts, and felt enormous relief when the ebb of procedures was well within sight. It had taken a lot to get here, but now we would just celebrate before our holiday in Morocco.

The party was a bit turgid to start with but as soon as people got oiled over dinner the inhibitions and the mood lifted. The band struck out over the charted seas and the sea-saw bodies went from side to side bleating and shaking. Many a regret would more than likely be brought to the surface in the morning hours, but for now, anything was allowed, anything went. It was carnival time. Somewhere in the midst I was approached by a very drunk young man whom I had never laid eyes on before and who, as is usual during such events as these, asked me to go and have a cigarette with him. I remember the incident in a haze and to this day am not absolutely sure that it did take place. Anyway, from what my maybe faulty recollection tells me, the young man was in his mid-twenties, he was dressed all in black, which upon recall seems a bit severe for the circumstances, and was speaking with a soft accent which suggested that he was perhaps of north African descent. He lit my cigarette whilst congratulating me on my beautiful bride and the magnificent party. I was feeling a bit wobbly from a long line of drinks of every caliber and colour, and remember staring at his hand as the match flared. He had a tiny little tattoo of a rudimentary bird in the corner where his index finger and thumb met. I asked him where he had got the tattoo and what it symbolized and he laughed at me saying that it had been done by a very talented man during very distressing circumstances. I was about to ask for him to elaborate as he dropped his cigarette and matches. We both sat down on our haunches looking for the slippery items when all of a sudden he seemed to sober up completely putting his hand on my knee getting serious.

"You understand why I am here, don't you?"

I stared at him with incredulity and whilst Denis' face did come to the fore, I kept on pushing it away, to remain reasonable and resistant to what was about to be said. My brain swayed and sitting hunched over like this made me want to go piss.

"I think I will have to go to the bathroom."

A hazy plan to get out of what seemed to face me.

"You know I will have to go soon. Just wanted to let you know that it is getting closer, much closer."

He paused for effect, as if that was needed.

"He wishes you everything. He wanted me to recite the

following to you: *Full fathom five thy lover lies; of his bones are coral made; those are pearls that were his eyes; nothing of him that does fade; both doth suffer a sea-change.*" He paused again before finishing, "*into something rich and strange.*"

Then he stood up, pulled me up with both hands, smiled and left. Why was it that every time I tried to forget, had been just at the verge of forgetting, someone or something came back reeling me in, the hook embedded in my soft brain tissue tearing at it and jerking little goops out with each tug?

We had packed our bags, the two suitcases on the bed like beached whales awaiting a deluge. We stood staring at them not comprehending how exactly we were to haul them from their station to the next point. Ciara then smoothly maneuvered herself out of the equation by wondering if I would not mind taking care of them whilst she checked the house one more time, and I agreed still gawking at them skeptically. My mind filled with a grayish mist of misunderstandings that were completely out of my control to deal with. I was forced to come back to myself as the only method available. It was how I chose to respond to the barrage of mysterious connections that was my sole saving grace. I could chose to pretend that it was not happening even though I was fairly sure that this was not the real truth. As I looked at it, it did not matter whether or not it was true as it actually had so little to do with reality as such that it did not really matter. It had too little reality coverage to count. My mental survival depended upon me being able to shut it out, so I did. I was pretending that this day was just as it was. We were the happy couple on our way to honeymoon ourselves silly. I could hear the quiet lap of waves and smell the moon-filled sand dunes in which strange little animals dug for time in the moving sand: my romantic ideas of Morocco soon to be confirmed or rubbished. I stumbled on the threshold and the suitcase went skidding across the driveway. Thank God it did not open but the movement had brought skid marks to bear

31

on the bag. Well now at least it would be a little easier to pick out on the line up parading down the conveyer belt. I wrestled the beast into the boot and then returned for the second one. As I started up the stairs I heard Ciara softly whisper to someone. Doubts crept in and I went cold. I stopped on the stairs for a while trying to strain my hearing to at least pick up a little meaning from the noise. I could not make myself hear anything else than a soft muttering of communication. I began to move slowly trying to make as little noise as possible. However, it was impossible to make my steps do anything but announce my being there as the floorboards played and swayed underneath me. Ciara went quiet. Then she appeared at the top of the stairs casually enquiring whether or not I had managed to get the bags into the car yet, as I blurted out,

"That sounded like a very mysterious conversation."

I was trying to give her the impression of that I had indeed overheard some of it.

"Oh no, Siobhan is just getting a little jealous of our holiday" Ciara laughed. As I got up to her she kissed the top of my head and said that she just had to plug in the timers and then she would be ready to go. I felt overwhelmed by my imagination now involving my wife in a huge conspiracy against me, shook my head feeling the weight of it in each turn, and then concentrated on my breathing going over my chosen philosophy that life was not that complicated. The heaviness of the bag grounded me again and I let my body collapse into its own weight balancing the weight of life against that of matter.

At the airport, after having parked the car in the long-term car park, having checked in, having braved the queues, Ciara and I hurried off to the restaurant for an early champagne lunch. Life was feeling alright as soon as the alcohol hit my gullet. No more worries for now. In Morocco life would be different and far away from all that caused me consternation here at home. I was beginning to relax and was intent on making this as pleasurable a holiday as possible for us both.

The front page of the man's newspaper across the aisle spoke of fires almost reaching Olympia in Greece. Olympia, where the fire for the games is kindled, where the flame is gathered to be brought around the world. It was strange how fire and floods could simultaneously be the bane, albeit in different parts of the world. This global warming situation brought out the worst in all there was, any element. Imagine a fire eating up the place where fire is created. Poetic justice of sorts. Life eating itself. Almost as if he had heard the thoughts rumbling through my head the man turned around to face me. His dark eyes were calm, not expressing any emotion that I could read. Yet a moment of surprise and unease passed before he decided to smile. Then he turned back to his paper. Obviously I got terribly suspicious. Why had he turned? I shifted in my seat. Why had he looked at me like that? Why had he smiled? I kept staring at his profile as discreetly as possible as if the way that he looked and the way that he carried himself would reveal his true nature. I was hoping to overhear him speak to the person sitting next to him, or to the airhostess, but he seemed fully engrossed in the paper, not recognizing anyone at all, except for me, for that specific moment earlier. Ciara started up a conversation which took my focus away from the man, but when she decided to snooze a little I turned back in my seat only to notice that his seat now was vacant. Nothing had been left to mark his seat. Thin air was what he had turned into. I sat up and looked around but could not see him anywhere. I tried to stop myself from going over and over this moment and its meaning, but I could not. Finally I had to get up. I unhooked my seatbelt quietly and eased Ciara's head off my shoulder. She did not seem to take any notice but simply curled up in the other direction. I wanted to use the toilet anyway. Two birds. One stone. All of the toilets in the front of the plane were vacant. I crammed myself into one of them, pissed, washed my hands, and checked my appearance. I looked tired. Rest would do me good. I scratched my stubble underneath where a dry skin patch lingered. As I opened the door one of the airhostess' obstructed my path. She said sorry, smiled and tried to move out of the way. The other toilets were still vacant around me, although a largish woman was making her way towards them. I decided to take the other aisle whilst I looked down towards our seats. The man still was not there. Where could he have gone? I walked down the aisle looking for his face amongst the passengers, but nothing. The plane hit an air pocket, shook and threw me forwards and upwards. I landed clumsily and stepped on a man's foot. Profusely apologetic as I was he managed to keep his annoyance in check. I moved down the aisle and when I got to the back, one of the toilets was locked. I decided to wait him out. I was certain that this must be him. Even though I had no intention of really confronting him I still wanted to just have another look to see if he was hiding anything, to see if I would get a gut feeling of some sort. After ten minutes watch an air steward came to ask me if I was ok. I mumbled that I was just stretching my legs, hoping that the man in the toilet would not hear my presence being revealed. A few minutes later the door very slowly opened and a woman in her forties made an appearance looking very embarrassed by my presence. I was so taken aback by her coming out of that cubicle that I must have embarrassed her even more with my mouth ajar ogling her unabashedly. I gathered myself and let her slink away before I returned to my seat. He was still not there and Ciara had now woken up. She was sitting reading and looked up at me questioning what could have kept me away for so long. I said that I had just needed to stretch my legs a bit; she took me on my word and leant over her book again. I reached down into my bag to get my book out and as I bent back up there he was, sitting in his seat, reading the same paper, unfazed by me, or anything. Where the fuck could he had gone to? I was tempted to ask Ciara if she had noticed anything weird or unusual about the man, but then as I did not want her to become suspicious or involved in the mystery of all of this I decided against that line of enquiry. There was no use in involving her in this. It had nothing to do with her.

The tires touched down like a spider considering a hot surface, we bounced ineptly on the runway, shuddering and yelping. I closed my eyes and tried to think of something that was to come. The beach. A bed. A sunset. Siestas. Eventually we came to a stop. The man had refrained from turning around again. I followed him closely, almost losing Ciara in the process. At the passport control I had to slow down as Ciara had our passports. The man dissolved in the thick stream of holidaymakers. When Ciara reached me I was leaning on the wall feeling very pensive and sullen. She gave me inquisitive looks that barely hid a supreme annoyance with my hurry. We did not say a word. Before we left she had accused me of being 'out there' and had asked why I was seemingly preoccupied elsewhere. I had told her that I was feeling overwhelmed by the changes in our lives and that she should just bear with me as I was surely just trying to adjust. Hence she was doing her utmost to keep her cool with my foibles. We were picked up from the airport in an air-conditioned saloon car. The man driving us was all smiles although brief in his communications. This suited me fine. Both Ciara and I now just wanted to get rid of the bags and consider the early afternoon. The door to our room opened up to a luscious space filled with light, flowers, chocolates and refinements that promised to make our stay as relaxing as possible. We undressed, lay down and did our sweaty duty as newly married. Afterwards we rested in the strange heat laughing at the impulse towards the predicted act, before we fell gently into an unplanned siesta.

When I woke the room was dim and the space next to me on the bed empty. I called out for Ciara but there was no response. I wheeled over to a sitting position but as my bare feet made contact with the cold marble floor I retracted them a couple of times before I dared full contact. I wandered into the bathroom but it was empty as was the rest of the apartment. Ciara's suitcase lay open on the floor but she had not emptied it out. Rather she had thrown her old clothes over a chair and then simply dressed herself right out of the suitcase. I looked for my watch and was surprised to see that it already was seven o'clock. I had a shower, dressed and went in search of Ciara. When I found her she was sitting talking to a man at the bar in the hotel. I walked up towards them, but as I came closer the man left and I realized that it was the same man from the plane.

"Who the hell was that?"

"Hi babe to you too."

Ciara smiled at me.

"You are not getting all jealous like that now are you?"

"No, seriously, who was that? I saw him earlier and found him a bit creepy. What did you talk about?"

Ciara was bemused by my urgency and desperation.

"God, babe, he just asked if I was on my own. It was a harmless attempt at chatting me up which was derailed by you entering the bar. You timed that just right. Gave me a perfect reason to decline."

Ciara laughed at my morose look.

"Where have you seen him before anyway?"

She looked down towards the table and picked up a cigarette, lit it whilst turning her face towards me.

"Oh, he was on the plane. Seemed a bit suspicious."

I heard how stupid it all appeared as I let the words form themselves into sounds.

"Suspicious?" Ciara showed her flummoxed state by sucking on the cigarette a little too long.

36

"What do you think our life is? A mystery drama? Are you waiting for Samantha Burton to come stealthily up to our table at any moment now?"

Ciara attempted a Northern Irish accent, which she butchered so badly that we both burst into laughter. I ordered a drink and then we planned the evening in a fairly rosy mood. We visited a specialist fish restaurant where the fish was served enveloped by a salt caking that had to be broken open by the white clad waiter's experienced hands. We ate and drank well. The previous feelings of unease were soon smoothed away. The rest of the evening passed in a white wine vapor that saw the bleached beach contrasted by the sucking soughing black of the sea in which the creamy moon bopped fishing for stars.

A couple of days passed like this. We were taking full advantage of the fact that we were on holiday and that this meant that we were not required to do anything in particular. We swam, ate, drank, dozed and fucked. We were both getting so relaxed and used to this that we were considering moving down here fulltime. We could live like this till our dying days. Nevertheless, the fourth day in we started to get a bit anxious to move. I wanted to go and see the desert, have an adventure, and Ciara wanted to go shopping in the souk. We sat down for breakfast and tried to appease both our needs, ending up with a perfect arrangement. The air permeated with the call to prayer, whispering secret songs to us from the minarets. We would go to the souk today and then plan the coming day's outing into the desert.

The souk was soaked in a thick molasses of light. The heavy air was punctured by dusty, but still sparkling, sun shafts, and sprinkled with the smells of spices, sweet oily perfumes and the exhaust fumes from a steady trickle of mopeds of all variations. All of it alive in the heat, one huge body in which we played bit parts just like everything else, moving life and light on. The amount and types of things for sale were endless. We looked at the fresh food, the boxes filled with every strain of fish that ever swam the waters, eyes bulging confidently with recent death, pictures of the deep still etched on their retinas. The raisins, lemons, dates, apples, figs, peaches, oranges, limes and rainbows of grapes that one could imagine just bursting out of their own fullness, ripeness, drenching the rest of the world, leaving a world dripping with colour and sweetness, a slow moving world constantly overflowing. Ciara bought a roughhewn wooden horse that lay on top of a pile of similar monsters of all different sizes. The artist factory in which it had been made must have paid all the workers by the amount of objects that they completed, leaving the objects with a charming hurried square look. There was something un-thought about them. There was a necessity to the made object, but it had no function other than to fuel the imagination with something just hinted at: a horse, a power, a mode of dream travel, a gesture of the enormity of it all, the innumerable opportunities, the never end. We dined in a nook of the souk, pointing at plates that other diners were delving into hoping that it would be something eatable, as there were no menus and no common language that could be used to control events. We ended up with plates of fish and vegetables that fit just right into our tired, hot and empty bodies. The plates of fruits that followed astounded us, as having a number of peaches in a row was something that we had never really tried or considered. Yet we did our best at completing the experience in as appropriate a mode as possible. We wanted to fit into the life in which we now holidayed. We took part. We let life change us even if only temporarily.

When we returned to the hotel we were saturated with our environment in every single way. I wanted to lay down, put a blanket over my head and try to hold on to the feeling in which I was now swimming, but was unable as another couple from the western part of the world entered the bar where we sat and demanded attention which we as civilized citizens could not deny them. She was wearing a red dress that barely covered her arse, and he was in a dear looking double-breasted suit. Completely overdressed, considering place and climate. Perhaps this was why we felt a twinge of intrigue and left the excuses in our back-pockets just for the moment. Within a very short amount of time it seemed we knew more about them than we did of each other. He worked in the oil business somehow, and she was his mistress, his wife having been left at home with the kids in Nova Scotia. One could safely say that he was way out of his element here in the desert, yet he could not be anywhere else. He came to Morocco as much as he possibly could, partly because it was the opposite of his usual environment, partly because Flavia, his mistress resided not too far away, across the water in southern Spain, and then there was work. The set up suited them it appeared. We were shocked by their revelations but pretended that it was all rational, swallowing our amazement when they weren't looking. After a couple of drinks we agreed to have dinner with them that evening. When we got up to the room we both wondered why, but saw no way of decently pulling out. However, we were also a bit enthralled, marveling at how the evening would pan out. We showered, changed and got ready to find out. I told Ciara that I had a nagging feeling of having recognized the man from somewhere else, but she brushed away my foolishness with clear and simple reasoning. It was impossible. I had never even been to Canada. But, I argued, I had always wanted to go. Ciara and I laughed at the logic, and she suggested that perhaps I should ask him to invite me over.

The air had cooled down ever so little, and the lanterns around the edges of the restaurant barely moved in the still evening air. Pools of light lay stock still, hiding from the dark. I set my feet down, as I should, in each halo, whereas Ciara daintily tiptoed through them without being aware of their being there. They were obvious. I was obvious. We were. No, perhaps that is not a fair statement but there was something simple about our being there even if the circumstances themselves were a bit strange. There they were, the couple, still in the same clothes only a bit more tipsy perhaps. We smiled on approach, and the man rose as we got there.

"Flavia thought that you would not come."

Flavia looked admonishingly at her man but then faced us with a smile which was to smooth over the admission to a possibility of disappointment. Will was beaming at us, well pleased with being right no doubt, but also well pleased with the fact that now the evening could really begin. There was something in the air, something pungent, something fermenting. I mentioned the smell, but none of the others could make it out. The menus were brought over and the small talk stopped momentarily as the company considered their choices, eyes scrutinizing the text, mouths sampling imagined tastes. Fennel sounded just like what I needed. Yes, definitely. Ciara leaned towards me with her menu and pointed questioningly at a dish with an extravagant name. We discussed it in hushed tones, and Ciara then nodded back into her seat. As the menus closed the conversation took a little time before it got started again. Will was saying something to Ciara, and she bent her head down and laughed shyly but evidently amused. I was daydreaming a bit when Flavia in dry slurry tones asked me if the wine that they had already chosen was to my liking.

"Yes, yes, very nice."

I was a bit preoccupied with the fact that Will was now really entertaining Ciara and she was having all of it. She continued that shy sexy laugh of hers, sometimes pulling at her napkin to cover her lap properly. With all the background noise swelling along with crowds arriving for dinner I could not hear what they were saying and this made me feel uncomfortable. Flavia kept trying to drag me into a conversation but I was distracted in my answers. The food arrived and just as it did Will put his hand on Ciara's whilst it was resting bird-like on her lap. I did not like this at all, although I saw that she did pull her hand back a bit from the touch. What did Will want? Another mistress? Perhaps they were swingers and found us a good catch? Probably. Probably that was it. Will then eased off his charm and concentrated on his food. Flavia leaned in to him and they consulted for a while. Will looked up at me, and a moment of distain swept over his features which then transformed into a warm looking quick smile. Ciara finished her food first, excused herself, rose and maneuvered her slight body dancelike between the tables, waiters, chairs and diners. A kid came running and almost collided with her but she just laughed, tussled the kid's hair and continued on whilst the mother of the child looked very cross and apologetic.

"So."

I had tried to remove myself by putting all my attention elsewhere but now here I was alone with the couple. I had not realized how little I had wanted to be in this predicament until it happened.

"So."

Will opened up the interaction with a repetition of the word he'd just uttered. I had to say something. Anything.

"What are your plans for tomorrow?"

As I said it I realized that this almost sounded like an invitation to some plans that we'd already made, but it was too late, I had let the sentence slip in desperation and now I would have to steer it in some other direction that I would actually be able to deal with. Will obviously turned the question back to me, asking if we had suggestions for them as they had done little in preparation for the trip.

"Ah, certainly you both have done it all already."

Which, again, as I said it I realized made it sound a bit perverted and I tried to cover this up with;

"Coming here so often, I mean."

41

Will was amused by my fumbling ways, and chose to let me dig my hole a bit deeper yet.

"I guess, but we usually come down only for one thing."

Flavia blatantly slid her hand on to Will's crotch and he looked at me very proudly as she moved her hand back and forth across his genitals whilst she remained in eye contact with me. I tried not to seem to notice the behavior. God, they were after a good time weren't they? There was no doubt now, we would simply have to explain ourselves out of the situation and run for the hills. I got up.

"Toilet. Back in a tick."

I was going to catch up with Ciara so that we could plan our getaway together.

I called into the women's bathroom but Ciara did not seem to be in there. I peered around the corner to see if our paths had crossed each other somehow but she did not appear to have returned to the table yet. Will and Flavia were sitting very closely, she probably rubbing him still, if he had not already come, and he, whispering further adventurous ideas into her soft furry little Spanish ear. I began to walk around the back of the restaurant wondering where the hell Ciara could have gone to. Then I saw her approaching the table from the other end of the restaurant, smiling at them as she sat down without as much as a lookout for me. Will leaned back in Ciara's direction, then leaned back and pointed her attention to something in his lap. Ciara laughed and so did Flavia. I could tell by the way that her back shuddered. Who are these people! I got angry at the whole situation and had to think quickly, on my feet, to be able to get out of it now. Strangely, Ciara seemed either oblivious or taken by the whole thing. Will seemed a bit of a dick to me, literally, but maybe that was what Ciara would not mind a little of. Where the hell did she go anyway? How could she have ended up at the other side of the restaurant when she had gone in the direction of the toilets? I was getting pissed off with her now as well. I really wanted us to leave. However, by the appearance of Ciara's amusement I assumed that this would be a difficult point to convince her of. I walked over to the table as slowly as possible, my thoughts blurred with rough useless ideas. I had a smile for all as I sunk back into the seat no more prepared than I had been at the beginning of the long journey across the room. Ill! That was it, I was ill. A terrible migraine had just attacked me and it would demand of us to leave immediately.

"I am feeling awful."

My whispered words to Ciara weren't discerned by the others. She looked at me as if a little annoyed but a slight shimmer of concern also made its way up her face.

"What's wrong sweetheart?"

She raised her voice a little as she uttered this, which I hoped to mean that she was with me on the escape plan. Will leaned closer over the table.

"What's wrong?"

"He's feeling sick."

Ciara was dealing with the situation without sounding overly worried. This was not good. I now had to look up and deliver the end of the evening to our company.

"I am feeling very shaky, just got hit by a horrific migraine. Think that we will have to excuse ourselves. Sorry."

Will looked very put out, sat back in his chair with both of his arms resting on the sides of it, his frown obvious to all. Things were not panning out as he had planned. I was smiling inside to myself: there you go you perverted fuck. In a way, I thought to myself, I did not see too much wrong in what he was trying to do, if it had not been me sitting there as the fool who was being robbed of his precious bounty. I mean, I was not against the idea of changing partners and all that. However, I felt that the whole game plan was leaning in Will's favour and I was not going to be in anything but a lose/lose situation.

"Do you need a doctor?"

43

Will was trying to catch me out.

"No, no. I'm sure it will suffice with a little rest."

What the hell was Ciara up to? Her silence suggested that she did not seem to want to get involved.

"Am so sorry to have cut the party short, but sure we'll meet up again soon."

She couldn't miss that cue now could she? She slowly turned her face up towards me and wondered:

"Would you mind if I stay on? You don't seem too bad, and I would like to get some coffee and dessert."

What could I say? She had made the request so openly that I was forced into retreat. I could not risk them thinking that we were of different opinions, as they would surely think that she would be an easier quarry then.

"No, no. You stay. However, don't forget that you had to make that phone call at eleven." Surely Ciara would not misread this obvious hint at that I wanted her to come with me, that something was amiss.

"What phone call sweetheart?"

She looked puzzled. Shit.

"Your sister wanted you to give her a ring in regards to her interview today."

It was possible. Siobhan was jobless, she was looking for work, and she always wanted to feedback the events of the day if she had been to an important interview. Ciara still looked at me completely nonplussed.

"Oh, I am sure that it can wait until the morning. We are on our honeymoon after all."

Yes, the fuck we are, echoed in my tight red skull. This fucking shit. Now I had to think of plan B, because I could not simply let her wander off with these obviously dangerous fools. God knows what they would do to her. And she might even like it. I went off out of the restaurant as soon as I had made sure with Ciara that she had enough money to carry her. Will had waved his hand dismissively at me, but I had pretended that I did not see him. That would make his bloody day wouldn't it? I stood around the corner of the restaurant, limp in thought. I was trying to figure out a way to spy on them without them having any opportunity to see me. I looked around the neighborhood, found a suitably sheltered café with a window to the restaurant. I installed myself and kept intent watch. They behaved fairly civilly, at least from this perch. Bird eye keenly trained on every little nuance, or what could perhaps maybe be a nuance. They gently meandered through coffee, aperitifs and desserts, smiling and laughing for a while before the mood seemed to change quite dramatically. All of a sudden Flavia stood up, her chair falling back to the floor, bowled over. She stood there just looking straight ahead for a while as Will and Ciara spoke to her with apparent concern, yet without her paying them any mind at all it seemed. Then she took her shawl off the fallen chair and walked off towards the back of the restaurant. In a daze I watched Will and Ciara begin to giggle like two little school children. What the hell was going on? Neither of them reached for the fallen chair or followed Flavia as she disappeared. Once more a curtain fell and the two of them began what seemed an earnest serious discussion. What could they possibly be talking about? And what could be so much more important than the sudden disappearance of both of their partners, under very suspect circumstances I might add? They baffled me with their lack of either sympathy or care. A hand on my shoulder brought me back into the reality of my own situation. I looked up. Flavia smiling sweetly, as if we all were caught up in perfectly normal circumstances that needed little probing.

"Who's the peepy peepy Tom then?"

I squirmed in my seat, feeling an undeniable guilt of some ridiculous sort. I smiled a fretted smile back at her and motioned towards the seats available.

"Do you want anything?"

Flavia moved into the seat simultaneously as loosening up her joints and muscles with snakelike movements. Then she just sat there quiet in her own little world. I was feeling slightly uncomfortable to start with but then the strangeness of the situation made me laugh. I chuckled quietly at first but then the sensation crept up from my churning stomach and proceeded to attack my whole body. Convulsions wrought every fiber into vibration, which caused loud loud noise to erupt from my throat. Flavia did not join in the merriment. She continued to live elsewhere. When my laughter abated and my eyes became clear of tears I realized that the table, which my eyes had been trained on previously, now was empty. The debris of the dinner laid morbidly still and untouched. There it was, the evidence of the reality of the evening. All the waiters seemed to avoid it like the plague, no one getting close enough to clear it away. It disturbed me. I felt an urge to go down there myself to help them out. Erase the scene. Flavia was humming to herself. I got up without a word, threw some coins onto the table, which clinked against the glasses, and walked out.

At the hotel our room laid bare, hidden in a soft creepy dark. I got out of my clothes in the bathroom and stood under a sticky hot shower for a good while. I watched the water race down my body and jutted out my hand to see it speed off in new directions before a dive towards the drain. The tendrils seemed to magnify the areas over which they spread. The hairs on my arms working like bulwarks. If one was as tiny as an ant these rivulets would seem like tsunamis, one would not have a chance in hell. The door to our room opened. I stood still in the shower without turning it off expecting Ciara to come into the bathroom carrying some sorry excuse for how the events had unfolded. My stomach jumped and rearranged itself with anger. I heard some scuffling and then the door again. I jumped out of the shower and ran for the room. Naked in the middle of the floor I realized that whoever it was that had been in the room had now left. I dashed for the door, flung it open but only to an empty corridor with a flickering light. I heard someone coming and directed my naked body back into the room and closed the door. There was a puddle by my feet that dripped itself larger by the second. Maybe Ciara was eloping? Maybe she had picked up her belongings just now and was on the way to the taxi in which Will sat cradling his hard-on. I searched the room for her suitcase but could not see it. Then I realized that of course it would be in the bloody wardrobe if it was anywhere and flung myself at the piece of furniture, a terrible and terrifying sparring partner. In haste I tore the door open, staring into the innards of the wardrobe's body, my eyes scanning the contents of the beast. Her suitcase was there, and her clothes, nothing obvious missing. I stood stock still for a long while until the cold crept up my legs and into my navel. My stomach jumped and turned, my innermost prodded in a flash by an icy needle. I shook out of my stupor and walked into the bathroom. Dried myself and then worked myself under the sheets. What else could I do? If I started walking the streets now, it would not only be futile, it would be bloody stupid. I would not find her, but if I did, I would have nothing decent to actually say right now. I was too angry and confused. Against my will I fell asleep. Fell like a brick into oily water, sinking heavy, clammy and deceptively soft edged.

In the morning I woke with my eyelids desperately clinging to each other. I forced myself to open them in slow stages. The first was a glimpse of the way that the light fell from behind rather than from in front of me, which confirmed the direction in which I was facing: away from the window towards the bathroom. The second was a haze, which suggested the shape of the half open door that led into a hollow dark. The third was a confirmation of just that. The fourth was my breathing retracting into my chest, keeping itself absolutely still in there, trying to judge any possible movements in the bed space behind me: A person sleeping contently, perhaps sighing with a depraved sort of heaviness? No person? I could hear and feel nothing. I watched the light move to open the bathroom space up. Still nothing. I decided that she was not there and abruptly turned around.

Ciara looked at her hand, which lay still beside her in the crinkled bed sheets. She found herself lifeless, like a mannequin, like a puppet. She looked over at the sleeping man's body next to her. So far and yet so close. An enormous gentleness seized her. She looked and took her hand, a maximum effort was called upon, she raised it, and as an odd dirge it traveled towards the man's body, the stagnant air in the room rising in little waves at the bow. She often had these feelings towards inanimate/animate objects and animals, as well as people. However, with objects and animals it was considered alright to touch no matter what one's relation. A perfect stranger could caress a dog for example, or a book on a shelf. When she got overwhelmed with belonging to, and understanding of, other people, especially other strangers, she wanted to touch them, let her hand run over their cheeks. She did not have to say anything, it was not that kind of understanding that took her over, it was more that kind which just is, that kind that says that we are all the same. There are no boundaries other than those that we make up ourselves and conscientiously try to keep to. Laws, which try to keep us frozen in time, but that never really manage, because life forces change by it's very nature, it never stops waving. A breath away from the sleeping man's face her hand stopped, hovered, and then retracted back to the safe nest of her sleep-warm body. She moved around in the bed, pushed the pillows up and slid into an upright position against the headboard. This time her hand traveled towards the bedside table and brought the menu back to her. She knew the menu inside out. The same crest graced the leather bound cover of this menu as in the other room, in the other bed, on the other bedside table, by the other man.

An overpowering sense of relief poured smooth weighty sand into the hollow of my bones as I saw her head on the pillow next to me. Nevertheless I also felt enormously angry about the fact that she had taken herself to a point where she meant this much to me. She was not really that important. She was outside of me and could never be "inside" of me. Here with me, inside of this my body. I fell helplessly asleep right then and there without actually touching her as I would under normal circumstances. A mossy stone I sunk to the bottom of sleep, nestled in between other dormant debris.

The day leaned heavily on the buildings bending them slightly, ageing them dramatically, and then they closed in on me. I had flash backs of the jumble of the Zimbabwe elections, and the recently crashed small airplane into a row of very ordinary houses in England, jumping around in my head along with the recent mess of my own. News from so far away from where we now were, we were somewhere in between I guess, but we were still in it, in the midst of history: self-made and imposed upon. I was walking again. I had woken up, looked at her hard, meaning all that I meant, whilst she did not seem to want to take anything in. She just sighed and turned around feigning disinterest and boredom. We did not speak. I got up, got into my clothes and left. I walked for hours before my body demanded of me to stop for something to drink. I sat in a café, got a small coffee and some strange bread-like thing, which I had pointed at with a pleasant little baring of my teeth. It filled part of the hole that was eating away at me. I watched the bustle of the city flood by in whimsical twists and turns, planets bending space to their fit. My coffee had the density of a black hole and I imbued it. I was ready to explode, only I did not have anything concrete to focus my explosion on. I should have talked to her before I left. God knows, she might not even be there when I got back, and the whole bloody thing would start again, with me none the wiser. I was trying to punish her, but was taking most of the punishment myself.

When I got back an empty room greeted me just as I had feared. I had been gone for hours so it was perhaps not so strange. I lay down and took a siesta just to push time ahead of me into some space where we could be together again, talking things through. When I came to she was not back yet and it was already going on four in the afternoon. I got up, showered, got dressed and went down to the hotel bar. There she was, at a table in the orange glow, calmly reading a book. I stood for a while looking at her, but she did not notice my presence. I walked over and sat down after having grabbed a couple of drinks for us. She did not look up when I arrived, but mumbled a "thanks" to the drink. Then we sat there, speechless, for nearly half an hour before I began. I tried not to sound too accusatory and angry, but it was a hard job.
"Were you safe last night?"
She shook her head at me in disbelief, and answered equally cryptically:
"Sure."
"Where were you? I was terribly worried about you."
"Worried" she spat at me, "more like stupidly jealous and idiotic."
"Perhaps some of that as well, but mostly worried, and confused."
"So fucking confused you behaved barbarically towards those new friends of ours."
"Friends? Hardly friends. But yes maybe my behaviour was a bit childish and erratic, but I had reason."
"What reason? Have I ever done anything to hurt you in that way? Something for you to base your erratic behaviour on?"
I slowly shook my head at her but said:
"You were behaving strangely yourself."
Ciara whispered to herself:
"Some kind of honeymoon this is."

"Yes, I agree." I retorted, very much angered by her words, and continued:

"Some kind of honeymoon, where the bride takes off with another man and does not return until the next morning."

Ciara looked up at me with her eyes now blazing.

"Where the hell do you think I was! Do you think I was fucking Will through the night? Is that what you think? Well then think that, if that is all that you think of me! You think that I would go with just any old man do you? Well then I should. Just to spite you. Just so that you can prove yourself right about me. Why would you marry someone that you thought so very little of? Why!"

She now began crying uncontrollably. I took her in my arms and held her without another word. How stupid was I. She probably had been so embarrassed by my behavior that she had asked for another room in the hotel for the evening, just to punish me. Just to teach me a lesson in civil behavior. I cringed at my stupidity. Of course, my lovely wife would not mistreat me in any way. Why would she have married me in that case? I held her closer as I felt my embarrassment rise and ebb. She stopped her crying and just lay there, seemingly exhausted from all this madness. I looked up realizing that we were the main performers in this fairly empty bar and that from the bar itself the eyes of Will and Flavia were upon us. I panicked a bit. Quick, how the hell would we get out of this now? They had obviously observed our argument, and thrilled with themselves they would hardly have the courtesy to leave us on our own. Sure enough Will soon cockily strode towards our table with Flavia tiptoeing behind him concentrating and smiling, hoping to seem a confident semblance of herself.

"Babe, let's do something on our own tonight." I whispered to Ciara who was unaware of the impending crash.

"Yes, let's." She answered as she got up out of my embrace. Her face paled at the sight of Will and Flavia, but it was a fleeting shade of pale that quickly rose pink and recovered. She greeted the two of them generously with a kiss on each of their cheeks. Will looked absolutely pompous swimming in his own importance, nursing an obvious feeling of having conquered our petty marriage. He shook my hand with a fake condolences look on his grinning face. I dried my hand on my trousers as soon as he had stopped squeezing it as hard as he could muster. I smiled back at him as if I wanted to spit in his broad North American features. They tried and tried to convince us to join them tonight again but this time Ciara was on my side and comfortably maneuvered us out of their equation for the evening. They took the defeat hard but as Ciara promised that we would be free to join them any other evening they slowly released the grip on us and let us slip away. I brought Ciara away from the table with my arm around her waist.

"Thank God."

"Oh come on, they're not that bad. I find them quite entertaining actually."

She looked up at me smiling.

"I know you do sweetheart, but not entertaining enough to have to spend all our time with them I hope?"

"No you're right, this evening we will get some time to ourselves. Who knows what plans we could come up with?" She said with a glint in her eye.

This was alright now. I had been a complete idiot. Of course we could meet up with the clowns again, if it amused Ciara. Who could possibly be threatened by those two imbeciles?

The next morning Ciara was set on going shopping and I indulged her without a complaint, my embarrassment still going strong. In an indoor shopping mall the same old shops greeted us as we knew from home, and thus were transported into normality for a little while, with exceptions from the covered women that browsed the aisles mechanically. I wandered off from Ciara in distracted boredom. I found myself standing in front of a shop window that offered tobacco and its paraphernalia. I thought of nothing in particular, not even smoking, when a voice behind me uttered

"So you're thinking of going back to it are you?"

I turned around to face a Moroccan woman.

"Pardon?"

She smiled and repeated herself. I shook my head at her, thinking that she was a distortion of light, a figment of the heat.

"You did smoke once, did you not?"

She was trying to be friendly, but I was not convinced of her as real.

"Everybody smokes once."

"But you have the look of someone that nostalgically gazes, almost licking your lips for the taste of it. Layers of some old you, resurfacing."

I decided that of course she was just being sociable, caring for a poor visitor to her land so I smiled back at her.

"Don't think I'll return to that old me though."

I turned around thinking that our banter had come to an end.

"You can't shed any part of your past. It layers you, stays there, forever, like on a hard- drive of a computer. The black box of an airplane."

I did not turn back to her, wishing that she'd go away. There was something odd about her interest in me, and my past.

"Why don't I go away?" she pondered to me.

I did not answer, I was pretending that I did not hear her. She let her voice run over the question again, revealing it, like something washed up by the sea on a clean deserted wide beach. Finally, as I decided to face her and her question, her purpose of this interrogation of me, she was no longer there. I could have sworn that I had heard her breathing just prior to turning. I looked around me but the swell of shoppers remained unhurried and did not contain even a fragment of someone in a hurry away from me. My mobile purred in my pocket and I found Ciara's voice reminding me of that we were spending the day together. Where could I meet her? At the coffee bar in ten minutes. I set my sail for the place by following a faint whiff of roasted beans in the stagnant mall air.

Ciara was already there with a cushioning of bags around her feet. How the hell had she managed to gather all those in such a short time?

"I got a few presents for you" she let the corners of her mouth rise and her eyes crinkle.

"I can't wait to see what" I said, and pulled the chair out next to her.

Once the coffee was finished we slowly pulled our booty together. As we were about to rise the woman, or wraith, of earlier made a second appearance. This time she greeted me like an old friend and before I had had time to blink she had introduced herself to Ciara claiming that she and I knew each other from some work training programme which sounded so plausible that my jaw just dropped. My eyes must have grown so huge that they nearly popped but Ciara did not notice a thing. The woman kept smiling and laughing at me, keeping jolly with Ciara who had clamped down on the bait, hook, line, sinker. All of a sudden the woman, claiming to be named Nada, had been invited along to dinner tonight, with her partner if she liked, Ciara emphasized. My shock and horror had frozen me completely and I had no comeback to anything. After Nada had left, having kissed us heartily, I still took some time to come to. Ciara noticed nothing. She gathered the bags, left some for me to carry, and asked me to hurry on as we still had a few shops to do. I followed her dumbly, amazed at how complicated life could become even if one just watched it go by.

The evening scooped itself up into present time, placed itself safely like a bet on a dead horse straight in my lap. I had said nothing to Ciara about the earlier run in with Nada. What was there to say? Ciara would not believe me. Why would I not have said anything earlier? It would wet Ciara's appetite for intrigue if I said anything now. At least if it rolled gently by, she would notice nothing, and I could perhaps figure out how this strange woman seemed to be intent on getting closer to me and my wife. I was a bit worried about the fact that Ciara had said nothing to me about Nada, no questions, no silent reservations. I got dressed whilst watching the news in the bedroom as Ciara was putting on her makeup in the bathroom. The phone rang. I picked it up and a whispered voice demanded to know if Fidel was here. I did not reply, put the phone down, and continued dressing. Ciara called out to find out who that could have been. I told her it was a wrong number.

"Is it not strange" Musa said, his hands close to mine on top of the table "how finger prints, the rings on a tree trunk which has been cut down, and different solar systems, all look the same?"
I was looking at his hands. He wore a silver ring on his left middle finger. The ring had jagged edges and some kind of inscription on a circle in its middle. Nada sat next to him, but was paying all of her attention to Ciara's seemingly exuberant story. His hands were strong in a bony kind of way, they looked as if they would leap off the table at any moment, seize the chance to dance, hold my shoulders tight to his in an embrace. I shook myself out of the mind game, which was leading me down old routes. I knew what was homoerotic, and I did not mind it as such, but life was mine here, with Ciara, and that to me seemed a good life, one worth concentrating on. One could spread oneself too thin if one let oneself get carried away with every possibility, every fancy. He looked at me after just having put the punctuation on his last sentence. His lips briefly shut, and then parted again.
"Do you believe there is such a thing as something completely new, that you could chance upon, and that would revolutionize your life? I mean, do you think we would be able to see it as such, or would we immediately turn it into something recognizable, just to be able to link and understand it?"

55

I must have missed quite a lot of the conversation; my reveries had sent me floating off, although I could perhaps try to string it together.

"Well, like you said there are coincidences, correspondences, like the ultimate depth of the oceans and the height of the mountains being the same distance from the earth's surface for some reason, same numbers that come back, which seem to indicate some purpose. However, maybe it is not so strange if it is tied to gravity somehow? No purpose, just the only way that it could be."

He was paying close attention to me, but shook his head as if I had missed something, which was entirely possible given the amount of reverie time that I had drifted around in earlier. Nada and this man, Musa, had shown up at our hotel restaurant just as we ourselves walked in. Ciara had greeted Nada as a long lost friend, and treated Musa, as Nada's proclaimed partner; partner of what, partner in crime perhaps, with equal generosity. I had felt the absurdity of the situation brush against me, but did nothing to clarify it, nothing to dispel it, just went on living in this fantasy, in these theatrics. I just let the situation lead, hoping that it would take me somewhere closer to an explanation of itself. Musa's heavy head of dark hair had turned away from me, exchanging some information with Nada quickly, almost imperceptibly. He turned back to me swiftly, smiled a big smile, his teeth glimmering by the light of the candle halos, then he hoisted his symmetry out of the chair and it struck me how certain male bodies are all angles apart from the bottom which disturbs the exactitude by its muscled roundness, a demand for caress, opposed to the rest of the body which is drawn in violent straight lines. My eyes on Musa's behind were uncovered by Nada who nodded with a little leer although she did not let that stop her conversing with Ciara.

"Oh, here they are."

Ciara abruptly rose and forced all eyes to turn to the door. In come the waltzing Will and his flavour of the month: puke.

Nada rose to her feet as well, welcomingly smiling at Will and Flavia, patiently waiting behind Ciara to be introduced so as to perpetuate the stories that she seemed to have come fully prepared with. I had nothing to do, other than to keep quiet to let the games continue. I might as well not have been there. I was useless to the story. As Musa returned, Will's eyes lit up with a new vigor. Will shook Musa's hand as if he was greeting a long lost friend. Musa did not seem quite as taken with Will, but did not shirk away from him in anyway. I watched, ever the sour impotent night-watch man. I felt jealous of Will again. Jealously rose quickly from my toes, and burnt in my stomach and on my tongue, like acid. Here he was, taking all the attention from both Musa and Ciara, whilst Nada a silent smirking black widow in the corner abided her time. No doubt she could slaughter Will. She had more rage in her bones, more cunning and stealth. Will just was as he was, over done. Again I slipped into the background. The back of my head cradled in my hands as I balanced the chair on its hind legs. Nobody paid me any attention until Musa suggested that he would show me his car. He had made the offer so slyly that not even Will had an opportunity to muscle in. It pleased me that I was the only one invited. We moved out quickly before anyone had the chance to query us.

We sat in Musa's car, me at the wheel, and he in the passenger seat, small talking for a short while. Then Musa asked if I would mind if he smoked. I looked at him and asked him that it depended on what he was about to smoke as sternly as I could. He laughed and lit up. The hash cloud was heavy in the car. With the windows still closed against the fresh evening air, it was a veritable steam bath of hashish. I began to feel drowsy and giddy. Musa chuckled himself and handed the smoke over to me. I took it, had a toke, and let my hands rest on the wheel staring at the ember. Had another toke, and then handed it back to Musa. We sat there speechless for the while that it took for the joint to be smoked. As Musa put it out in the ashtray I burst out laughing.

"I do not even know Nada! I've never ever met the woman until today at the mall when she approached me."

Musa was staring at me, momentarily puzzled but stoned enough to just think me pissing about so he let his chuckle come pounding out.

"I know, it was all part of the plan."

The daze that I was in was not letting go, even though Musa had answered my claim with those words. I was fighting with myself, trying to filter clarity into my head. I rolled the window down to the background noise of Musa's continuous chuckles, which I could not help to mimic in bouts of stoned conscience. God, make me sober, I cried in my head during lucid flickers, but I was unable to maintain them for more than a nanosecond. The fresh air did nothing but add to my state of mind. I rolled out of the car amidst louder bursts of laughter from the two of us. We were creating music. I was dancing like a rag-doll to the tunes, and my inner lucid man was only a helpless audience to the carnival. The lights were spinning, the sand was swirling, and my hands in the red dirt made me mad with joy. I begun digging in the dirt and throwing it up in the air, screaming at Musa to come join me, that I had something to show him too. He came lolling around the car, got down on his knees with me and watched me work my hands. We were being drenched in red dirt, laughing all the way, until he put his hand on my knee. For a moment we went quiet, staring at each other whilst the last of the dirt rained down on us. He put his finger up to his mouth. My eyes quizzically opened and he just held his finger against his lips looking down at the ground. I listened for something, which could tell me what this was all about. I was looking up at the stars, but could hear nothing. Next I heard a car starting just next to us. There was some loud shouting that I was unable to make out but Musa seemed to be fully aware of and intent upon. I struggled up towards the window in slow

58

motion it seemed but Musa immediately and almost soberly pulled me right back down. I looked at him and grinned, but he was somber as he told me that "they are looking for you." I paused in my stupor for only a wink and then giggled softly. He did not budge from his serious manner.

"Why the fuck would they be looking for me?"

I shook my head at him as if he had mistaken me for somebody else.

"They've mistaken me for somebody else."

Musa responded without looking back at me.

"No, it's you who they're after alright."

I continued letting my head rock from side to side.

"No, no, no, no. That's not the way it is."

This time he did not entertain my negation, but still kept a hand on my shoulder to ensure that I stayed put. I wriggled a bit, but his grip was too tight to allow me to move. I leant over towards him as if to say something to him quietly and then kissed him on his cheek for some unknown reason to me. He did not flinch, but continued to listen for my inquisition. When most close and immediate sounds had died down his hand fell off my shoulder to the ground and lay there lazy and muscular in the beautiful red dirt. Musa turned around and leant his back against the car breathing a sigh of relief.

"They're gone."

My hash haze had slightly dissipated by now but Musa remained as much of a mystery, if not more, to me.

"Why and who would be looking for me?"

Musa quietly told me "Local men."

"Why would they be looking for me?"

"I think that they think that you've been involved in some illegal activities here."

The sincere shock on my face must have surprised Musa.

"What! You are joking with me?"

"Not joking with you in the least. That is what they were saying as they got in the car."

"Do you know who they were?"

"No, not sure. They were locals though."

"What, like police, or, or jobs?"

"Jobs?"

I corrected my question.

"Like just criminals or hooligans?"

"Yeah, criminals I suspect. They sounded like that I guess. Like small-time criminals."

I was staring into the sand.

"How the hell would they get that impression of me? I'm just here on my honeymoon, not hurting a fly. Even my lovemaking now legal."

I searched his face for a smile, but none was forthcoming.

"It's serious you know."

"But what can I do about it?"

He looked at me.

"You ought to go to the police to report the incident."

"What incident? I heard nothing, saw nothing, nothing happened to me, even though you are suggesting this absurd story. I mean, what the hell would I say to them! You'll probably vanish into thin air soon, and then I'd be left ranting to the cops about you and the incident with them laughing their guts out at me. Very funny."

Musa remained serious. Then he got up and stretched his hand out for me to use to get up. I chose not to take it and got up by wriggling myself up along the side of the car. I brushed the dirt off me as best as I could, and Musa involved himself in the same cleansing ritual. Then Nada was next to us. She'd appeared as out of thin air. Perhaps she was a ghost or an apparition after all.

"Where did you guys go? We've been looking for you everywhere."

She mistrustfully looked at our red dirt marks that still spoiled part of our appearances.

"Ah, we were just having a chat and a smoke."

60

Musa all of a sudden seemed carefree and amused again. Nada looked at me, smiled. "Ciara was getting worried about you."
"Oh, I see. I must get back to her then."
I bowed to Nada and mocked her apparition with an insincere smile.
"To my lady's side prompt."
I galloped a few steps and then reverted into a slow amble in the direction of the restaurant. Nada and Musa could follow if they must. I did not turn around to check. As I walked into the restaurant Ciara stood up and did really look a bit concerned but as she clocked my unhurried steps she sat back down again.
"Sorry I got a bit distracted by Musa's company, and a wild adventure right out of thriller, which I will tell you all about later my sweetness."
Our fellow tablemates took the outlandish behaviour of mine in their stride. I suppose that Will and Flavia expected nothing but strangeness from me by now anyhow. I sat down and ordered a fresh beer. Ciara leaned into me and whispered:
"Where did you go?"
I whispered back at her:
"Ended up having a smoke with Musa. Interesting guy, but I am not sure what he and Nada might be up to."
She looked at me:
"Up to?"
"I'll tell you later."
I stopped short as the waiter returned with my beer and leaned in to put it on the table next to me. Simultaneously Nada and Musa came walking back in. They looked a bit flustered with each other but were smiling all the way. God how peculiar this was. Will and Flavia likewise feigned reality in our world of weird calling out to Nada to hurry to their rescue with another bottle of wine. Nada nodded towards the waiter who produced up a bottle from what seemed like thin air. We all settled at the table again. Musa looked over at me still grave in his manner, but soon let go of this demeanor joining in the merry making.

After dinner the whole lot of them wanted to go dancing and I tagged along because what else could I do? I could not leave my wife in the clutch of a bunch of Patricia Highsmith characters. The rest of the evening flitted by without anything else to really mention. Ciara kept to my side and was not inappropriate in any way with Will or anyone else for that matter. I was certain that I had made the whole thing up the other night. I felt like a fool and tried to make it all up by being as amicable and carefree as I possibly could. Now, if I had misjudged the situation, like that with Will and Flavia, surely there must be some logical reason to the appearance of Nada and Musa. I assumed that the thing with Musa earlier on in the eve had been a hash-imposed reality, which evaporated as the drug left our heads. I said nothing more about it to Musa, and he said nothing to me. It was as if nothing had happened. As if all was right with the world.

The light filtered through the curtains and arrived at my bed gently buffeting me, nudging me towards wakefulness. I smiled at myself as a vapor of last night's dancing rose in my mind. I turned over towards Ciara, snuck an arm around her warm waist and pulled her close; my hand nestled between her breasts, whilst moving towards her; distant planets moving through the conjugal space of sheets and pillows. Ciara followed my lead without waking. I laid there looking at and over the back of her neck, an angle very particular, very much stuck in this moment for some reason, even though the perspective hardly was new. I guess it was the air, light and time that made it so special. It perhaps also was the fact that the last few days had been very insecure, and now it seemed that life had come together again. There was nothing that I needed to fear. There was nothing that could rock this simple straightforward understanding world of mine. Sure things never were absolutely perfect. Naturally they would alter or veer off in a negative direction at some point, but not now. Now was good. The curtains fluttered in the warm morning breeze, the sun were pleasantly hot, my skin at one with the cool sheets and the soft female body pressed up against me. Ciara began her phases of waking, stiffened, groaned, relaxed and pushed herself into my body with soft little circular movements. My body responded with pride and my hand slipped over her breasts, fingers circling her nipples, pinching them for her to increase her pushing against me. Her hand slid behind her and she touched my hardening cock, guiding me. I maneuvered myself into her very slowly. Afterwards we lay looking at each other in silence for quite sometime, not saying a word, before Ciara moved away and showered. The sound of the shower was a comfort to me, I could almost taste the sweet water on my tongue, but I waited for her to finish before I went in there myself. She kissed me, a tongue flickering between her wine-roughened lips, before I stepped into the falling water.

On the streets we made our way through the maddening crowds without getting too stressed out. A lazy laissez-faire thickness clucked inside of our heads, limbs and hearts letting us remain staid. We'd decided to take a trip up the mountains to visit a village that laid claims to extraordinary beauty. We found the bus and managed to get a couple of seats next to each other. Ciara rested her head on my arm whilst the landscape swept by. I could not close my eyes, as was usual with these sorts of journeys for me, in fear of missing views. For me each adventure seemed so unique that a second of shuteye would mean a monumental loss, which I never would be able to recoup, never. Hence my eyes wide recorded the shifting nature, the passing people and animals obsessively. I remembered as a young boy being caught up in an existential moment, which still colors my life in many, many ways. At a particularly magical point I ventured to keep my feelings and awareness forever, store them somewhere inside of me. The irony now being that I do not actually remember the event as such only my absolute belief in that I would be able to keep it somehow, forever. I think that already then I did suffer from Alzheimer's type moments, in that I tried to make this experiment on numerous occasions, yet each time pointed back to a moment that already was lost to me. I simply could not regain or retain anything of my life, it was slipping away underneath me and all I could do was to keep slipping with it. Yet at the same time I was a firm believer in that all that happens to me, to one, is layering and saturating one's life to an impossible point, like the endless universe. So that memories of forgotten events, emotions, sights etcetera can, and do, come back constantly helping form the now without our awareness of it, even the way that we are able to take it in. I observed a goat in a tree and shook Ciara a little to steer her eyes to the animal. She laughed, looked at me, and turned back to the goat gymnastics for another briefly allowed second of our lives. I sunk back into my seat. When I had been only young I had also tested the possibility of a belief in what was called God. I, as I was preparing for bed, decided to give God a chance to prove it's reality by offering a very real dare for it. I thought, because obviously if God was a god then it would evidently; or so it seemed claimed at least, be able to hear what I was thinking. So I thought: prove yourself to me. I will hold out my hands, close my eyes, and would like for you to put a cake into them. If you do so you will have my soul and devotion forever. A trembling moment in the dark I saw nothing, but waited holding my breath for a weight of something to reach my hands. I prayed for it. I wanted it. However, my eyes opened, my hands still empty with air, I had to reconcile myself with that life was more lonely and complex than I would have liked. My soul would have to wander alone through life and the grave to a beyond, which perhaps never was. Tears formed in my eye as I recalled this instant of horror. I had never felt so alone. Even in my middle age I found this thought profound and I had not come that much further from it, other than that now I thought that it did not matter whether god was real or not, it could be useful and comforting anyway, belief that is. It could still serve its purpose if one just let it. However, I never spoke of this with anyone of course. It would make me seem like a softheaded fool, and life nowadays was callous towards those that emitted a little faintness. Hard cold facts, results and tangibility were the orders of the day. Logic had won out, or what masqueraded as logic at least. I laughed a little to myself but Ciara did not stir. The bus scrambled up another hill and all of a sudden the view rested on the village occupied in a dip of the earth. So far it looked impressive but the colors were not coming through just yet. However, as we lumbered in at excessive speed; children and adults flinging themselves out of the way of the noisy whale on wheels, gradually the turquoise, whites and blues arrived. We were well stirred, and still vibrating from each bump in the road up the mountains as we stepped off the bus. The ground felt comforting in its stability. Hawkers of goods gathered around, pressing up against us, as we moved down towards a place to sit down for a cold drink. Then in the shade with the drink we regained energies and enthusiasm. We got up and began wandering the village. As we were ambling through the slightly foggy appearance of the place, due to the coloring and heat I suspect, it made us dream and loose focus. It was like a meditation of sorts. We were lost in ourselves, hardly aware of each other. We lunched contently and as the day declined minded the time that we would need to get back to the bus. We did not speak much. It felt unimportant to word anything.

It was quite late as we walked back into the hotel. We planned a quick bite to eat in the bar and then off to bed. There were a few people in the bar but none whom we knew, which was a relief. However, as we did install ourselves at a table near the bar, who should come walking in, but Flavia; her buxom being lit up at the sight of us and made her way towards us positively shining with joy. My stomach sunk. I could do without her tonight, and the rest of the vampires who surely would get dragged up by the swell that Flavia brought on. We should have ordered room service as I suggested to Ciara, but she had been so absolutely certain of that the others would not be up at this time that there was no reason for me not to acquiesce to her suggestion. It seemed a bit simpler to eat at a table rather than in bed. How stupid of us. Ciara did play down her disappointment though. It was barely noticeable. She greeted Flavia graciously and bid her to take a seat with us. It turned out that Will was off playing poker somewhere and she had not wanted to go along. Hence here she was all on her lonesome eager for company and entertainment. Ciara told her all about our day trip and Flavia feigned interest just for us to remain I think. I hoped that after our second drink Ciara would come up with some good excuse so that we could retreat, but a third drink was ordered and now I seriously started to worry that Will would return and a long night of inane conversations would ensue. I suggested to Ciara that perhaps we should make an excuse and leave; when Flavia had gone to the bathroom for a moment, but with the flow of alcohol in her veins Ciara had come to life again. She claimed that it would be mean of us to leave Flavia on her own like that.

"She's a grown person, who surely could use one night of early sleep just like we could"

I gently put it to Ciara, but she would not have any of it. By now she was ready for more light entertainment, and which two fools better suited for that pursuit than Will and Flavia. I begun to lose my temper a bit, I sat back in chair glowering at Flavia hoping that she would read the cue and go. Naturally this did not happen. She had no intention of letting "a party-pooper" like me take away from whatever wicked plan was hatching in that Moor head of hers. I would have gone to bed, leaving Ciara there on her own with Flavia if it had not nagged at me that imminently Will would make his re-entrance, and that I needed to be there to keep an eye on his intentions towards my wife. I rested my head in my hands with the realization of that I know was in for an excruciating eve which might not end without some pain. After quite some time of mental self-flagellation I thought fuck it and sat up in my chair. I attempted to join in Ciara and Flavia's conversation, tossing in a witty comment here and there, which seemed to be a move in the right direction according to the smiles that this elicited from the women. Even Flavia every now and again sent me those types of looks that, to me engendered little rushes of spiders all over my back, but which I think she meant to be looks of a sexual nature, or at least something to that effect, and maybe every now and again they did complete their purpose, in a creepy crawly sort of a way. I'm sure it sent Will wild. I was smiling to myself as I got up to chase down another round of drinks.

"A penny for your thoughts."

Musa had just materialized in front of me. I stopped to look into his smooth eyes, almost creamy, from which black lashes formed a fan or fence trying to contain his being. Warmth was spilling over. We were close enough to kiss. My ears were shells in which the world collided, muted and too dense. I got a bit groggy, but recovered by shaking my head and managed to keep my smile going.

"Hi there. Nice to see you again. I assume you guys got home ok the other night?"

Slowly the night began to return to me. In fact seeing Musa now threw me back into the pit in which we had been dancing, sweaty, close and hot. I swear he had been coming on to me, and that all I had done was to laugh at him, yet allowed for him to continue dance that close, feeling his hard-on against my thighs, against my butt. God, I do wonder if Ciara clocked it? No she must not have given that she had said nothing, not a thing. Come to think of it she had in fact not even mentioned Musa at all, which was a bit strange considering she was the self-elected spy of our honeymoon. She kept a close eye on all details that we later could go over and ponder upon. Why Flavia had mentioned her children only when Will did not hear. Why Will claimed to be living in a city yet seemed much more of a country type of fellow. Why Nada had a long scar that stretched across her back, which she was trying to cover up with make-up that must be terribly awkward to apply. Perhaps Musa did apply it for her? All this Ciara had suggested but I had only laughed at her, saying that she was crazy, that she was spying in vain. What you saw was what you got. That was that. She had got a bit thick with me, but it did not last long. She told me that I had no imagination. But I did. Here Musa was and he kept flooding back into my head along with the night that had passed by fairly unremarkably just recently. It was a lot more complex than I had given it credit for. My intentions of keeping things clean and simple, of not jumping to conclusions or ideas, of not getting embroiled in the mystery, were evaporating. Perhaps it was the alcohol, I thought, and tried to slip out of the space in my head where life became unmanageable, entangled and confusing. Musa raised a corner of his mouth at me, bent over closer, and whispered

"I would rather have gone home with you."

Yes, I was right. He had been coming on to me, and here he was, doing it again.

"Sorry." I pretended that I had missed his come on and called out to Ciara: "Look who's here!"

She let out a little cry, got out of her chair and arranged for a chair for Musa whilst enquiring where Nada was at. Musa kept looking intently at me as he answered Ciara "She's coming, she had to have a shower, and you know how you women are with showers. You take all day."

After finishing his answer to Ciara he turned away from me and settled into the chair that Ciara had secured for him. He looked at her with appreciation and friendliness.

"The drinks" I spoke to myself, and returned to the task I had

68

meant to complete when Musa had appeared. After a couple of steps I realized I was not sure what he would want and turned around to return to the table. He was staring right at me whilst the women nattered on with each other.

"Rum and coke" he mouthed at me. I winked at him, immediately realizing that this had been the wrong gesture to offer a man like him. I hit my forehead with the palm of my hand as I made my way to the bar. The bartender had been watching me and asked if all was ok, bemusement riddling his face.

"Yeah, just forgot something. You know how it is."

He seemed to understand and went about fetching the drinks. I avoided turning around to face the table, instead I was staring at the bar not noticing the sticky rings left on the glass surface, not even noticing my own reflection that dimly stared back at me, another self dreaming me here in this perplex situation. I was running away in my head towards some normality, some reality where things usually were just what they seemed. Indeed in some way I was looking for my own obscured image, the one that grimly remained hidden from view by panic. In some ways I was very flattered by the behavior of Musa. Yes, it did make the evening much more interesting. I did not mind staying now, which was something in itself I guess. All of the sudden I was ready for something more than just going to sleep. My enthusiasm surprised me. What was it about Musa that changed everything now? Well, he was an interesting character. As far as I could remember of the evening before he was a great fan of rugby, he even claimed to support a local team, which was very odd but amusing. He knew the names of the players and all. He had spent some time in the UK and hence his interest. He had spoken of entropy as well, and the fact that he thought that life and death were intermingled to such an extent that it would be unfair to celebrate life as much as we do and not do the same for death. In fact, he had said, there was perhaps little difference between the two. We might be getting a

69

lot more than we currently are bargaining for once we kick the bucket. His words had had a profound effect on me, although I had not allowed myself to think about it until now. He was interesting, that must be it. None of the others interested me like him, in fact it was the exact opposite I could not wait to get out of their company. Nevertheless, and this was the big obstacle in the way of my allowing myself to enjoy this moment, and Musa, he was after all the partner, or something of that ilk, of Nada, who herself was utterly detestable. I mean what was she? She was not real. For all I knew, Musa might be in on the same insane plan to drive me round the bend. Why in the world would anyone pretend to know someone that they did not know? Maybe when one was younger, as a dare, this might become something that could be 'fun' momentarily. But, as an adult, to go to the lengths that they already had gone, was no longer 'fun', it was just bloody freaky. I mean what kind of psychopaths were they? I caught a glimpse of my absurd stare in the bar and cocked my head. The bartender was standing right in front of me waiting patiently for me to pay. I excused myself and fumbled for my money. As I turned with the tray carefully balanced in both of my hands I found Musa still looking at me, as if he had been trying to figure out what I had been thinking whilst in wait. He was serious but I seemed to catch a hint of concern as well on that handsome face of his. What made him so handsome? He was not so in a classical sense. He had big nose and a certain awkwardness but this mingling with his confidence ended up being peculiarly attractive. It was thoughtful somehow. He seemed carefree in the way that he was put together, yet every word, piece of clothing, and look was probably calculated. Calculated carefree, like an actor. Perhaps that is what this life was, a real replica of Fowles' *Magician*? This amused me. As I got to the table Musa got up to help me by taking the tray out of my hands. He divvied up the drinks and almost as soon as he got a hold of his drink he swallowed it in one big gulp. He got up, returned to the bar for another. Was he nervous? I minded my drink until I found that he had been missing for longer than seemed usual. I looked towards the bar and found him there, conversing with Nada. She was dressed in a dark blue summer dress with white patterns, which very much became her, a light scarf in green draped her neck. The two of them seemed to be having a little bit of an argument. Maybe Musa was trying to convince her of that they should come clean? As they noticed me watching them they became a little less animated and turned their backs, but Musa kept sneaking a peak every now and again, as if he felt he needed to defend me by staying aware of that I was there, that I was real, that I was watching. Ciara spotted Nada and called out for her waving. Nada seemed a little frazzled by the attention, the argument still not completely cleared up, but still she managed to simulate genuine contentment in recognizing her newly found friends in the bar. What a surprise! It was our hotel bar after all.

"My dear friends"

Nada exclaimed as she came up to the table with Musa right behind her, a hand on her back. Now I was certain of that she was an actor. Nobody got that dramatic unless it was part of one's daily makeup, or an assignment. It did not really matter however, as it was kind of interesting somehow. This was the point of view I now decided on. It was like some acquaintances you keep simply because they amuse you rather than that you believe everything they say. One such person in my life, for example, was a fellow called Christian. He usually made up the most fanciful stories, believing that I believed in them without a doubt. With a mischievous smile he would embellish the stories to an absurd point and I would smile and ask questions, letting him be where he was. It obviously made him feel good about himself. Just like that it was with Nada, or was the manner in which I decided to deal with her anyway. Musa was not really in the same category in that he did not seem to actually make that much up, but rather just went along with the lies without

71

correcting them, and without referring to them. Nada sunk into the girl chatter without even saying hello to me. Musa tried to take away from her rudeness by nudging at my interest in rugby. He pushed some statement towards me and I reluctantly took the bait. Nada really got my goat. I slowly relaxed into Musa's friendly banter, and then my other least favorite person of our honeymoon showed. Tensions rode high again. Will stood there with his hands in his pockets gyrating his hips as he laid into the women with something akin to humor. The women giggled at him, welcomed him into their midst where he comfortably descended garlanded with their undivided attention. The only one that did not seem to unthinkingly take him in was Nada. She could not be all bad so.

"What do you think of that mad Austrian guy who kept his daughter in the basement for so many years? What a nutter!"

Musa was drawing me back into a conversation as soon as he sensed my irritation.

"Yeah it is strange how people can be so bloody weird. But then again there seems to be a lot of them around, don't you think. Every damn day we hear something new in the papers about incest, rape, child abuse and so on."

Musa nodded his head at me.

"It sure seems that we can't trust anyone."

What was he doing? Was he trying to warn me? I watched him closely, quizzically. He squirmed a bit in his seat, perhaps realizing that he had got out on thin ice. Ciara saved him.

"Honey, do you think that you could get my cardigan from our room, it's getting a bit chilly."

I thought it a nice break to get out from the present company, recompose myself, and think of a plan of some sort so I hurried to Ciara's request.

"I'll be back in a moment."

Musa looked relieved. Now he would have some time to reconsider his angle, breathe a little and perhaps have a quick word with boss Nada about the next move. Nada watched me move away from the table.

I got into the elevator and inspected my image as the metal cage ascended. I looked a bit fraught. I ran my hand through my hair, grinned at myself, and straightened up hoping that the impression that I left the others with was one of strength and self-confidence. Somehow it seemed that this was not the case right now. I felt a bit under the weather, not from an impending illness, but rather from the unawareness of intentions of others. Usually this would not bother me at all, but the circumstances were far from usual. I kept telling myself that it was amusing nonetheless. The whole situation was a bit like a comedy of errors, and never would we, or I, be able to forget a honeymoon like this. I mean, who would. I laughed to myself, gathered Ciara's cardigan from her chair by the table and went to stand by the window. The ocean was black out there and in no way discernible, through the glass, from the sky. I tried to catch some distinguishing feature of a promise of a horizon but no matter how hard I strained my eyes there was nothing there. I tensed as I heard the front door, which I had left unlocked move a little on its hinges. A sliver of hall light appeared on the windowpane that I was facing. I stood stock-still hoping that it was the wind that was softly nudging the door. However, the light that had gently sprung leaked larger and a human stain of dark was revealed in the mist of that illumination. My heart skipped in its skeletal pen, and started throwing itself relentlessly towards the cool white bones, causing scatters of crimson droplets rain into my empty pit of a stomach. I swear I could hear the vibrations in my frame; my eyes shook with each breath that rose to the surface of my being against my will. It was a blur. The dark human form entered the room without a word, gained in size as it drew closer to where I was. Time was frozen both in me and for me. A fly buzzed around and around above somewhere, constantly knocking into the lampshade. My skin was melting. I felt myself falling and if I had been conscious I guess I would have felt the arms of someone catching me, carrying me to the bed, and then softly leaving the room. However, I was not there.

When I woke I found myself on the bed still clutching Ciara's cardigan. My forehead was damp as I wiped my hand over it. I labored into a sitting position and let go of the cardigan as I did. I looked over at the bedside clock and noticed that only twenty minutes roughly had passed since I had entered the room. It felt more like a lifetime. My feet on the floor sobered me. I looked around for my shoes. They stood side by side at the window facing the same way, outwards, as I had, prior to fainting. I found this gesture slightly sinister. Why would he do that? And could I be certain of that it was a he? I mean I assumed that it had been either a complete stranger or, Will or Musa, but then again it would be very possible, I surmised, that it had been creepy Nada. After all she was the one with the strangest reasons for being here, in the middle of my life. Only she would be weird like that, as well as, only she would try to freak me out with the positioning of the shoes. Nevertheless, I had been more or less convinced of a male presence when I had stood there. I don't know why exactly. My attention was drawn to a fly that seemed to be doing its religious circuit over a forgotten morning coffee cup. Round and round he scrambled, perhaps picking up sugar crystals as he bounced off surfaces. He hypnotized me. My eyes followed him in his orbit until he started to become fuzzy. He became fuzzier and fuzzier. My hands searched for my face to knead my tired eyes. It must be the drinks, I thought to myself, or just pure tiredness. I blinked and blinked but my surroundings stayed fuzzy. Then a curtain fell, and what had been unclear became an unswerving darkness. Not a speck of light reached me. I felt as if I had disappeared. However, I could hear the fly that seemed to have been the cause of all this now continuing it's circles somewhere around my head. The room grew louder and louder as my

74

darkness continued to make itself at home inside of me. It enveloped all my organs. It returned everything to a single mass: me and my environment, my neighbors, things and insects. I did not move for a while, waiting for normality to return, waiting for what I perceived to be a panic attack to be over. I was trying to think of positive and pleasant things, tried to ignore the dark. But out of it came a spiraling madness. At first it was a hot splinter in my toes, but quite quickly, a tsunami gathered in the very spot where the splinter had begun. It grew and grew and rushed up through my legs, through my stomach and chest, and at almost the same moment that it had become, it was in my mouth. I threw up violently. It was a strange feeling throwing up without actually seeing the outcome. I knew it was there in front of me somewhere though. There was probably a breath of steam above it, hanging there over the contents of my gullet. I tried to avoid going forward. I felt another wave come hurrying up my body's murky corridors. This time it was sound. I cried out in a manner that absolutely frightened me. It was a sound I never ever thought possible to utter, unless perhaps you were an animal in the abattoir. When the cry ended I found that my body had collapsed backwards on the bed. At least I assumed that it was the bed, it was soft, it stood where the bed had stood in my previous life where there had been light as well as shadows. Then sleep came over me, took me, and completed the dark.

Ciara's voice gently spoke to me. A hand, very likely hers, was stroking my arm.
"My love, wake up. Try to wake up now."
She kept repeating the words, kept stroking my arm. I heard no one else in the room, but had a feeling that there was someone there anyhow. I stirred but as I came too properly I decided against opening my eyes just yet. It was too early for that. It could all have been a nightmare, but I did not want to perpetuate it by facing reality too rapidly.

"How are you? What happened to you? Open your eyes please. I want to see that you are ok."

It was funny that, I thought, as if she would be able to see me better with my eyes opened, as if she would understand me better with my eyes opened. In a personal morbid joke I hummed *Georgia on my mind* in my head and smiled.

"Oh babe, you are smiling. What happened to you? Please do open your eyes, will you?"

I smiled and thought it all a stupid nightmare. My eyelids slid over my eyeballs. I could feel them. No light, no contours appeared though. I was shuffling my eyelids repeatedly up and down over the sockets but nothing. Nothing. Then I burst into tears. Whilst I was sobbing I heard Ciara somewhere in the background, she was also crying whilst she tried to keep communicating with me.

"What is happening? What's happened to your eyes? Can you see anything? Babe, please answer me."

Her words were delivered staccato, a cry, a word, a cry, a word, until sentences were built. The tears ebbed after a while. Ciara was now lying on top of my chest breathing with me.

"I can't see anything."

She stiffened.

"I can't see a thing."

Ciara pushed herself off my chest.

"What are you saying?"

Her unbelief made her voice shiver.

"'I think I've gone blind."

She rushed up.

"I'm calling a doctor."

I did not protest. Of course, we should call a doctor. That might clear things up. But as I heard her on the phone I started to falter. What the hell would a doctor do? Make my eyesight come back from that black hole where it had disappeared into? Not really possible now was it? I felt the warmth of the tears build up and brim my sockets, and then roll making cold tracks on my cheeks and neck. Ciara was chatting away to the concierge explaining that we would need a doctor immediately. She hung up and assured me that somebody was on their way, somebody that could give us some answers. Ciara started to clean up the room. I could hear her on her knees scrubbing at what must have been the vomit. Where she had got cleaning supplies from I had no idea. After maybe an hour of listening to Ciara cleaning, babbling and helping me shower and change my clothes, there was a knock on the door. Ciara's light little footsteps softly made their way across the floor. I imagined that I saw the outlines of heated footprints that momentarily, fuzzily, wavered on the cool tiles. I went into a fit of shivers and returned to a horizontal position on the bed. Then hands were all over me. I was sat up. Questions in broken English fell over me. By the sound of his voice he would have been around fifty or sixty I thought. The fact that one had to surmise a whole lot of things when blind suddenly interested me and I began to pay attention instead of panic. I returned into my darkened body and world a bit more alert.

"What happen right before you realizing you no longer see?"

Now I needed to be on my toes for real. I did not want to divulge anything that would suggest that I was paranoid as well.

"I was just sitting here looking at a fly that was walking across the bedside table. My vision just gradually faded. I don't know anything else. Nothing else happened."

The doctor asked me to open my eyes, and only then did I realize that I had been sitting with my eyes tightly clenched, my face probably stuck in a horrible grimace. It took time to relax myself sufficiently to let my eyelids rise, but I did it. I felt the doctor fingers around my sockets and heard the click of a light; he must have been shining a torch into my eyes but not even a dim glint passed on into me. My darkness was absolute, it consumed all definition. The doctor fired more questions at me: whether or not I had felt any indications of my eyesight

77

worsening prior to the accident (what accident!?), whether I had any allergies that might have brought this on, whether I had experienced a severe trauma recently, etc? I said as little as possible but obviously thought of everything, checking with myself whether or not he might be on to something. I guessed that the scare that I had had with the person in the doorway could have been seen as a real fright, but never could I imagine that it would have made me blind. Never. Circumstances had been very strange lately, people were strange, but surely that could not bring a person to a point like this? Perhaps, I thought to myself, I was simply going mad. I had acted very madly lately, and it all, even the strangeness of others, seemed to be more in my head than elsewhere. Maybe I was going paranoid? Maybe I had a brain tumor that was playing my head? I asked the doctor whether or not a brain tumor could cause blindness. He hemmed and hawed for a bit, but admitted reluctantly that of course that could happen. However, he said, there was no other evidence of this at this point. In general, I was in good shape, but perhaps when I got back home I should go and get proper tests done. He suggested that we would go home immediately and that I should try to get the tests done as soon as possible.

After he had left Ciara and I sat on the bed in silence for a good half hour. She was holding my hand in hers stroking it absentmindedly. Then, she got up and said that she would go down to organize a change of our tickets. I asked her what time it was and she told me nine.
"Nine what?"
Frustration rose and spread through my body.
"Sorry. Nine in the morning."
I had had no idea. Time seemed to have gone with my sight. I felt absolutely no difference between hours, night and day.
"Don't go."
She stopped in her tracks.

"Don't go," I implored her.

She came back to the bed and sat down again.

"What are you saying? We need to get back home as soon as possible. You heard the doctor. Even if your own diagnosis is a bit fanciful, this is serious."

"Yeah, I do understand, but I think that we should give it a little time. I think that maybe it is just a bit of scare."

"A bit of a scare! Are you mad? You're fucking blind babe."

Ciara was getting a bit hysterical. This suggested to me that she might not be part of this madness that seemed to surround me. She must be an innocent bit player I thought to myself. I then explained to her what had happened just before I lost my sight. At the end of the story I suggested to her that it might have been that scare that had brought on the blindness and perhaps it would go as soon as I relaxed properly. Perhaps I would only need a few days of doing nothing but sit in the sun, swim, eat and sleep. Ciara reluctantly tried to come around to the way I was thinking. I think that the thought of just simply relaxing would do her good as well, so maybe there was a way of justifying it.

"However, I do not want any of the others around over the next few days. I feel that they'd only aggravate me."

Ciara understood and eventually agreed that we would give it a few days, and that we would avoid the others to ensure that I got the rest that I needed. The whole thing was too strange anyway. Possibly I was right. We should try to wait and, see.

That day we spent for the main part in the hotel room, getting room service and sitting on the balcony. Ciara was at my beckon call, leading me slowly from space to space in our quarters, paying me undivided attention. I loved it. It was just the two of us finally. I milked the circumstances a bit, but then again I was incapacitated by my darkness something horrid. I thought to myself that if this would continue it would be a right struggle to gain independence. Although I loved the

79

dependence momentarily, this was solely due to the circumstances and recent events rather than it being part of my makeup. It would drive me absolutely around the bend if this were eternal. I tried not to think of this though. I kept trying to really really open my eyes. Really really stop this hiding of my head in the Moroccan honeymoon sand, but it did not work. The blackness remained, even if it started to shift within itself. It was shades of darkness now, but it had nothing to do with light in anyway. It was more like a taste of the dark I guess, some parts or sequences tasted or sounded less dense than others. And then inside of my head I was still able to visualize things and this became my new obsession. I would try to recall as much as possible of my sight-full existence, turn the scenes over and over, distinguishing colors and their variations deliciously, tasting each layer of a melting luminous ice-cream. It seemed that I had never actually seen the world properly, in its totality, until I went blind.

Days went by. Ciara and I continued our seclusion. She hardly ever left the room, except for the occasional swim in the pool, or a gathering of items that we could not get from room service. Otherwise, she spent the day ferrying me across the apartment, having siestas, and lazing in the sun on the balcony. One day she got me a pair of really dark sunglasses, so that people could not actually see my eyes and so would not get suspicious of my sight, or lack thereof, just incase I wanted to venture out. However, I was not keen on the idea and reminded her of that most likely my sight soon would return and then we could go out to her heart's content. Here and there she would fall back on the idea that we should really go home as this strange ailment had gone on far too long, but soon upon that idea she instead set about thinking of ways that would ease my gloomy unease. It was strange, and I said so to Ciara, that none of our gang had come by to enquire about me, or of our disappearance. She thought that the reason for this was the fear of illness, the contagiousness of whatever I had attracted. She was probably right. They were a useless bunch anyway; one would not expect any grand empathy from that lot. I knew that. It seemed Ciara had not run into them outside either, and this I found a little more confounding in that she was much more part of their circle than I had ever become. Perhaps, she said, they had gone home. After all we had no idea when their departures were due. Ah, but Musa and Nada lived here I pointed out. Ciara made some kind of noise, which suggested that she had no idea, and why should she have had.

Eventually even I got bored of sitting in. Ciara suggested that we would go to the doctor's office to get an idea of if we were idiots or not. I firmly refused her inspiration. The doctor would probably not even see us as we had gone against his prescription. Ciara then suggested just going down to the pool to start with, and this to me was a bit more feasible so I agreed. It was strange leaving my world, which by this stage had become so familiar that I had no problem with moving about in it on my own without mishaps, without bruises (the colors of which I saw in an almost fragrant manner, and which I indulged myself in so intensely and joyfully that I sometime would knock against something quite hard just to be able to perform this strange new ritual), whilst now I was forced to fall back on Ciara's prompts, pushes and pulls again. At points I could feel the globules of warm water that would bubble up out of my eyes in frustration, but I hid them as best as I could from Ciara. The elevator in particular felt all of a sudden claustrophobic, this even though it had less of reason to feel like this now that I could not actually see the walls, I thought. We got down to the pool and I ended up feeling so uncomfortable by what I imagined being the icy chills of people's pitying stares, but also strange perceptions of that I heard Ciara talking to strangers in hushed tones; which she promptly negated with a laugh, that I only lasted half an hour. What I did not tell

81

Ciara was that I also thought myself to have heard, I could have sworn it, kissing noises which I believed have come from her as well, but it all seemed so fantastic to me that I had to bury it. Soon we desperately trotted back up to the safety of the room. I slept for hours from sheer exhaustion.

Nevertheless, the next day we tried again, and this time I lasted a good while longer. Ciara said that she was proud of my progress, and I was too. The following day again I was out for almost the whole day although confined to the space around the pool. I even went for a long swim, which was so delicious that I hardly wanted to get out. Ciara told me that I was getting bleached and all wrinkly, like our wedding cake, and I had to take her word for it and reluctantly ascended, dripping like an Orpheus, unable to bring my love of sight, back into the living world. We had dinner out as well, but did not stray too far from the hotel.

The next day the same pattern was repeated and I had a feeling that I could get used to this. It was not that I would like to remain blind, but as I had never believed that this would be the case, the panic of it always seemed possible to deal with. Towards evening my skin sensed the moon, leisurely sipping up whatever there was of the light. We had just got over to the restaurant as I saw a flicker across my retina. I held my breath, staring hard into what I thought must be the back of my head. The flatness of blindness teased me, I concluded, as no other flickers crossed my path. It had been a mirage. I sucked upon a giggle and felt Ciara's hand on my arm.
"What are you thinking of hon?"
I did not mention my recent blip, but pretended that I still enjoyed a joke that we had shared earlier in the day. Ciara read the menu for me and we were soon installed with aperitifs and munchies in wait for the main meal. I had relaxed into my chair and we sat quietly. Suddenly another red-hot flicker tore

through my perceived facade. I sat up quickly and Ciara obviously reacted concerned.

"Oh just a shooting pain in my back, must have been slouching at a weird angle."

I did not want Ciara to get ideas of false hope. Nothing had really happened yet. That was that. Nothing else happened that evening other than that the food got served, eaten and digested in a relaxed atmosphere. By the end of our night I no longer thought of the flashes, but instead was planning another day of being led around. We returned to the hotel room, impatient to tend to our horniness. It was incredible how enhanced I felt that the sex was now that I was unable to see. I told Ciara this and she confessed to me that for her too it was a sort of freedom and a definite turn on that I was unable to see. I asked her what she was getting up to that I could not see, and she laughed whilst pulling at my zipper. Soon all superfluous thoughts were erased.

I woke up with my ears ringing, and the sides of my head sore, as if I had been given a good boxing. I heard the call to prayer, Ciara in the shower, and sat up in bed rolling my head on my shoulders thinking that I had slept wrong. My neck hurt me a bit as well, so it might have been a nerve or something. Unexpectedly, as I let my head dip back on my shoulders, I must have opened my eyes as a definite, if fog clad, picture of the ceiling appeared before me. I sat there with my head tilted back letting sight pour into me. I heard the shower turn off and groped for my sunglasses on the bedside table without letting go of the ceiling. I was afraid that the picture might go if I moved too much, but at the same time was prepared to hide my new ability from Ciara should she walk in. I was not sure why I was reacting like this, but assumed to protect her from a joy that might be very short-lived, as had been my earlier reaction. As I heard her footsteps on the bathroom floor I raised my glasses and slipped them into place. She walked in and I noticed that the blur that had begun gave way to release a dark form of her naked body to me. It was delicious, although reminiscent of the moments before I went blind in the first place. I tried to remember what I had acted like without sight, what I had done with my eyes behind the dark glasses, what I had walked like, what I had reached for on my way to the bathroom, how I had dressed awkwardly, and all that, to ensure that Ciara still would believe in my blindness. She laughed at me as I went into the shower with my dark glasses on and helped me pull them off. I closed my eyes as she did this, and she did not seem to take notice. I began to plan how I was going to conceal my sight until I was certain of that it was staying. We only had about four days left of our honeymoon before we would return to a very possibly dreary rainy life. I decided that I would 'come to' only on our last day so that the positives of my now pretend dark could be properly utilized, especially for Ciara's pleasures. It was also of interest to me to see what the world was doing when it thought that I was not looking.

Again we went down to the pool. Little by little the lucidity of every angle, shape, and line solidified. Depth and vibrancy of color tumbled on and completed themselves. The bodies of others that I, just the night before, had sensed only by warmth and cold now frizzled within their own limitations of skin. I found myself turning my head around a little too much, froze and looked sideways at Ciara who reclined in the sun-chair next to me. Luckily she was dozing. I must, I said to myself, really remember not to move my head around so much and then only move it to noise if I was to move it, or she and everybody else might cop my new reality. I laid back. I opened my eyes to a sound of shuffling that came closer. In the corner of my eye I saw the pool boy at Ciara's chair, she looked up and raised herself a little. He bent over and whispered something in her ear. I lay perfectly still. She looked over at me. "Do you want to go in the water for a while?"

Her voice nice and calm, not a mention of the recent information that she had received.

"No, I'm ok thanks. You go ahead if you want to."

I closed my eyes and heard her get up saying something about that I would fry if I did not get in the water soon, and that she'll be back to at least wet me. I laughed at her, opened my eyes again, and then got terribly suspicious of her as she walked off into the building rather than getting into the pool. About fifteen minutes went by. She had had only her towel tied around her hips as she'd left, and she had not brought the keys for our room with her. Her handbag was still sitting on the table. That was a bit stupid of her, I said to myself, as the only one to guard it was her blind husband. Then she came back out to the pool area, this time with her towel thrown over her shoulder. She might have gone to the toilet? She left her towel on a railing and lowered her body into the water. She submerged herself quickly and then came right out again. As she came up to me I closed my eyes pretending to be sleeping. She squeezed her hair over my stomach and although I was prepared it jolted me upright.

"What the hell!"

She burst out laughing and sat her whole cold wet body on my lap.

"Bet you want to get in the water now my roast chicken."

I tried to feign boyish anger turning to merriment but it was very stilted. She sensed that I was upset somehow, and drew the conclusion that perhaps she had woken me out of a deep sleep. I agreed with her that that was probably it, but the thoughts inside of my head were veering around each other, screeching at every turn. Before she settled in I asked her to help me to the pool. Whilst in the water I let myself feel every sinew and muscle in my body as I stretched out for a good half hour's spin. My thoughts calmed down with the cold, and I was able to regain some semblance of reality. Most likely she had wandered in out of the heat for a while, went to the toilet, chatted with the staff, looked at the events planned, and so forth. That made the most sense. As for the pool boy things were not as clear but if the whole time away were explainable then surely this boy's little whisper also would be. I blushed at my stupidity but the cool water effectively washed the flush off my face as quickly as it had appeared. When I was done I swam to the ladder and called her name. She rose quickly and came to help me up.

A well-deserved siesta after an arduous day's faffing about was rent by the telephone signaling to me through a stark gray contour-less landscape. I imagined the instrument pregnant with voice, a voice dangling at the end of wires, a voice, almost equal to a heart, ripped out of its container and sent barreling through fiber wires and satellite connections. Ciara climbed over me towards the signal's home. I came back into the world with her great breasts rubbing against my face. They had not changed. I mean at an age like hers any day can become the day that it all flails and falls. I stuck my tongue out to brush the left nipple lightly but she pulled away to listen seriously to what was being said. I could hear a male voice but could not decipher what was actually said. She answered in curtly, giving nothing away. She hung up.
"The concierge, wondering if we were to join tomorrow's excursion. They're off to the big smoke shopping."
I saw her allow her face to show the disappointment that she felt being stuck here with me, although her voice remained full of tones comforting me with her disinterest. How quickly she had adapted to the new circumstances. For sure, she would not be one of the dying breeds. I was quiet for a while but then encouraged her to take a day out. By now, I would be fine here on my own, and we only had a few days left. She should make the most it.
"Do you think?"
Her joyous reaction to the encouragement was real. She really

would love to see a bit more of the country before we went home.

"You could come babe. I mean, you don't have to be able to see to get a sense of the difference and excitement."

I laughed at her, and said that I rather stay here whether or not I could see, as I would simply like to lay back and relax.

"My idea of fun for now is not to have to lift a finger. God knows soon enough we'll be back at work, back in the mundane."

I saw Ciara gasp and then put her full brakes on her immediate reaction to what I had said. She closed her mouth that had prepared itself for a panicked speech. Most likely she was caught up in my blindness. She was whirling inside the sudden realization of the bottomlessness of it. With it, I would be unable to go back to my job. She looked positively shocked by what she had hid from herself until this moment. What would happen to us! I would have to come to with my seeing very soon, so as not to let her drag her pain around too long, but not yet, not just yet. I hugged her to me and said that she should definitely go, and that she was not to worry about me. I was a grown man who could do with a little time of my own. I was secretly thinking that I could get back into my book that had lain untouched for the last while. After a little more cajoling she returned the call to the reception and put herself down for the nine o'clock bus.

That night we took a longer stroll than usual hunting a particular fish restaurant that Ciara had read about. After many wrong turns, we took the right one, and were greeted by a very cheerful place indeed.

"I hope the food is as nice as the place looks." Ciara said.

Then she described the place to me and I followed her descriptions with my eyes verifying her perceptions. She had a good way with words. I wondered if my description of the place would have been the same as we got seated at a charming little secluded table overlooking the sea. I found myself turning towards the sea and so did Ciara. In a way I think that she was accustomed to me seeing and so forgot my disability as soon as she relaxed.

"How beautiful it is," she said.

I agreed with her and she turned to me and laughed.

"If I did not know better I swear you were just as able to see as I. Tell me, how does a beautiful place feel, without sight I mean. How can you tell it is beautiful?"

I closed my eyes to find the space where I needed to speak from. I saw nothing. I found no words. It was just dark inside of my head, now that sight had returned.

"I don't know," I finally admitted after a few false starts, hanging my head a bit.

Ciara looked like she was going to start crying. I felt awful and tried to distract by turning to the menu. How about this? I pointed at the menu at a particular point and turned the menu towards her on the table. She burst out laughing.

"God you are crazy."

I caught my mistake, and covered up by joining the laughter asking what it was that I had pointed out.

"Not bad" she agreed once she had looked.

"I'm a lucky man," I said as I sat up with a content grin.

Ciara reached out and took my hand. "I love you."

We ordered and enjoyed the evening fully. As we walked back Ciara was hanging on my arm uncertain of if we really were going in the right direction. It seemed so to me but at the same time I had to really control myself so as not to take the lead. She snuck into a shop to ask but came out with no new information. I ensured her of that she should not think too much. It felt right to me. She was emboldened by my encouragement and continued dragging me off in the wrong direction. Shoot. Ah well, I sighed in my head, and let her lead us astray. As I was waiting outside yet another shop a stranger approached me asking for a cigarette. I reached into Ciara's bag and pulled one out of her pack sure she would not mind. All of a sudden though she came running out of the shop screaming at the stranger and me.

"Get away, you thief!"

I twirled around seeing the stranger backing off in surprise and then turning on his heel running down the street whilst Ciara gave chase. I began screaming at her to stop, to come back, but she ran around the corner. I felt very frustrated. I started quickly walking in the direction of the corner that she had rounded.

"She is crazy", I said to myself.

Not only was the man not a thief, but also she had put him in such a strange situation that god only knew how he would react once he had come back to his senses. Women could really drive a man mad. As I got to the corner I saw Ciara in the distance standing talking to the man. They both seemed very calm now and the discussion almost jovial. She gave the man something and he shook her hand. I backed back around the corner unaware of my next move. I put my head around the wall and saw the two of them say their adieus, and pulled back quickly. I was leaning on the wall and decided to walk back to the spot where Ciara had left me. She came up around the corner, still looking a little incensed but confident. She called my name as she got closer and I lost my head. What the hell was she doing chasing strange men down deserted streets? What did she think she was going to be able to do? What did she think would happen to me if she disappeared like that? She tried to calm me with words and explanations but I was caught up in the game that I was playing. I was a blind man stranded in the middle of the street whilst my crazy wife ran after strange men like some female Rambo, and if anything was to happen to her there was absolutely zilch that I could do about it, or know about it. I could start kicking and hitting the air about me, but that was it, there was nothing else that I could do. Nothing! I was absolutely impotent. Eventually my words ran dry and I fell quiet and deflated whilst Ciara tried to give me a hug. I held her at arms length away from me.

"Sorry. Babe I am so so sorry. Let's go home. Please babe calm down. I won't do anything stupid like that again. Let's go home."

I finally relented and let her take my arm. We did not speak again until we found the hotel. I said that I wanted a drink in the bar before we went to bed, and she agreed without any hesitation. We had it quietly and then made our way up to the room. As we were turning in to sleep I asked her what had happened as she ran after the man.

"Oh he just ran off."

I tensed up a bit involuntarily.

"You did not get him?"

"Of course not, he was way too fast."

Ciara was up getting ready as I woke.

"Hey" she came up and kissed me.

"I'm leaving in fifteen minutes. Do you want a coffee before I go? Is there anything that you want me to do before I go, just to, like, prepare you?"

"No, no, I'll be fine. A coffee would be great though, and toast, and a grapefruit juice"

I said, as I sat up in bed. Ciara immediately got on the phone and placed the order. She seemed in a jovial mood as she packed the last things that she would need for the day and then sat down on the bedside looking at me seriously.

"You know I could still pull out, stay here with you, if you've changed your mind? I don't mind."

I thought about it for a split second, no, I needed a day of no drama.

"Of course not, you go on now."

As she reached for the door room service knocked. She brought the tray in and kissed me again. The door clicked close and I took off my glasses. God how tired I had got of wearing them. I heard the noise of the bus leaving in the distance, brought the tray out on the balcony and then went back into the room for my book. The morning sun was light and gentle on my eyes. I stretched out on the chair reading and ate my toast. Life was good. I woke out of my reading around midday realizing that there were quite a lot of things that I would like to see before Ciara came back and so set about preparing my exit from the hotel. It dawned on me just how tricky it would be as I stepped outside my door. The cleaning lady gave me a thorough look up and down, made blunt by my supposed blindness I was sure, but she did not stop to help me out thank god. However, I stopped for a little while. I had secured my sunglasses on my face and had made the plan that I was simply going to get into a taxi outside ask to be driven to the next town where I would step out on the beach, aim for the waves, sit down, in case the taxi driver was keeping tabs, and then wait till he had left. Thereafter I would shed my darkness and return to life. To go back I would do the same thing. Chances were, perhaps, quite substantial that I would run into someone that would know of my predicament, but I was up for the challenge. I had planned escape routes in that regards as well. I knew what to do. I was ready. Worse come to worse I would come clean with an excuse of that my sight was not fully back yet and that I did not want to inform my wife in fear of if my sight would revert into itself again. Yes, I was ready. My plans reviewed emboldened me and I continued into the elevator, out of the lobby, and into a taxi without too much hassle. I did get a few strange looks, but was gone before they could try to figure out what was going on. When I got to the beach the taxi driver hesitated a bit, but again I did not allow for him to become too detailed in his observations by hurrying the situation. Anyway it was very likely that this taxi driver would not be seen again, either by a blind or a seeing me. I sauntered out on the beach as my plan had it. I kept my sunglasses on just in case I would have to improvise something, in case I ran into someone. I felt strange, almost high, from the madness of my excursion. I walked for a good half hour and then sat down in the warm sand. I took off my shoes and jacket, leaned back on the crumpled pile staring at the sandy sunny break in time of freedom. After a while I got up brushed myself off and walked towards the town. I entered the souk to get out of the heat, and found myself coasting through the jumble. There were no awkward moments of getting caught on the wrong foot, in the wrong lane, dancing side to side with a stranger to make the difficult decision of whether one should veer left or right to get out of each other's path. As I perfectly operated the space I found a very intense looking fellow traveler, with an old fashion but expensive camera, who swayed a bit ahead of me. I could see his shoulders rise and fall, a man on the sea, and the camera likewise was being brought up and down with the swell. I let myself drift up alongside him and was caught up in his haunted look, concentration and aim. His dark hair fell in two waves, which he ritualistically pushed back behind his ears although it never really obeyed him. His pale face was carved into shaded darks where his restless eyes laid ready to pounce and the hollows of his high cheekbones squared to frame a hungry if narrow mouth of the palest pink. He made me feel something akin to want, and I was lured in against my better judgment. Skulking in the shadows that he recently had excavated I followed at a very close distance meaning not to lose him. As he would stop and sink to his knees to get the shot he wanted, I found myself trying to imagine the image as if developing it then and there by circling the space he moved through carefully and seriously. Of course it was only a matter of time before he realized that I was there, but instead of simply turning around to confront me, he started walking backwards including me in his frame even if only as a prop in the background. Eventually he trained the lens right at me clicked. As he lowered the camera my heart skipped a beat. How striking he was. I stopped in my tracks and returned the look that he was reserving for me alone.

"What are you doing?"

His words hissed at me even though he drew out each letter, sucking on the shape of them. Momentarily I was speechless; stunned by his being, but eventually I mustered the individuality of responding.

"What are you taking photos for? I mean, for yourself?"

He looked at me incredulously.

"What the fuck are you talking about man? Why the fuck are you asking me questions like that?"

He paused in his rant, straightened up and then, a little less defensive in his tone, said more matter of factly:

"Who the fuck are you?"

I looked down slightly embarrassed.

"I, uh, I did not mean to offend you. Honestly. Just was intrigued by what you were doing really. I'm just here on holiday."

There were still a fair amount of glare in his eyes but he seemed to have calmed down. He swallowed and stubbed his foot on purpose against a wooden box.

"Sorry. Guess I overreacted a bit. It's the heat."

He looked up and as his eyes met mine there was no anger left in them. Now he looked positively civil, if a bit wild.

I laughed and said, "No sorry it was my fault. I should not have been stalking you like that. I had no right to. Just got carried away with curiosity."

We stood quiet for a moment, locked in this space of mutual embarrassment.

"Sorry, can I buy you drink or something, to make up for my rudeness. Please."

I was salvaging the interruption and then hopefully would get a bit of time to get to know the man.

"Sure. That'd be good. Just to get out of the heat for a while."

We found our way to a bar and settled down with a nice cold beer. His name was Luca. He was an independent photographer that at the moment was working on a book on North Africa. He'd been in Morocco for over three months now and liked it a lot. He had been all over North Africa before, but it was a long time ago, when he was a teenager. At that point, he told me, he was hitchhiking across the whole continent. I was so intrigued by him that I must have looked star struck. His stories were plentiful, and they all had so much color that I felt my own life drain beige in comparison. Morocco was his starting point and from here on he would be traveling eastwards. He estimated that he would spend at least a few months in each place before moving on, to make sure that he got the right shots. Here and there in between he said that he would return home, to tend to life there. As our empty glasses gathered Luca's life rolled out in front of me. He had no partner, neither here nor at home, and said that his life style really was not conducive to regular relationships. What about me? This was the first question that Luca had thrown my way and it really put me off my guard. Me? I began hesitantly explaining that I was here on my honeymoon. This made Luca laugh. He asked me where my wife was and I explained that she had gone off on a trip for the day and that I had not wanted to join. He eyed me as if I had told him a stupid joke. I did no elaborate on my story, did not tell him of my blindness and all that. I mean there was no reason for Luca to know that. I did not know him. Our early afternoon ran into late, and I was shocked to see the clock behind the bar as I had gone up to order one final round. Shit, I really would have to leave now. If Ciara got home and I was off gallivanting she was sure to find me out. I exchanged numbers with Luca and thought that maybe one day we would meet up again, at home. It would be strange seeing him out of this context, but it intrigued me. I found my way out of the town, got onto the beach again, and then found the spot where I had started from. As I stood there looking for a taxi I suddenly spotted Nada on a corner across the way. She was animatedly discussing with someone that I now and then only could see the arm of. Her hands gesticulating wildly Nada seemed almost angry, but then again that was a bit of her trademark. A taxi pulled up to my side and I got in quickly hoping that Nada would not see me. However, she was way too concerned with her discussion to notice anything. As the taxi pulled up closer to her proximity I shrunk in my seat and tried to look in the other direction. When we had got a safe distance away I turned around to see whom it might be that she was arguing with. A fleeting split second tore at my sanity as the other person very much looked like Ciara. Soon the world was caught up in a flood of blockages, moving cars, mopeds, and people, all conspired to take my breath away as I desperately attempted to see through them. Why would Ciara be there? She should be on the trip far away from here, and not in this town arguing with Nada, who she did not even know. I demanded of the taxi driver to bring me to my hotel, but by the time he had fully understood, and we careered towards that spot, the sun seemed to have shifted a bit. The corner where Nada, and possibly Ciara had stood now lay bare and useless. I felt tears well up and confused the confused driver even more when I mentioned the hotel again. He shook his head, said something insulting probably, and then turned the vehicle around. As we drove off back home I rigorously scanned the streets and cars and taxis on tenterhooks for Ciara's face, eager not to see it, for that not to have been her, and set on her not seeing me, should I spot her. I did not see her.

I arrived at the hotel just in time. I secured my sunglasses, paid the driver and labouringly emerged from the carriage. I heard the bus pulling in as I entered the lift up to the room. Ten minutes later I was installed as if nothing had happened. The door opened and Ciara entered looking very excited. She cheerfully announced her arrival and immediately came up to kiss my forehead.

"I missed you."

I smiled at her. She took off my glasses and touched her lips to each of my eyelids.

"There. They'll be back in working order in no time."

Then she began telling me all about the trip. She undressed as she spoke and I noticed that unlike the woman that had been arguing with Nada, Ciara was wearing a light blue shirt. I sighed with relief. It must have been my eyes deceiving me. It must have been the drink and the heat. She could not have changed her shirt between here and the next town. She had not brought any change with her. Ha, there I go again, making things up like some kind of mad man. Inwardly I laughed at myself, mostly with despair, as relief poured over my paranoia.

"How about you, what happened here?"

She came up to me as she tied her hair back. She looked radiant. Her bronze tan warmed the whole room. Her blue eyes gave off a glow that threw me again. It could not have been such a fantastic trip. Nothing could be that exhilarating.

"Ah you know. I took off my sunglasses, skipped my blind phase and went on down to the next town cavorting and causing mischief."

She laughed at my attempt at a joke. "Really?"

I sighed. "No, in reality I stayed here philosophizing on life until boredom hit and I wandered off to have a beer. Helpless as a little babe, and a drunk little babe too at the end of it."

She looked seriously at me.

"Ah, I thought you smelt of beer."

"You would too if you were stuck lonesome in the dark."

She came back up to me and sat down on my lap.

"I'm here now. I'll take care of you. No more loneliness for you."

As I sunk my head to her chest I wondered how long I would continue with this stupidity of mine. I decided that I would start seeing tomorrow morn at breakfast, or as I woke. It would be the fair thing to do, and we could enjoy the last few days in semi-normality. Only, I would prefer, without the rest of the gang. Perhaps I should make that part of the recuperation deal. I would see tomorrow.

Tomorrow arrived. I woke very early to an empty room. I assumed that Ciara had gone off to pick up washing or something. After half an hour there still was no sign of Ciara and I begun to worry. Typically we would sleep in quite late, and given the hour, it was unusual that I was awake, and definitely that she was not here. I called down to the reception to see if they had seen her. No, was the cold unwanted answer. The receptionist sounded bothered by my query, as if I had taken her from some important task by calling, especially with such a ridiculous question. Of course it was way too early for her, and for any guests to be wandering around. How could I be so silly. I got up, got dressed, deciding for myself to take a chance. I would get a taxi to the next town to see if I could spot her anywhere, thinking that there had been something to yesterday's vision. Should I get caught I had already resolved to come clean. Surely she was up to no good anyway disappearing like this. I hurried off. As the door slammed behind me I realized that I had left my sunglasses behind. I went back into the room and rummaged for them. I could have sworn that I had left them on my bedside table. I looked everywhere and just as I had given up I took one last desperate look in the bin. There they were. I wondered how the hell they'd ended up there, and bent down to fish them up. With them I brought up two halves of a ripped note upon which something was scrawled in unintelligible writing. I automatically stuffed the note in my pocket, not thinking much more about it. As I rushed through reception there was no one around to see me. I got into a taxi that quickly bore me off in the direction of my choice. I found the taxi man staring back at me at regular intervals, but not a word crossed his chapped lips. The back of his silvery head seemed a comfort to me and I found myself entranced by it now and again. He must have felt my idle meditation, and those were the moments when he uneasily threw himself into the mirror. For the rest of the time I was keeping a concentrated vigil over passing cars, buses, taxis and walkers. I swore to myself as I realized that I could have made things a little easier for myself by having quickly scanned the leftovers in Ciara's wardrobe. I could have had a bit of an inkling of what she might be wearing, maybe. The taxi swerved and coasted. There was little traffic to hold its movements. In no time we were in the next town. I signaled to the driver to drive around and around. He checked my signals three times, even stopped to confirm what he was seeing, and then did as I bid. We rolled slowly up and down the calm streets. The heat was rising incrementally. The streets gathered speed and one by one objects and people miraculously developed in increasing numbers. A fruit stall got stocked by a severe looking woman clad in black, the sidewalk outside the barbers was swept by a grey bearded man that kept wiping his forehead from a task that seemed a little too much for him, and a little food stall was prepared by a boy that could be no more than fifteen. I got caught up in the preparations for the day but was called back by the taxi driver who stopped and turned around saying something to me. I kept showing him a circle with my right index finger. He heaved a sigh. I think he would have preferred for me to get out, to the fare that he would get. He was bored of me, or maybe thought that I was a nut job and so wanted to get rid of me as soon as he could. He paused between the sigh and the car moving on as if weighing up his options. Financial gains won over fear. We looped the town again. It was a puzzle that gained strength with every orbital progression, gained pieces fitted themselves together, yet nowhere to be seen was Ciara or any of the other people from the group that we had got to know during our vacation. Ciara was not being jigsawed into place. She was still moving way outside of the picture, to some other music. I brushed away a quick needling thought that suggested that she was now at home in our empty room worrying herself silly about my whereabouts, and at the same time touched the drivers shoulder saying our hotel name. He looked relieved and sped up as best as he could in the, by now, busy morning streets. The world flushed by, and my head was positively spinning trying to keep up the watch. Not until we came close to the hotel did I get rewarded with a sight that was to confirm my fears. There in a café I spotted Ciara's gentle face. I asked the driver to pull up across the street where we were shielded by passing traffic. Ciara: and this time it was definitely she, was sitting at a table by an open door. She was concentrating on the table, it seemed, as the two people across from her; with their backs towards me, continuously talked and talked. I could see their heads swivel on their necks animating and twisting sounds out of themselves, but it was unclear as to who they might be. One, a man, was wearing a dark blue djellaba whereas, the other, a woman, was wearing blue jeans and a white shirt with her veil-like long dark hair loose over her shoulders. As the woman, after a little while, got up to leave she kissed the others in an off-hand manner and then stood at the entrance of the café for a moment. Of course it was Nada, and so the other person must be Musa, but why would Ciara and Musa be meeting up like this. Why would any of them? Unless Ciara perhaps had been seeking solace with them through the difficult times that she was experiencing with my disability, and lack of will to address the same. It seemed possible that this could be it, but why would she not have said something to me. I would have understood. I would have encouraged her to keep that sort of contact up for the sake of her sanity. She had nothing to fear from me. After Nada had left Ciara raised her head and spoke to Musa with what looked like candor. Musa leaned forward and took her hands in his, comforting her or something. She leaned forward as well and all of a sudden they kissed. Right there, right in front of me. Clear as day despite the heaving traffic. The taxi driver distracted me by muttering something,

99

which I totally ignored. It was a definite kiss on the lips even if only light. Fury boomed through my blood, inflating me like the hulk. I could feel the tightness of the shirt on my back. I reached for the car door but the taxi driver hollered at me, grabbed my arm, and I stopped mid movement. I think he was afraid that I would do a runner. I looked back at him still caught in the moment of anger. He flinched and pulled back rapidly but was at the same time not ready for me to go. I rooted through my pockets for money, flung it at him, and tackled the door. Then I stood on the sidewalk being jostled by passersby. I raised my head and saw the two of them still engaged in soothing words but now sitting back from the table and each other. Perhaps it had been misconstrued. Perhaps it was only a kiss on the cheek. No it had without a shadow of a doubt been a kiss on the lips, even if good friends that would be inappropriate, especially with a Muslim man. I watched the traffic and made way to cross the street to confront them, but as the cars would not let up I came to decide that this was not the moment. I needed more evidence, an assurance. This had far too much riding on it. It would probably break our brand new and raw bind. It would alter the world as we had it figured out. I held back. I backed up to a bench that had been strategically placed for this moment. Shielded by the traffic I watched as Ciara and Musa got up. Musa paid, and then nuzzled up behind Ciara in the tight space of the café. I could have sworn he was way too close. As the sun hit his face I was surprised to realize that it was not Musa at all. There in the sun light Will proudly stretched his thick hairy body, all dressed up as a Muslim man, as Ciara turned to him. He grabbed her by the waist and pulled her against him. She offered little resistance, but Will let go off her as quickly as the moment had overwhelmed him, as if he was aware of that it was a stupid move, at least here in the broad daylight. They spoke for a little while longer at a civilized distance and then parted. Ciara headed off in the direction of the hotel. I stayed seated on the bench for another half hour crushed by what I thought was happening. I could understand if Ciara was having an affair, but how did Nada figure into it all? Was she some kind of chaperon, some kind of organizer? It did not make sense. Then, I walked up to the café, ordered a coffee and sat at the table where it all had happened. I tried to hear the echoes of the conversation, but could only see and taste the dust stirred up by the traffic. I thought out a plan for myself. I would keep the blindness until a moment of revelation. I would catch Ciara in the act and therefore not prolong the agony for any of us for any longer than necessary. I assumed that she was as keen as I was in getting out of her bond. I left a couple of coins on the table and steered my husk towards the hotel. I would say that I had been out for a walk and ask nothing of her. I would leave her to explain herself if she chose to, but would do as little as possible to raise suspicions within her. All was fine. All was ok.

I entered the lobby slowly. I could see the staff eye my procession with slight ill comfort. Cautiously I crossed the threshold to the lift. I ascended. I arranged my hair and appearance in the mirror so that when the lift bell chimed I was cool and ready. The door to the room was slightly ajar and I could hear Ciara on the phone. She sounded upset. I stood for a few seconds trying to make out what she was saying but to no avail. Silently I slid the door open inch by inch but she hung up and the room went quiet. I stumbled in.
"Where the hell have you been?"
"Just out for a bit of fresh air. What's wrong?"
She looked positively disheveled.
"What's wrong! Are you insane! Where the hell were you? You can't just disappear like that."
Tears of frustration and very likely guilt streamed down her cheeks, down her neck, and down her cleavage.
"'I've called everyone attempting to find you."
I laughed and said "I'm just blind, not an Alzheimer's patient."

101

She came for me. I grabbed her arms that were ready to pound me. She did not notice that my instincts had been a seeing person's, she was too upset. I held her to me, and gradually she began to calm down.

"You can't just waltz off like that. I was so worried."

"How long was I gone for?"

She looked up at me.

"At least three hours. I thought you might have got run over or something."

I was thinking to myself that it was strange that she might have kept track of me whilst being out herself.

"I did not realize that I had been gone that long. Sorry babe. I lost track of time."

She wiggled herself out of my embrace and walked over to the mirror fixing to remove the desperation off her face.

"Where did you go?"

I found my way to a chair and was about to sit down, but it was like the act of talking kept me from fulfilling my battle with gravitation. I remained hovering just in front of the chair.

"I went to the next town to take a walk on the beach, and then ended up sitting there for a while."

"Why did you not wait for me?"

She turned to me.

"I did, but then as you did not turn up I thought that you might have had the same thought yourself so I decided to just go for it, like an adventure. I've got to start broadening my invisible horizons."

I laughed, but she was not amused.

"You could have left a note, or a message, with the concierge, or something."

Finally, I let my body fall into the armchair.

"I forgot. Sorry."

Ciara began organizing the things in the room, finding a space for everything. Then for a couple of hours I pretended to nap whereas she sat and read on the balcony. It was taking a good while for us both to calm down. My head was full with scenarios and lies that I imagined had been told to me, but I was forcing them aside, trying to focus on more useful strategies. Soon, I imagined, she would be tempted to keep some appointment with Will or Flavia or something of that ilk, and then I would be ready. I would follow her into her lair, and reveal her for the lying bitch she truly was.

A couple of days dragged by without anything spectacular or revealing happening. There were no strange absences, no surprises. It was almost time to leave. The evening had just drowsily caught up with the digit six on the clock on the wall in the reception as we returned there after having cleaned up from the pool and having had a siesta. We were both fresh and clean, and by this time I had almost talked sense into myself as to the suspicions and the facts that I had gathered. I was returning to a universe where strangeness was only in my head. Ciara looked great in a white dress, thin straps slipped over slender shoulders, although it was a tiny bit too short for my liking. Yet, as I could not see it I was unable to comment on it. We stood for a moment at the entrance to the hotel before a taxi arrived. The balmy air clutched at us and I could not help smiling at Ciara, and she seemed to return my sudden sense of connectedness and wellbeing. I had been a fool again. There was an explanation for everything. Among all the scenarios that I had gone through in my head, the most logical one, to me, was that there was some type of blackmail going on, for what reason I had no idea. At least Ciara was simply protecting me from something. Especially as I could not see, as I was more fragile than she had ever known me, her sense of protecting her mate had been pushed to the extreme. The taxi swept us away further and further from the hotel. I felt a sense of relief in leaving it behind and imagined that tomorrow, on the plane, this sense of relief would be even stronger. It made me smile. Ciara looked at me, reached her hand to my face, caressed it, and then put her hand on mine, which rested on her knee, and returned to gazing at the dimming landscape.

The yellow awning of the restaurant glimmered in the sunset, and the twenty meters to the beach seemed a little indiscreetly planned given the propensity for storms and such in the area, but it was said that the restaurant had been there since at least fifty years back. This was our grand finale to our honeymoon: a dear restaurant in an incredibly seductive location. Ciara went with me to the bathroom, waited outside as I tended to my bodily functions. As I undid my zipper I felt something caught in my pocket. I reached in and found a crumpled piece of paper. Unfolding it I realized that it was that paper I had found in the bin the other day. I stared at it but it did not make any more sense than it had then, must be Arabic. The door opened and a guy in a very blue, almost neon, shirt came in. He drew up next to me and began loosening his belt a little. I distractedly kept an eye on him as you do in the company of strangers. He looked like a local, but perhaps made of money. How else would he be able to dine here? I said "hi", and he responded easily, which suggested that he might have good English. "Sorry, I know this is a bit strange…."

He looked at me quizzically. I was, after all, standing there with my trousers unzipped and holding my hand flat out at him, a little wrinkly piece of paper on my palm as the focus. It must have seemed bizarre.

"Would you know what this note says?"

My hand trembled a little with the awkwardness of the situation as I handed him the paper. With his cock in his left hand pissing away, he took my note into his right reading it as if he was sitting in his office. Somehow, the situation did not seem to baffle him.

"It's a bit badly written but it says that someone should call Fidel as a matter of urgency, but there's no number."

A sharp red-hot sting punctured my breathing. Just a mention of his name still got to the core of me. All of a sudden he was real again. He was a living breathing being that somewhere in this world pulsated along with the stars, this being radiated all the way to me in this toilet in Morocco. In my head I saw the obedient waves lying down to die on the beach outside, still laced with particles of his breath. I scrambled to reassemble him; hands full of sand that poured between my fingers. The guy handed me back the note. I stood there crestfallen and occupied with the shimmering gurgling silvery urinal. The guy looked at me bemused, shook, and put himself away neatly, zipped up, and rearranged his trousers and shirt. I heard him wash his hands in the sink behind me, and felt him give me another look in the mirror as he said "Bon Appetite" and disappeared out the door. My electric hands were painful on my cock when I did the deed I had come here for. As I splashed cold water on my face at the sink I imagined that I removed the residue of this upset, of his name as well. This was my life. I could not allow myself to be a prisoner of a blink of a past that did not exist. As I exited Ciara gave me a look of annoyance. Guess I had been a while. We got led to our place. The exquisite placement of the table made it feel like we were alone on the beach. Ciara positively frizzled with excitement. We ate, the moon dressed up. With each bite there was a lap of the waters and a rustle of the palm trees. Satiated and a bit delirious we wandered hand in hand out on the beach after having paid up. Barefoot we could feel the sun still remembered in the sand as our feet made smooth prints in its frustrated enamel. Soon also these would be whisked away by moonshine, as our honeymoon would be confined to a couple of photo albums gathering dust in a study or an attic. It made me sad and regretful. What had I done with this once in a lifetime moment of my life! All I had done was acting idiotic, paranoid, jealous, brutish and to top it all off, blind. My poor love. What had she put herself up for? She might have had an inclination, but the full extent of my foolishness, thank god,

105

was still a mystery to her. I hoped. I took her in my arms and she fell gently in. We stood sharing the perfect end to a perfect dinner and evening.

"I wish we would never have to leave" Ciara whispered into my chest.

As the taxi dropped us in front of our house I think that we both felt alienated by the normality of the situation. We became awkward and almost a bit testy with each other. Bumping into each other, as we began to rearrange the house back into working order, we bristled. Gradually I began to see again. I had confessed to Ciara that the last night on the beach I had seemed to have been able to distinguish moonshine, but, I said, I had been too scared of it being an illusion that I had refrained from telling her then. Now as we were home I told her that the shape of things was returning to me, but I still kept my dark glasses on because the glare felt too painful to start with. She believed me. I avoided going to an optician, or indeed the eye hospital. Within days my eyes were restored and we marveled over the incident and the body's capacity to heal itself.

Life had changed now. I went in to my office with a deeper sense of dread than ever before, and I came home with similar stones in my stomach. Ciara and I led careful lives, well planned, but not trusting and warm. I felt that the honeymoon in some way had ruined us. Things were not the same. Days carried a deep melancholy, a sense of that perhaps Morocco had been the zenith, and that we now partook only in the dying days of us. It had been a rapid rise, and now all we faced was the long decline: a star dying, a swan song. A horrid perforating whistle in the back of our heads, just barely audible, that pricked and pricked and pricked at our vapour. Neither one of us mentioned it. We just let it slide. Coming and going. Every now and again lifting our heads up to have a look at what lay ahead, but never really recognizing anything. Our sex life dried up fairly rapidly along with the other developments. We did not talk of this either. But I could pinpoint the moment for some reason. At the time it had not been a particular moment, but in hindsight, it was glaringly obvious. She had just gone down on me and all of a sudden stopped, as if she'd thought of something else that she rather do, and that was that. I pulled up my gray corduroys, she wiped her mouth and the lipstick smudged across her cheek. We went to watch television. Not a word. I was thinking that maybe if we did not mention it we would fool the drive, but I had no dream of what it would be like to have it back. I did not really want it back. Not with Ciara. Halfheartedly we tried the usual remedies, but forgot to carry them through. New toys, new spaces and fantasies, fizzled and died. We both looked longingly elsewhere caught up in a dry thorny conjugal web, which was draining us of our blood with every movement we made. I sometimes wondered if Ciara was having an affair, and linked it to the time in Morocco. Yes, sometimes I was thinking that perhaps Will would come fly in, do the dirty, make her sing a little, and then lift off out of here, for some more, somewhere else, cocooned in his deceitful and sleazy self. However, these sorts of thoughts did not make me jealous anymore. They just slipped over me, like in the shower, and I watched them disappear down the drain. I watched the droop of my prick point in the same direction, and had to really strain myself to remember what a sexual being was, and how I at points had been just such a being. It was tough work. I started to think that maybe I had gone asexual. That there really was nothing out there that could be exciting enough to get a rise out of me. I knew though that if I really let myself, that night with Fidel would have been the closest to reality in that sense that I had ever felt, the only moment in my life that I had felt really truly loved by another human being. I did not know how or why this could be, but it was like that. It was simple. But it meant absolutely nothing. Then Ciara and I parted in a nearly thankful atmosphere. Our marriage dissolved, and life went on as if there never had been a bond there in the first place.

One morning I was lying watching a spider carefully thread its way upside down along the hem of the curtain. I was wondering what the world would look like, climbing around like that, being small like that. I followed every movement of the see-through spider, worrying it would drop into my slippers that sat as goal posts at the end of the hem. It worried me. I was transfixed. I thought it was a bit of an epiphany, and wanted to go get the camera to take a photo, only I could not tear myself away. When the spider had stopped on a corner of the hem where I could not see it, I began to think of photographs, and managed to get up out of bed, away from the spider, and rummaged through a press at the end of the stairs. Ah, I found it. I dragged out a box filled with the albums from the honeymoon; other things fell backwards into the press with loud bangs. I ripped off the seal, the duck-tape that we had used to make sure that the photos would be well kept. As I began to rifle through the photographs I was overcome with sadness, just as I had been during the actual honeymoon, over that this is what it came down to, a dusty forgotten box of photos. This is what it amounts to. Faded images that momentarily brings one back to a time passed. A time that doesn't compare, not even to itself, not even then. Sweet poisonous utopias. There we were, dancing, eating, squinting naked at each other, filled with champagne bubbles in the gushing sunshine. There they were: the objects and clothes that belonged to that time alone. How light life had seemed. Yet, I knew that this was not the case. But even Will's and Flavia's faces seemed friendly and caring. Nada looked like the dear old friend she had claimed to be. It seemed real. It seemed we had been there, had had a good time. I felt like slapping myself, but bit my finger instead. When the pain pierced me I stopped, stared at my finger for marks, for blood, for unmistakable presence. My eyes were going blurry. I rose quickly and a bunch of photos burst forth from my lap raining down like snowflakes over the carpet. Some landed face down whilst others kept their faces turned to the ceiling. I stood for a while staring at the blurry mess, and then went in to the kitchen to open a bottle of wine. I would need fortification to get through this ritual I had begun. I returned swirling a ruby red body of liquid in my right hand. I looked at the pictures again. Now they seemed a bit clearer. I sunk to my knees and studied them one by one whilst sipping the wine. There was one photo in particular that caught my interest. It was taken the night I had gone with Musa to look at his car. It was from the bar where the others were drinking. It revealed Ciara, Will and Nada in an odd embrace smiling at the camera. I could not say exactly what was odd about the photo, or the manner in which they posed, but something there gave me the shivers. I stared at the photo for a solid fifteen minutes but nothing. I left it and began rifling through the other photos in a panicked manner. There was something there that I needed to understand but I did not know what exactly it was that I was looking for. Then all of sudden I stopped at a photo which depicted me posing outside of a shop in a market. The photo must have been taken from one of the trips that we had took before I had gone blind. Behind me I could see a crowd that was aware of Ciara taking the photo, many of whom therefore stared into the camera as well. However, there was one person there who seemed keen on not being caught on her camera but had at the same time not had time to fully conceal himself. It looked like Fidel. I was trying to get my eyes to focus and get a sharpness to the image that was not there. It could be Fidel, I was not at all certain that it was him. How could I be? It unsettled me enormously. Why would it be him? It was a very unlikely scenario, but I began to try to gather the other photos from that trip scanning the backgrounds of each photo meticulously looking for a similar shape. Every photo in the box thereafter got the same treatment but yielded nothing other than an interesting exercise in actually properly looking at the photos. That is, until I was almost at the point of relegating the whole heap back to where it had came from. The next to last photo displayed the closest beach outside of our hotel, a beach that we had spent little time upon as it was in no way comparable to the one in the next town, and because it had a tendency to be populated by sex tourists, both male and female, that either were about to procure, or had already done so and were then parading their trophies back and forth along the waterfront, whilst every now and again stopping to grope and uncomfortably snog. I did not remember taking a photo of the spectacle, but do remember having gone down there a couple of times disgustingly intrigued by the goings-on. I had wondered to myself whether or not I would have partaken in such a thing, when I had been a bit younger, or indeed, when I became older, but could not reconcile my ideas with my emotions. I thought of those who accessed whoring as having a desperate habit which only befell people that could not get it elsewhere and under less sleazy circumstances. However, at the same time, I envied the finger up at the establishment and behavioral rules, at least for the westerners. It seemed to me that a poor person had fewer options. Neither did I believe in the supply and demand argument. I did not think that one needed the other; I thought that supply and demand existed separately in this world of ours, and sometimes came together more by accident than anything else. Thus, it was a divided discussion in my head, one that I rather avoid because of that, because there was no final solution as far as I could see. On the photo in my hand another suspicious doppelganger of Fidel's lurked in a near distance, he was again in a twisted profile as he was turning away from the camera reaching into in a bag by his sun-lounger. Sharing the seat was a young dark man who obviously did not have the same issue with avoiding the camera. Defiantly and with a definite omniscient smirk he faced the camera as full on as possible. There was an out and out challenge in his look and

110

pose, as if he willed a fight for his territory. Perhaps, he was staring at someone else, someone behind the photographer's shoulder, someone that had nothing to do with the photograph as such. I wished that I could ask Ciara about the photo, and tried to scribble a nervous wobbly mental note about approaching her at some point in the future when things had settled a bit, had become less complicated. I picked up the last photo envelope, tried to stick this and the other Fidel-like photo into it, to place it apart from all the other ones. Something was keeping me from being able to secure the photos fittingly into the envelope. I tried pushing them in a bit harder but something was obstructing my aim. I took them out again and looked into the envelope, there at the bottom of it was a crumpled note of some kind. I dug a finger in and fished it out. As I unfolded it became clear to me that this was the note that I had found in the hotel room that day, the one that I had tried to get the stranger in toilet to decipher for me. It made no more sense now, but something made me neatly fold it up and stick into my pocket. I put all but the photos of Fidel back into the box and managed to squeeze the box back into a corner again. Threw some loose stuff on top of the box and slammed the door shut before the order would begin to shift.

The screen flickered blue on my naked chest as I leaned forward typing deliberately slow letters into the greedy google mouth. I was searching for everyone that I had known in my life. Some appeared in the ether, some were lost. Bit piece biographies painted up scenarios that sometimes made sense. This person had become a lecturer at a university, that one had gone into the prison services, and the one that you least expected seemed to have been able to make a career out of journalism although he was hardly able to write in the first place. I marveled at the way that life and people slipped away and developed independently and so far apart from where they had started. Childhood friends became real people with real

111

problems. Childhood enemies must have developed skills outside of the violent and vicious, in that they now seemed to have relationships based on other things than making other people feel like outsiders. Then again maybe they continued in the same vein, and were now torturing poor souls in a more adult manner. I guess that was more likely. Certain people in my past embarrassed me still. They were so greedy, false and empty that I could never foresee anything good or useful ever coming from them. But you never knew. A tableau gained colour as the faces gelled on the screen. Amongst the pixels I was looking for a particular face. Nowadays one could find almost anything on the net. I popped in names and watch the developments. There were millions and millions of Wills and Musas none of whom seemed to fit the templates of the Will and Musa of Morocco. No one named Nada came through either. Messing I put the name Fidel into the machine, but of course nothing of what I was seeking came out from behind the web curtain. I searched through images too. Then I felt the note in my pocket, scanned it, and decided to see if I could find some random stranger to translate it for me, just for fun, just to see if there was anything else to it. The scan flew through, and I blew it in the direction of a chat room of a well-known university where Arabic was studied. It took no longer than maybe five minutes and a ping was heard and I opened a message from someone going by the name of Raz. Raz told me that the Arabic used in the note was Moroccan, which hardly was news to me. Thereafter Raz ventured out on a limb where he (or she) explained the ins and outs of Moroccan Arabic, it's particularities etc. I yawned and typed an exasperated: but what does the note actually say? The answer came through within seconds. It means: *which straw will break his camel's back?* I looked at it with contempt: bloody wanker, having me on like that. My fingers raced across the letters to combine letters forming an insult. There was no answer back. I left the chat room. The door clanked loudly behind me as I stormed off.

There are some real idiots out there in cyber space, I thought to myself, and logged on to a porn-site for a little stress release. Nevertheless, there was no escaping the bad taste the joke had left in my mouth. I worked myself in vain, and then had to turn the computer off. Why would anyone take the time out just to play with me? It had no purpose. I mulled over the perceived insult. Hours later I realised that perhaps it had been someone who actually had something to do with the note itself, in its inception. But then, what were the chances of that? Next to none, I would guess. But what if? I turned the computer back on and then waltzed off to the same site desperately and apologetically asking for Raz. There was no response. I began making up excuses saying that I had misunderstood and that the note had been very personal, but still not even an echo returned. I was alone in my dimension. I laughed at myself but stopped midstream. Of course I would go down to the university to see if I could get someone to translate it for me in person. That way the anonymity would be taken out of the equation and I would be much more aware of what exactly I was dealing with. It was already late in the afternoon. I would not be able to go until the morning now.

There was no trickle of sunlight. Instead the sun just came flooding in. From nothing it gushed me to waked life. I came to overwhelmed. I sat up staring incensed at the wide window wondering why I never put up a curtain or blind. However as my routine faded I rose to the task at hand. I jumped up, tossing my body into the clothes of the day before. A hand through my hair and a quick brush over my teeth and I was ready to go. I shoved the note into my pocket again and strolled towards the subway. I crossed the threshold from sun to dark at the orifice of the subway and was struck by the particular smell that erupted from the bowels of the earth, somewhere between soot and soil. I was struck by a thought of the particular smells belonging to different nation's subway systems, such as, the

Paris metro, which has a sweet perfumy smell, very seductive. If those crafty Parisians could bottle that, I'm sure it would sell. The turnstile caught me just above the crotch and I lost a little of my height as my body adjusted to the discomfort. Then the giant silver grater offered a little tongue for me to step upon and this rough little lash ticked and tocked me down into the ground. I felt the black rubber strip that covered the sliding banister heat up under my hand. The platform was fairly empty except for a lost smelly shadow skulking here and there. I sat down on a seat that seemed almost without stains, at least recent ones that might not have dried just yet, and contemplated my self-imposed task. I was sitting with my head in my hands staring at the cold floor when I heard the steps of someone edging closer. Instead of looking up I kept an eye on the floor should this somebody get too close to me. A white clad foot entered my visual space. Then the other one arrived, but the body to which these shoes belonged turned and bent to sit down a few seats away from me. I sniffed the air a little, felt a sudden nostalgia, and looked up lazily. There she was, just an arm length away. I looked away and considered what my next step should be. Why would I talk to her? No better just get up and go. I stared down the tunnel and silently raised myself off the seat. As I began moving as inconspicuously as possible away from her I heard her move a little but I refused to look in her direction knowing that she would not let this lie should she spot me. She cleared her throat with a little deliberate cough. She had seen me. Sure, that was why she had sat down where she had as well. I kept on walking though. Then she called my name loudly twice. I did not hear her. She called again but this time much more decisively. She had me. Short of running out of there, there was nothing to do but to turn to her, recognize her, and then enter into an inane conversation with her. She smiled as usual as I fell into the trap.

"Well, I'll be damned."

She grinned and replied:

114

"Maybe that is the way it will turn out if you don't behave. You might want to check your hearing with a specialist. I called you three times before you heard me."

"Sorry, my mind was elsewhere. How are you? And what are you doing here in the middle of our great big city? I mean what are the odds that this should transpire."

I tried to seem as merry as she, hoping that this painful encounter would be short-lived. Nada pulled at her skirt a little but then gathered herself as some kind of cold-hearted assassin.

"It is great to see you again. How is Ciara?"

"Oh, she's fine thanks."

There was no way that I was going to start sharing with this psychopath in anyway, not now, not ever. For all I knew she had followed me here and probably was more than aware of that Ciara and I were no more.

"Good. Good."

She seemed amused by my answer. Bet she was. The train, the great tattooed saviour rushed up. I began feeling my pockets with sudden inspiration. She looked at me, and then looked at the train, hesitating as she stood up to get on.

"Sorry" I mouthed at her. "Think I must have left my phone at home. Gotta get back."

She took another confused step towards the soon to be closed doors of the train, swiveled, and then punctured my get away.

"Of course, I'll come with you. Would be lovely to see your place, and perhaps catch up with Ciara as well."

She had turned the situation around completely and I needed to come up with the next step. The doors of the train closed their mouths as if disappointed by my foolishness. The train slunk out and away. The platform seemed emptier than ever before. I could find my phone. "I better have a thorough look through my bag first," was my excuse.

It would be better to get rid of her in the subway system. That way she could not follow me. Lo and behold, I found the phone.

"Sorry to have made your miss the train for nothing."

"Oh that's ok" she said as she sat back down again.

Five minutes to go until the next train now: five grueling fucking minutes. She patted the seat next to her and I went to sit down like a good little boy.

"So what are you doing in our fair city?"

Nada cocked her head and looked at me.

"Here on business."

"Ah, and what kind of business could that be? The narcotics business?"

She gave me a look of irritation.

"Something like that."

She took a deep breath.

"It would be great to meet up with you and Ciara. How about dinner tonight? For old times sake."

"Sure, sure" I nodded at her.

What kind of fool did she take me for? Well, I only had myself to blame I guess. Best just agree with her and let her go off happy to have arranged something with us.

"Musa is here too."

I turned my head to watch her face.

"Musa, huh. Great stuff. And how is the old rogue nowadays?"

"He's fine. Nothing has changed really. Still has not found the love of his life."

I nodded again.

"I know what you mean. The poor sod."

She looked bewildered.

"What do you mean?"

"Oh nothing, nothing, really."

She continued.

"He would be so happy to see you both too."

"It would be wonderful to see him too. Very nice guy."

"So come meet up for dinner tonight then."

"Yes definitely."

We were quiet for a few minutes and as the next train rolled in we got up and Nada said, "Where should we meet?"

"Let me think."

We wandered onto the train. I looked around for seats as the other passengers looked us over briefly, making assessments of hazards. We were nothing to worry about.

"How well do you know our city, here? I mean should we meet at a subway station, or would you find your way to a restaurant if I gave you the address?"

I said, as I turned towards Nada elegantly swinging into a suitable pose, not too close to her.

"Oh, I'll find it no problem if you just write it down for me."

She was certain and apparently more familiar with my city than I had expected.

"Sure. Let me think."

We stood quiet without looking at each other for a while whilst I thought.

"Where are you getting off by the way?"

That surely caught her off guard I thought to myself. Now all I had to do is get off elsewhere.

"Not sure, it's in the middle of town. I know when I see it."

She smiled at me again with an air of victory. There, now what would I do? She most likely would get off on the same station as me, knowing just then that that was it. Then I could pretend that, oh no, I better go somewhere else first. Now for that restaurant, I better make it a real one so that she would not cop too early.

"And where are you getting off then?"

Of course, she would go retaliate to further whatever evil plan she had.

"Riverside."

Nicely smack in the middle where she could get lost easily.

"Great. That's the one for me too."

Obviously. I had a hard time not laughing.

"Good stuff. I'll wait to write the address for the restaurant down in that case. You're more likely to find the place if there is some kind of aid for my sloppy handwriting."

It was strange that she had said nothing about my blindness. Perhaps she had forgotten? No, that was unlikely. A person of her caliber probably never forgot anything. Indeed the reason for her being here was almost certainly because she never forgot. For all her intent on being there with me she had precious little to say. We swung on the silver railings, blurry images rattling in dark windows. The voice over the PA system announced our arrival at Riverside. We squashed ourselves out of the train along with the throng, and for a moment I blissfully thought that I had lost her. But never would such a thing happen. It was Nada, or whatever her real name might be, that I was dealing with after all. She put her hand on my arm. We went to the wall and waited for the rush to dissipate. Without much further ado I wrote an address down. We kissed each other on the cheeks, and parted. At least I hoped we parted. I kept looking behind me thinking that I could see her here and there in the mass of wriggling waves in my wake. However, as I had took a long detour before at a leisurely pace arriving at the university, the streets more or less emptied behind me and if she still were following me she would have to be quite far away. Once I entered the university itself it would be easier to lose her. The steps up to the front doors had just been washed and glimmered promisingly in the sun. I tread resolutely. The woman at the reception instructed me how to get to where I wanted to go, and once she had finished I decided to say something stupid just to cover my tracks. One could never be too careful. She looked at me with tired disgust but agreed, after persistent explanations, that she would not let anyone else know where I might have gone to, even if that person might offer her money. She evidently thought that I had some type of mental health issue as she agreed readily with everything I said whilst looking around for possible help if needed. She looked relieved as I left. The door to the office that I was after was closed. I knocked softly not wishing to completely disturb what ever was on the other side. A gruff voice summoned me and an airless little room swamped by piles and piles of papers and books revealed itself as my hand pushed the cold handle. A grey bespectacled man with hunched shoulders blinked at me with huge eyes.

"Yeeesss?"

The one word had been dragged out to make its way all the way to me. I was standing ossified in the doorway. I felt as if I was back in school. I stammered and spluttered.

"I, I, was looking for someone to help me with a short translation."

Still barely woken out of his reading the man responded with the same word.

"Yeeesss?"

I shifted my feet.

"See, I have this note here. Not sure if you can help me. This note, it's in Moroccan Arabic. I think. Uh, I mean, I have been told."

The man crept closer over his desk by the way of his hands nearing me in a crablike manner.

"Then you have already had it translated, yes?"

He cleared his throat.

"Surely nobody would be able to clarify such detail of language for you without being able to read the damn thing."

He sounded fed up. I was not going to hold his attention for long. He pulled his hands back towards his decrepit body, curling up within himself. He reminded me of fern furls. I thought the best thing would simply be to hand it over and thus with one step I moved to stand just opposite his weighed down desk, at least one had to assume there was a desk there somewhere. The supposed object was suggested by the arrangement of the items upon and around it. The note lay crumpled in the midpoint between us and we were both looking at it as if it belonged elsewhere. Silence. Then his hands moved out again gaining and gaining on the note until they grasped it.

The sound of the paper opening laid vast rivers of cold into the room, and although the door was open there was a sense of the room being hermetically sealed from the rest of the world. The man glanced long at the paper, and then at me, and then back at the paper.

"It is Moroccan Arabic."

I did not chance a smartarse comment. I waited and waited but he did not say anything else. I could not wait any longer.

"Sorry sir, but what does it say?"

He looked up as if he had heard an annoying insect or something.

"It is a line of poetry."

God this was not going to be easy now was it. It was my turn for "yeess?" He was searching the note for meaning.

"Well, you see, given poetic license, it could mean quite a lot of different things."

"Like what, sir?"

"Like, *in silence the gates give themselves away*, or *barriers extinguish their being*, or something like that. But you should really take this to Raz. He is the expert here in this particular vernacular."

I froze. That must be the same Raz of the Internet. The liar. It'd be a cold day in hell before I went to that asshole to get this translated. I felt confused as it was anyway. I had no idea who in this wide world was actually speaking the truth, the real truth, nothing but. So far my bets were on this old man. He was too outside of life in general to have anything to do with the games that people were playing with me.

"Oh, and where could I get a hold of him then?"

Unexpectedly a curiosity crept up my bones. What if I would confront him, just to see if he remembered me? Just to see if he would change his story now. To see who he was and why he had thought that it would be ok to tell me such bullshit. I got the directions to find Raz but had to quickly move back around a corridor corner as I saw Nada walking into a room. As I walked by I realized that she had entered Raz's office. I stood

120

outside the door listening intently yet could not distinguish anything from what might be happening in there. A woman walked by looking at me funny. If I didn't move on she probably would contact security but I could not leave. There was something that needed to be discovered, and I felt sure that soon I would get some clue to what all of this meant. I had to stay around. I did the most studenty thing I could think of. I sunk down along a wall a fair distance away from Raz's office and hid myself behind a newspaper. I did not have to wait that long before the door opened again. There they were, Nada looking very pleased with herself, and Raz, a lot younger than I had expected, all dashing and smiling broadly. They laughed at something that Raz whispered in Nada's ear, then Raz, in a very baritone timber, said;

"I'll check with him, and get back to you. Alright."

Nada nodded with a smirk and then sashayed down towards the elevator close to where I was sitting. I did not move a muscle and made sure that the paper wholly concealed me. Nevertheless I held my breath. I imagined that he had stood leering and watching her ass as she walked off. What if she would recognize my clothes or something? She might be on the lookout for me skulking somewhere, but then again she in all probability thought that I would not be aware of her following me. She passed me without any hesitation and when I in the corner of my eye observed her by the elevator she seemed absolutely calm and collected. I did not believe that she had spied me. I heard the door of Raz's office close. I waited about ten minutes allowing for Nada to have left the area for sure, as well as considering my next move. Then the door to Raz's office opened. I thought that I would have to act immediately. Raz might know about me, but now was a good opportunity to check to see if he knew what I looked like. I folded up the newspaper and began walking towards his office where he was standing fiddling with his keys to make sure that his valuables where beyond lock and key. However, as he noticed me walking up the corridor he seemed confused and began rearranging the books that he was holding instead. Naturally he dropped them. I got up to where he was standing and got down on my haunches to help him gather his belongings.

"Seems you've got too much to carry my friend." I said.

He gave me the impression of being very nervous, and only mumbled in response. Once he had it all in his arms again he rushed off to the elevator. I heard him press the button and drop part of his burden again whilst I calmly walked down the long corridor pleased with myself. Just as I was to walk through the door at the end of the corridor I heard the doors of the elevator close and I turned around. The corridor was silent and empty again. I waited a little while to see if he would return. He did not appear. My thought was that perhaps in the confusion he might have forgotten to actually lock that room of his. With the coast clear I tried the door handle and was thrilled to notice that my surmise had been correct. The door opened to a very similar office to the one I had been in not long ago. Books and papers all over the place. However, Raz had the good sense of having his window a little ajar and the blinds at an angle to emit a lazy thick light. I began rifling through the top layers of the stuff closest to his desk. Nothing but Nada's number seemed of interest. I stuffed the note with the number into my pocket and went through the drawers. I heard footsteps in the corridor and froze for a moment until the echo died down at the other end from whence they had come. Raz was probably off to lunch, and most likely with Nada as well. There was something going on there. I just did not know how the hell I had got involved in any of this. It was plain stupid if it wasn't for the bad taste that all of this called up from my guts. I drove this thinking out of my head and concentrated on rummaging until I noticed that Raz had left his computer on. I started going through the emails. Lo and behold, an email from Nada as well. I clicked it open and read out loud to myself:

"Yes, and if there is contact it is important that it is kept short. There is

no information there. No information to give".

My lips pressed hard against each other I stood shaking my head at the text. It meant nothing either, just as it said. I quickly browsed over the other emails in the inbox but there were no other ones that caught my eye. There had surely been more from Nada, but they had been erased meticulously. The slate was clean and gave nothing away. Again steps were heard in the corridor. This time they seemed to have stopped right outside the door of the office. I stood stock still trying not to breathe. The person on the other side seemed to have done the same. Then the footsteps moved on.

As I held the phone to my ear and heard the ringing of Ciara's number take hold there wasn't any clarification of this that I expected, but for some reason I felt that she might be the only clue to what I had just experienced. The phone rung out, I left a message.

"Please call me as soon as you can. Just wanted to forewarn you about something."

It took Ciara a good few hours to respond and when she did she sounded bored with whatever I was going to say, no matter what is was going to be, already from the start. I explained the strange meeting and the restaurant date that was organized but which I was not even remotely thinking of keeping. I left out the stuff about the university. That was going a bit too far. Ciara took the news completely wrong. Now she was going to go to the restaurant herself to meet with Nada. She looked forward to it. Thanks for calling. Click. Great. Now Ciara was going to link in with the snake in the grass to complete any blank spaces. I had officially now made my situation worse just because of not thinking before I acted. I banged my head a couple of times against the tree against which I was leaning.

About the time that I should have met with Nada the telephone rang. I did not pick it up.

"I should move." I thought to myself.

Now that Ciara would have passed on all the information to Nada I would have no peace. All the stuff that had started in Morocco would start up again here at home. I was almost certain of it. I switched on the television and settled down to a barrage of Olympic sports, the bottle of beer almost emptying over the sofa as I made a rough landing.

"Time to go blind again" I mumbled to myself and coughed on a giggle, and peered into China.

Sure enough shortly thereafter the phone began ringing in the middle of the night. I never bothered trying to pick it up but instead took the phone off the hook. There would be no one on the other end. I knew it. Or if there were they would have nothing sensible to share. I changed my number, and for a while the calls stopped. Then they started up again. I cancelled my landline and bought a new mobile phone. Peace at last.

Buried behind a pile of paperwork I diligently plowed through the necessary tasks. My work was not the most exciting but it paid the bills and afforded me some luxuries. I could do the job blindfolded, and in a metaphorical manner did so. There were not too many surprises, although every now and again I did drop the ball and got a bollocking accordingly. I did not socialize much with my colleagues anymore. None of them really caught my fancy in that way. I did the job, had my lunch in haste, as I wanted the day to end as quickly as possible. There was no joy in it. It was, as it had to be. During appraisals my boss and I would play a game of progression and needs fulfilled. Neither of us believed a word of what we were saying. It was not the most satisfactory outcome of my idea of a working life, but then again few jobs fulfilled those childish types of dreams. I had not completed my potential, hell, I had not even come close to that which I had imagined, but neither could I see anything changing. Life was what it was. There was no luck coming my way. Life had dried in its shell, nothing would fall out to grow somewhere else, no tendrils would cross arid lands to find a crack which to fill. I saw my reflection stare stupidly back at me on the surface of the computer screen. Man, I looked tired. Sometimes I thought that the mishaps of Morocco were the only exciting things that had happened to me in my adult life. It was sad. Pathetic really. On the way home from work I stopped by the local bar as was my habit now. I read the paper with a beer going warm in my hand. I heard the door open, the parched outside gulped the dank alcoholic air until darkness returned. Whoever had entered stood still blinking into the dark disoriented. The bar man hollered "Come on in", perhaps to enable the person to steer their way by the sound of his voice, a fog horn to lead you further into the fog. The unsettled bat knocked in to a chair on the way, it rattled noisily. I sighed exasperated from being disturbed in my drinking time but did not turn to see who the idiot was. The person sat down a few chairs away from me. I could feel his presence but it did not interest me in the least, I just hoped the fucker would keep his trap shut long enough for me to finish my session. Naturally that did not happen.

"Thought I find you here."

The decisive voice did not match the clumsily manner in which the man had entered the bar. I pretended that I assumed that he was not addressing me and so kept reading.

"You not talking to me?"

Shut up, bounced around in my skull. The man went quiet for a while.

"This the way you treat old friends is it?" Surely the fool would be aware of that I was way too involved in my reading to have heard a word of his. If he didn't consider that scenario then he did not deserve an answer back.

"Yo fuckhead!"

That was it. The insolent idiot was going to get a taste of my fist right in his jabber wocky. I stood up off the stool in a hurry with the result of it crashing to the ground behind me. Very dramatic. I turned towards the voice and was ready to do some serious damage. Then, there, calm as anything, was Luca. I was caught betwixt murderous instincts and joy. The disorder must have been worn right on my skin as Luca burst into a merry laughter. The bartender, who had been on tenterhooks throughout the monologue, now returned to movement, drying the glasses from the washing machine, not paying us any heed anymore.

"Luca!"

I was still perplexed but gradually coming to.

"Luca. What are you doing here?"

I started towards him. I was genuinely overwhelmed to see him. We hugged.

"Great to see you man."

Luca patted me on the back, and I patted his.

"Barman, a beer for my friend."

I gesticulated at the beer and the bar by Luca. The barman understood sulkily.

"What are you doing here?"

I repeated my question that had been swallowed up by the surprise. "How did you find me?"

Luca was looking at me smiling and nodding as the beer was brought to him. He took a long sip and then replied:

"I rang your door bell and the old lady across the way told me that you most likely was sitting in this bar."

I recoiled slightly.

"How the hell did she know that?" I shook my head to get rid of the question.

"Never mind, my friend. How are you? When did you get back into town?"

Luca began chatting away about his finishing the series, at least for a while. We ordered more beers and the night rambled on.

When we parted we had decided that I would go over to Luca's for dinner and drinks at the end of the week. He had some photos that he wanted to show me.

I crossed the street into Luca's neighborhood leaning forward a little as I stepped up on the sidewalk. This part of town was very different from mine. There was a lot more money here. The careless, effortless presentation of the whole area put well off in bold letters for all to see. People here were different. Their cars were different. I had sensed this off Luca. I mean given his job and all, but at the same time he himself was different from this as well. Suntanned women gossiped on the front steps, drinking café lattes or smoothies, smiling as I walked past. Life was easy. Behind the women equally well-tended flowerpots, placed strategically unplanned, oozed with flowers and behind that doors ajar revealed content yelps from hoards of well clad if disheveled children playing in lush gardens. I found Luca's door and knocked. He took a while coming to the door.
"Sorry, thought you might be late."
A towel thrown over his loins, his hair dripping, the whole place smelt fresh and clean, Luca stepped aside to let me in.
"Here, let me just throw some clothes on. The sitting room is over there. Make yourself at home. There's coffee in the pot."
I ambled slowly, browsing the photos of landscapes and portraits on the wall as I made my way over to where he had suggested. Of course, he was good, that's how he got paid. I moved on. The living room was spacious and airy apart from the brown paper boxes of stuff that were stacked against one of the walls. I sat down just looking around as Luca returned dressed in a t-shirt and blue jeans.
"Coffee?"
He gestured towards the kitchen.
"Yeah, right. That'd be good."
He walked off into the kitchen but we continued our conversation in raised voices.

"I like the photos there in the hall. They all yours?"

"Yeah, all from North Africa, except one, the one with the miners, that's from China.

There was a pause during which his concentration probably was on the task.

"Glad you like them."

Another pause.

"Sugar and milk?"

"A couple of sugars but no milk, thanks."

Luca came back out with two cups of coffee. He settled down in the sofa opposite.

"I miss North Africa. Can't wait to go back. The only reason for my return was to see my mum, and perhaps, I hoped, a chance to meet up with you again. Hope you don't mind me being so forward, but I really enjoyed our booze up in Morocco. Don't know why exactly, but I did."

I got a bit embarrassed by Luca's frankness, but had to agree with him, there had been something about that day which had remained with me as well. I was very happy to see him here at home. Did not expect it but had thought about it now and again, wondering how I would get a hold of him, or if I would ever see him again. He felt like a mate already. We got on very easily. I felt I trusted this man. This was the kind of thinking that led me to blurt out that I had had a lot of trouble when in Morocco. I revealed that things there had been very strange.

"That country will do that to you my friend."

I shook my head at him.

"It wasn't the country as such, it had to do with something else. Not sure exactly what though." Luca looked at me with curiosity.

"Was it your wife?"

I was surprised by his question and a little too brusquely asked, "What do you mean?"

Luca's face contracted as if he was preparing to apologies.

"Umm, just seemed a bit strange that you'd be on your

honeymoon yet cavorting around on your own like that. You seemed bothered. Guess that's what I was trying to say."

I averted my gaze to the floor, and said quietly,

"I know what you mean."

He was encouraged by my words.

"You just looked miserable and lost."

My head nodded at what he was saying. I looked up at him again. His eyes were holding mine. His sincerity prompted me on. I started laughing.

"There were some very strange things happening during the honeymoon. Somehow they have not ended yet either."

"Like what?"

"Like, eh, like, my wife acting very weird, like, this strange woman claiming to be my friend from before although I'd never set eyes on her previously, like, I went blind, like, I was followed, like I felt that I was given messages from someone I'd met years ago, once."

I searched Luca's face for approval or disapproval. He showed no signs of either.

"It was all very spooky, and like I said, I feel that it has followed me on from there. Things are still happening. This even though my wife and I are not even together anymore. Makes me think that it did not have anything to do with her at least. Although this woman, the one that claimed to be my friend, showed up out of the blue the other day down in the subway, and now she and my ex-wife have been set in contact again. Strange stuff. Reality and fiction, and so on," I sighed "and on."

Luca was quiet. I don't know if he expected me to go on or not, but I remained quiet. I felt that I had said too much already. Not because I worried that Luca too could be embroiled, but because I was afraid of losing him. I was hardly surrounded by friends as it was, and family was scarce on the ground too, other than my dad whom I would call every so often, but with whom I had little to share. Luca suddenly sprang into action.

"Let me show you my photos from Morocco. There's some stuff there that might be of interest to you."

I got up out of the sofa and followed him as he walked through the house. He unlocked the big glass door to the garden and I followed him down an overgrown garden path to the shed at the bottom. As Luca stuck the key in the ramshackle door I said "this your bunker? Or where you keep the bodies of your large family?" Luca turned and gave me a grin. Inside, the shed seemed enormous, and in many ways as a completely different building from what the outside suggested, it seemed sturdy and well built. It smelt dusty and clean at the same time. I sniffed the air and looked around. Luca had fixed this whole space up as his dark room, but he also had an Apple computer in there for the more modern methods of dealing with photos. Luca explained that he still had a deep love for the chemicals and processes through which one once developed black and white, but that the slowness of that process often was incompatible with the demands of the business end of things. At my request he turned off the big light, switched on a diffused red light and took me through the stages of developing a photo. He got the negatives out, ran through them quickly against the red bulb and then said: "Ok, come look here." He stuck the negative into the enlarger and focused the image as clearly as possible. I could see the image he had chosen. It was a photo from the day that we had met. I recognized the street. Luca removed a photo paper from closed box in a drawer under the enlarger and placed it in the space where the image would be. Thereafter, he flooded the paper with the image for a little and then swiftly moved it into a tray that, he explained, contained developing fluid. Luca stirred the chemicals a little whilst intently watching the white begin to turn. Shadows clambered forth. I held my head close to the tray.

"Be careful you don't get anything in your eye"

Luca admonished my obvious intrigue. I lifted my head up a bit. The picture that wriggled under my eyes became increasingly clear and after just a little while I could see myself stand on the sidelines watching Luca watching me. What I had not known at the time was that Luca was not the only one aware of me. Not far behind me I could see someone that I knew very well obviously keeping a close guard of my whereabouts. It sent shivers up my spine. I stood up, looking at a red Luca remove the image. He shook it a bit, and then stuck it into the stop bath, lifted it and shook it again before tucking it into the fixer, telling me all about it as he went on. Thereafter he turned on the tap at the end of his table and let the image bounce around in the rhythm of the water to get rid of the chemicals.

"Who is she?"

I looked at Luca.

"She was my wife."

Back on the sofa in Luca's living room I sat nursing a glass of whiskey. Luca was leaning back in his armchair opposite with a similar glass of whiskey in his hand. We had looked at that single image, only, and that single image had ripped the ground from beneath my feet. I had trusted her. She, as far as I had understood things, was the only one who had lived in the same universe as me. She had been the only reality that I had known through all of this, and now she had disappeared in a puff of smoke. I could smell the brimstone. I felt hollowed out. The whiskey ran into my feverish body, which contained no guts, nothing but skin hung on its skeletal frame. The liquid moved like fire in the empty dark. The bone-dry splinters of my faith kept it traveling swiftly into each nook and cranny.

"If I couldn't trust her, then who could I trust? How the hell could I trust you?"

I swept the last of the drink into me, set my glass down on the table and calmly got up. Luca did not protest. I closed his door quietly behind me and made my way somehow back to my flat. Later I would have no recollection of just how I had got home.

A couple of days later; prior to which I had been locked up in the dark of my flat sitting like the living dead in front of the television, trying not to feel or think, I was back at Luca's door. I had not called beforehand, as I wanted to apologize in person. I knocked and knocked but no one stirred. I tried looking through the windows and knocking on them as well, but nothing. I sat down on the steps. At least I could wait for him for a while. Perhaps he'd just gone down to the shop. I took a book out of my pocket and began reading. By the time I looked at my watch next an hour had gone by. I got up, dusted off my jeans and knocked again. This time I heard quick steps and the door opened briskly.

"Hey."

Luca moved aside immediately to let me in. I thought this a promising sign. Perhaps he had not been too hurt or pissed off with me. Luca acted as if there was nothing wrong, and I did not want to start digging in it if he did not want to. He made me coffee and we sat quietly with Nina Simone playing in the background. The phone rang and Luca went into the kitchen to take the call. I sat looking around the living room and all of a sudden noticed that Luca had put the photo in question up in a frame on one of the walls, and not only that, it seemed that he had removed all the other prints he had previously had on the living room walls, which meant that the only thing really, at least photo wise, up there, was that single image. I did not know what to think. It was so provocative that I smarted. The image kept bringing me back to it, it was as if it was staring at me rather than the other way around. It was as if all reality lay in that image and all that surrounded it was stuck in a frame on its wall. Luca came back into the room and observed that I had noticed, but did not attempt explaining himself. I looked at him and at the image quizzically yet he did not do, as I seemed to bid. I was not even sure that I wanted it that way; perhaps there was a reason for him not to rise to it. He asked if I wanted to go for a walk, and I nodded at him getting my body out of the sofa simultaneously. It was a relief going out on the street. We walked in silence for a while and let our feet steer us towards the park. When we got in beneath the trees I turned to him and asked him: "Why?" He did not pretend that he didn't understand what I was talking about.

"I was so overwhelmed by your story in regards to the image that I felt that all I could do for now, in order to try to understand what you are going through, or, in fact, mainly, to try to help you understand it, was to put that damn thing up on an empty wall. There it is, as bare as can be. Maybe, I thought that it would open the image up somehow, with nothing there to disturb it from itself, if you know what I mean."

I was watching the ground grind by underneath me. I watched each piece of rubbish sail by. I loved the feeling of the muscles in my leg stretching and working. I strode wider watching my legs as if I could see right into them, could see the muscles and sinews roll around each other like clockwork.

"See there's lots that I could tell you, about, about all this."

Luca glanced at me through the corner of his eye.

"So why don't you? Maybe there is something I can do."

I sucked my teeth.

"It's already been done."

"You said that it was still going on."

Now Luca stopped and I stopped as well. I searched his face for reasons for his interest but it was unclear, he seemed sincere.

"Why do you want to know?"

"Just thought that I could help you somehow. You know, figure it out. I feel somehow caught up in this myself, because of that photo, and because of some other photos that I think that you should have a look at."

Anger boiled up in my throat.

"This is not a fucking joke man."

Luca remained calm.

"I know."

"What photos?"

"There are some other photos at home that you should look at. There might be more clues to what was going on. It seems that both you and your wife were in some other photos of mine. Really, you should have a proper look through all the photos that I have of that period, the time that you were there. It seems that our paths crossed repeatedly before the day we actually met."

We walked on. Before we got back to Luca's house I had begun telling him the story about the honeymoon. I tried to tell it with as much detail as possible but it all seemed disconnected without telling the story about Fidel and the park. I did not know why this was. However, I was not about to tell anyone about that, it was my own private business, and I did not want to scare Luca away thinking that I was a poof or something, so I did not even hint at it. I just left it out of the equation. It was dead and buried. Throughout my soliloquy Luca did not say a word. Even when I was done he did not ask any questions. This unsettled me and I put it straight to him.

"Why don't you ask anything?"

"I don't know. I don't know what to ask really. It's all very strange. Somehow I feel that I need for you to look at the photos first, and then maybe you can talk me through them? Guess I work better with images than with words. I can't think properly without the images."

At the house Luca gave me a heavy plastic bag full of photos.

"These are all the photos from that period. I've thrown in a looking glass so that you can have a proper look at them. When you're done you can bring them back here and we'll see..."

I walked home with the bag in my arms, full of misgivings. I felt as if I was waking the beast.

It took a week before I dared to tackle the images. It was a grey and helplessly drizzling Saturday afternoon. I opened a beer and sat down on the living room floor with the photos in a pile in front of me. One hand on the beer and the other with the looking glass raised. The first photo yielded an image quite content in itself, a bent little lonely tree silhouetted against a dramatic backdrop of towering mountains. It would hardly hide anything human behind one of its rocks and if it did I assumed that it would not have anything to do with me. The next photo was from a tour out into the desert. A road wound its way up an incline and at the ridge of the hill was a donkey drawn cart; the donkey's head just peeked up over the ridge although the large cart already was more than perfectly visible. The poor animal, dragging around things twenty times its own size and weight. Again there were no people in the photo, other than the top of the head of the driver. I decided to divide the photos up in two different piles, one for people and one for those photos without people. This exercise saved me from scouring at least thirty photos. I began again in the pile of people images. After a couple of hours I stopped my staring and slowly stood up. My body had almost locked in position and I felt my head heavy with imaginings and searing pain. So far the only thing of interest seemed to be the photos took in the street that day that I had met Luca for the first time. There was that ominous photo with Ciara watching me. Also, I thought that I had seen Nada in the background looking at something in a stall, but it might not have been her. Then; and this I almost did not even consider a clue of any sort other than an emotional kick in the teeth; I had seen a person strangely similar to Fidel. I put this down to stupidity on my part rather than anything meaningful. I mean, even if it was real, it wasn't anything. It was just this person that I had known once, briefly, and in truth did not know at all. We had no ties; all we had been was so momentary that it was outside of the real. I huffed at myself and went into the kitchen for another beer. I lay down on the sofa and watched some Olympic sports men and women battling it out it in Beijing. I fell asleep as they twisted and turned distorting their bodies right into my dreams. I woke again towards midnight with a really painful cramp in my left thigh. I sat up all turned around rubbing my thigh. The pile of photos lay still yet breathing like some kind of living being on the floor. I rolled over and crept up to the pile to stare at the photo of the Fidel look alike. As he had been slipping in the shadows when I first met him he was slipping here. I held out the photo at an arm's length and then turned my head to the window. Out of the corner of my eye I imagined that I saw him moving and smiling as if he had evaded me successfully. I quickly looked back at the photo and it stopped still. Ain't nobody there. There never was.

Her hands were rotating around each other as she sat there waiting for me in the café. I stood outside on the street for a good few minutes before I walked in. I was trying to read her tension and upset. Ciara had called me about an hour before this meeting urging me to come see her here as soon as I could, her voice quivering. She would not say why she was so eager and disconcerted, just that I should come immediately that she had something to tell me. If it had not been for the photo of Luca's I would not have gone, but now there was something that I wanted to talk to her about as well, and given the incident with Nada on top of it all I thought that perhaps there was something to glean from Ciara even if just more lies, which, turned on their head, could come to mean something. At least now I knew that that's what it all was, lies that is. I hesitated a little longer and then mustered the energy needed to confront her. As she noticed the sound of the door opening she turned quickly, really expecting me, needing me to be there. A broad if nervous smile sprung out all over her face and she stood up with excitement. Hell, she'd never ever been that excited to see me, even when we'd just started going out together. I guess I knew why now somehow. This was something else. She had other reasons for her animation. I scratched my cheek and crinkled my eyes a bit at the scene as I approached her. Her blue raincoat looked quite regal against her silver coloured shirt. She was an attractive woman there was no taking that away from her. In confusion I stretched out my hand towards her, like the stranger that I felt I was to her. It was the only tangible fact about her. She looked at my hand just as confused but then decided that it probably was best to just shake hands. We sat down a bit awkwardly, just as she decided that perhaps we should go for a walk instead. I got up and stood by the door as she went to the cashier to pay. Out on the street she did not say anything for a good while. We walked down towards the river and then turned to drift along with it towards the estuary. She unfroze and began talking only after a prompting by me that I did not have all day that I had to get back to work.

"I called you because I needed to talk to you about your friend."

I watched my strides intently, and started curving around things I could divulge, and things that I obviously couldn't, especially if she was now referring to Luca, whom she should not even know existed. Just take your time answering everything; I thought to myself, therewith giving myself license to think, something that I was not the best at, especially in tricky situations like this. I did not feed Ciara anything but waited for her to continue. I was not going to rush whatever lies she now was about to spout about Luca, if he was the one that she was referring to.

"I would not trust him if I was you."

I looked at her pretending not to have a clue as to whom she might be referring.

"The man called Luca" she said almost irritated.

A matter of fact temper seemed to be running through her cold veins. I cocked my head and looked at her out of the corner of my eye. She continued:

"I know that you have been hanging out with a man called Luca."

She stopped and leaned on the railing gazing at the river, knowing that she had got my attention, this forced me to make

137

my mind up instantly. Either I would walk on, or slow down to turn to her, that is if I wanted to remain in this discussion, something that to me by now was too shocking to leave.

"What are you talking about?" I retorted.

I was not going to give in easily, to have her toy with me. Resistance was the only way to get her to spill more.

"I know all about him."

She sucked on each word of that short sentence as if she was the conductor of my single bodied orchestra. Now I was supposed to go up a few octaves and then fall back into bass tones.

"My dear Ciara, whoever you are, I think that it was nice meeting you this afternoon, but as I am thoroughly convinced of that you have lost your marbles I will now return to my work. Please do not contact me again. This is just fucking absurd."

I pulled my coat around me and turned on my heel. Each step away from her brought relief, until I heard her thievish little hustle bring her up behind me. She was out of breath as she caught me by the arm.

"Listen."

I shook her off and walked faster, but she wouldn't give up. Again she was at my arm, tugging at me, begging me to stop for a moment. Extremely irritated I stopped and crossed my arms across my breast. "I give you five minutes."

She pulled me aside to a park bench and we sat down. Now the words came easily out of her, they practically poured.

"The man, Luca, that you met in Morocco is not what he seems. You might think that he is a friend of yours, but he's not. He's anything but."

"Who is it that you are talking about?"

"Luca, your friend, the photographer."

"How do you know about him? As far I was aware you have never met him."

"That is right, I have never met him, but I have heard about

138

him."

"And who might have whispered in your tiny little ear? You having me followed now?" I sneered at her.

"No. I do not have you followed. I heard about him when we were in Morocco."

"Then how come you know that I am meeting up with him now?"

Obviously she would have to fall now.

"Nada told me."

"Ah, so the lying impostor called Nada now is the one that we should listen to? The fucking freak from nowhere, that claims to have known me previously even though I've never ever met her before in my life. Perhaps she was referring to a prior life. That Nada?"

Ciara sighed.

"Just because you do not remember meeting her before does not mean that what she says is not true."

"Yes, sorry, it is. My recollection is what counts in my life as my truth. She does not belong there. Fuck she does not belong here. What the hell is she doing here anyway? She should be back in the skin layered bosom of her reptile home."

"She wanted me to warn you."

"Oh, that is terribly good of her. Now, I have been warned. I thank you for your concern, and let's hope that our paths won't have to cross again. Good bye."

I stood up and this time as I strode off she made no attempt at catching up with me again. With every step I regretted losing my temper as it had done little for my game. I was none the wiser now, not about her, not about what she saw the situation as, not how she could possibly have explained her appearance in the photo in Morocco. I had pretty much slammed that door shut. As I reached the park up by my work I had to focus on holding my hands in my pockets to avoid them from hitting my stupid little anger riddled head. When I got back to my desk the pile of work had built up and took me away from my preoccupation for a while. On the way home I stopped by the pub for a couple and the newspaper. I needed to be a little lulled before I faced the emptiness and phobia of my flat with all that had happened earlier still ringing in me. The night passed quietly enough and a film on television laid claim to my focus, although later I slept only in fits, due to the sticky remnants of irritation that coated my being.

Even though I did not want it to, the comments of Ciara's affected me. I felt estranged from Luca. I needed to rectify this. I called him and suggested that we go out for a few beers over the weekend. I needed my one ally. I was not going to let go of him that easily. That was what they wanted I guess. Luca was happy to hear from me and asked me about the photos. I explained that there were some major clues in the photos but that I still had a bunch to go through. We decided on a place to meet in the evening and I went back to the pile that now had been pushed into a corner of my bedroom floor. I scanned each image seriously but only found one more image, which fairly straight out showed Musa, Will and Nada dining at one of the sidewalk restaurants. Although it was strange that Luca would have captured that particular group; I would have to ask him about this, there was nothing out of the ordinary with the manner in which they seemed to interact. It was simply a dinner out. Yet, the more I thought about it, it seemed odd that just those three would be dining together. They had been friends through us, but I had not been aware of that they had continued that friendship outside of our company. I mean, it had never been mentioned. There were no dates on the photos but I assumed that the photo had been taken sometime after I had gone blind. This would fit the situation I guessed. They might have sought each other's company when we were out of the picture.

In the pub Luca and I were bending solemnly over our beers. The lights over the bar shimmered muddled in the foam. I glanced over at Luca and he glanced back.

"So tell me, what did you think of the photos?"

"They're great."

He scrunched his face up.

"I did not mean that."

"Yeah, I know" I said.

I turned my eyes back on the drink and then guzzling a little before I replied. What the hell, I should not let Ciara's stupid comment hold me back.

"I found a few strange coincidences."

"Like what."

He was interested.

"Like, people that looked like people I knew, but I can't be sure, no matter how many times I look at them. It could be them, or it might not."

The pub was spookily quiet and empty around us.

"And then, there was a photo of three of the people that I knew eating out at a restaurant during lunch hours. However, this might not have been so strange, other than it would be interesting to know when the photo was taken."

"That can be sorted. I have all my negs in order of dates."

"Good, and you must tell me why you took that photo as well."

"What do you mean?"

"Well it is a bit odd that you would have taken a photo of those three in particular, don't you think."

"I guess. We'll check it. Just show me the photo later ok."

"Ok."

He was behaving in a very understanding way. If there was something fishy about Luca I doubt he would have behaved like that. His behavior gave me hope. He was alright. Later on as we parted we were both a bit unstable and I felt a lot lighter too. We'd spent the rest of the evening chatting about anything

141

but Morocco and my particular predicaments.

There was still the note. As far as I was concerned it was unfinished business. I was sure there was something further that I could glean from it, if I'd just managed to get a more concrete answer. I did not want to bring it to Luca, although he had suggested that he had friends at the university where I had visited earlier for the same reason. Even if I gave Ciara no credit I thought it no harm to keep this to myself. Now, I would try to get a third independent interpretation of the note. I had figured that going to specialist places was not getting me anywhere; somebody else always seemed to have been there before me. Thus, came Saturday and I packed the car and ventured off into the countryside: the greenery in a slipstream outside my car windows. I swore I was underwater in some shallow pool upon a cliff somewhere tropical, soft muted greens and blues surrounded me. The sweet smells of grass and woodland wafted in. Serenity filled the car and the gentle music that snuck out of the speakers kept me enthralled. Just driving like I was born with the vehicle attached to me, as if I could bend the car to curves in fluid effortlessness. Every time I took a jaunt out of town I was struck by the same thought: I should do this more often. The shadow of my car chased me, not losing its focus until I entered long stretches overhung with leafy nets through which the sun here and there swayed drunk and giddy. A snapshot of myself; hurrying through the most picturesque of landscapes, hair tussled, elbow in the breeze, shades loosely on my nose, and a contended calm face glanced back at me every time I skimmed the mirrors. After a good four hours drive I stopped for the night for food and a night's sleep. I had been led to a bedroom through musty smelling corridors where the wallpaper peeled off at the top of the walls, damp ruled, and broken framed pictures of bleached rural landscapes were about to close their eyes. I was not at all surprised by the pokey plainness of the space that temporarily was mine. I

undressed immediately and walked into the shower without worrying about closing the curtains. Surely in the country nobody worried about the nakedness of strangers. The hot water worked wonders on my aching muscles that gradually loosened their focal point of speed. I got back in the same clothes and went out after getting rough directions towards a close-by eatery by the unhappy woman at the reception. As expected in the country the room I entered was lit by long neon spears that covered in webs and dead fly debris buzzed uncomfortably from up on high. A mechanical ceiling fan had been rudimentary attached next to the neon lights and sounded like a horde of machetes menacingly waiting for a massacre not far enough from the top of my pate. I ate my plate of what was referred to as food in an uncomfortable rush washing it down with a half carafe of house red. As I put the money down to cover the bill I got a long side-glance from the only other person in the establishment, a grey man slurping what seemed like pea soup, his raincoat still fixed to his skinny bent body. To him I was news. After having dined at the only eatery I found the only bar in the village. Again I was a curiosity to the two older men that mumbled and burst out in loud awkward laughs at the table by the door. I sat down at the bar with my back to them after having nodded at them as a way of acknowledging their existence and not causing any ill will. They had not nodded back but just gaped at me as if I had been a phantom. The barman was equally reticent but served me real drinks, perhaps believing in the possibility of a stranger in their midst a little more than the other two. Every time the barman went up to them they mumbled in unison and then I felt six bleary eyes scratch the back of my neck. I sighed deeply, drank the dregs, threw the money on the bar for one for the road and heard the shuffle of the barman's feet against the dusty sticky floors.
"You come far?"
Sudden interest on the barman's part felt more intrusive than under any other circumstances after their little coven.

143

"Just the city."

I was unwilling to share. I was leaving after this one anyway and then I would probably never ever see this little shithole again.

"Where you going?"

Obviously the man could not take hints. I closed my eyes to my drink and refrained from looking up at him. After a long pause I gave up and said that I was to visit my parents up the country. He continued wiping the same corner of the bar with a smelly rag not taking his eyes off me.

"Oh yeah?"

He kept wiping and I thought that maybe I had got away, he had lost interested but he must have just been thinking, for he paused mid wipe and said,

"How come you're here?"

"Just passing through. Leaving tomorrow morning"

I said through my teeth.

This time he must have got the hint for he moved on down the bar with his slimy rag. As I left I grunted at the barman and stared at the two as they stared at me as I walked by, not a word or gesticulation passed between us. Walking back in the dark I got a sensation of being followed but anytime I turned around I could neither see nor hear anything. It must have been the spooky atmosphere of the bar that had left an impression on me I told myself. As I pulled at the keys in my pocket there was a definite crunch down along the gravel path. I called out a soft "hello" but the night had swallowed the sudden fragment of noise and posed full and round in its gloom, satiated and soundless like a Buddha.

In the morning as my breakfast was slapped down in front of me I was exceedingly aware of something that I had done not quite right. I did not look up at the landlady as I half expected a barrage of abuse should I do so due to her manners on offer. Absorbedly I tended to my food, making sure that no stray crumb should offend. Eventually the landlady could no longer stand the distance between her physicality and all that which raced through that graying head of hers.

"It is good that you are leaving just after breakfast. The roads will be wide open."

I did not answer her, although I was wondering why she was so keen to get rid of me. The only thing that I was aware of having done to her was to lay my head on one of her stained pillows and soon was to give her some money for the pleasure. I had not asked her for any particular or peculiar favours. I could not stand the insulting conciseness that she used in speaking to me.

"Is there a reason for your rudeness?"

This time it was her turn to be taken aback. Once she had gathered herself the wild abusiveness that she had so hard tried to keep in check reared its whole gruesome body in one swift blow.

"You better get out of here now you sick sick man, or I will call the police."

She snatched back the plate, which still contained the breakfast that I sorely needed for the distance that I hoped to travel today. She stormed off mumbling loudly if indistinctly. As I let the car slip out of the tight spot in the driveway I could see her standing in the window still giving me abuse.

Soon as the road opened up, the tarmac gleaming with early morning rain, the trees and bushes at the roadside quivering at my speed, the bad feelings that the stupid little town had left me with were blown away, like every trace of me most definitely was removed from that dingy little room where I had had a taxing sleep. We erased each other: the night and the day. Our meeting removed pixel by pixel. That sleep had just been another night on a pillow, on a bed, under a blanket, my head in wait to be turned off, moments that never really were, but still became. It is past. The road is becoming hot by my tempo, red hot, and the sun begins to ride along, galloping, each gilded

145

rubber hoof hitting the scheduled spots like music. I turn on the stereo, shades back on, window down and elbow hanging back in the breeze. In no time I reach my destination. The towering building bends over me as my eyes follow its lines upwards. For a moment I feel like I am going to lose my balance. My gaze quickly switches back to earth. Standing in the mainly empty car park of the mosque I look around for any sign of life. I go up to what seems like the main door and knock. There is a steady silence greeting my attempt at contact. I try the handle and it gives way easily. I step out of my shoes and into the building. My feet leave heat marks that ooze off the cold tiled floors. I listen for any sort of noise as I walk through and eventually my stubbornness pays off. There is a sound of hushed voices trickling through the membrane of the building. I walk on and find them. I knock on the door and am greeted by a serious looking young man who obviously gets confounded by my appearance yet without missing a beat lets me in with a gracious gesture. I step in and find myself in the company of two older men seated at a wooden desk, my young greeter remains standing by the door. I nod at the men and they respond to me almost in unison to please take a seat. On the spot I decide not to actually use my real name but rather to introduce myself with a witty alter ego. They counter with introductions and ask me to tell them why I might have turned up here with them this afternoon. Again I think on my feet and decide not to make it too obvious as to the task that I hope for them to solve.

"I found this note in my room, a friend is supposed to have left it as a joke, and I was hoping that you would be able to tell me what it might mean."

I passed on the note with a slightly shaky hand. It struck me that my obsession with this note might be way out of proportion. Yet, here I was. They both looked at the note but agreed rather fast that there was another place I might need to try. I tried to ensure that the next place would not be a dead end by helpfully hinting at the possibility of it being Moroccan Arabic. They nodded in unison and agreed that they were sending me to the right man. One of them wrote down the address whereas the other one smiled benevolently at me without another word. The new note they handed me revealed an address and an impeccable map. I thanked them over and over whilst backing out of the room. The young man watched my odd behavior nonplussed and then carefully closed the door so that he disappeared little by little from my life. I stood staring at the door for a few minutes before I moved my hand a little and the map dropped to the ground. I bent down, picked it up, and shook involuntarily before I made my way back to the car.

The stairs creaked as my feet took turns balancing my weight on the well-trodden steps. The smell of sweat was overwhelming; it clung like melting salt to the walls and pressed itself fiercely into clothes and skin. I could feel it prodding me all over with sour stale needles, tattooing me. The grunts and regular bass thuds called me all the way up the stairs and I walked into the hall revealing a jumble of activity. People skipping rope, pounding sandbags, hammering outstretched hands and anything that wanted a beating. It seemed most people in here were Muslim. A guy hanging on the rope of the ring in the middle of the hall looked in charge so I aimed for him. After carefully stepping around each bustling hub I reached the man. He ignored me for a while as he concentrated on the two men tiptoeing around each other in the ring. Every now and again one of the men would break out of the dance for an avalanche of roughness directed at his sparring partner, leaving the other swollen, bleeding and scarred. It seemed to me a combination of two extremes, the graceful and the crude. It fascinated me more than I would have expected, never having set foot in a boxing hall before. I hung back indulging in these opposites. The fight came to an end and the man turned to me with raised eyebrows.

"I was sent here from the mosque."

Eyebrows remained raised, almost accusatory.

"See I have this note. They gave it to me at the mosque. There's a name on it. And then there is this other note."

I started digging in my pockets.

"Just wanted it translated, that's all."

I stretched the notes towards him and he took them gruffly.

"It's Moroccan Arabic."

I continued explaining. The man looked around and called out to a young man that was skipping in a corner. The young man immediately responded and came over.

"You Moroccan aren't you?"

"Yeah."

"This man here wants help with the meaning of this note."

The note was handed over; the young man glanced at it seriously, and then glanced back at me equally gravely.

"You want this translated?"

"Could you tell me what it means?"

He looked back at the note and without looking back at me said: "It is a threat." He continued: "It says, *not to look for meaning here*, in the note, I guess, or wherever you found the paper."

He swallowed and looked up at me again.

"It is the tone of it, it is threatening, it puts emphasis on that you should not be reading anything into it, into this, or you might end up in trouble. Serious trouble. Does that make sense to you?"

I shrugged

"Don't know."

I grabbed the note as he returned it to me, thanked him utterly dejected by this hunt for meaning, and wound my way back to the stairs. Nothing of this made any sense. I had traveled all this way, and it was completely useless.

In the car on the way back my phone rang. Luca's name was displayed in the scratched murky little window. I hesitated but then answered. Luca wondered if I wanted to meet up in the evening. I told him that I was out of town. We decided on tomorrow eve instead and hung up. I came up to a railway crossing where in wait for the train I grabbed the note that now was lying on the passenger seat, crushed it in my hand. As the train had thundered by and I moved again I rolled the window down and tossed the damn thing to land somewhere between the tracks. The last I saw of it the wind claimed it and danced it off in the same direction as the train that had just passed. Looking the other way I could see a raptor circling the roadside caught on a swell of heat. I turned the music up and drove on. The night crept up over the bonnet and the road became a silent tunnel. I was pulled all the way home by a thin metal wire fastened to the rising morning; which eventually slipped in under the tires.

Falling into my unmade bed I expected my stiff body to unfurl into a sleep so thick and heavy that nothing could disturb it. Instead I was wrecked by intermittent signals from built up stress in my psyche. I saw the bloody note everywhere. It was carried by children on a slide in a playground, a dog was chewing on it in the shade under a tree, it was preached from the pulpit by a transvestite under a black veil, a slight woman I was just about to mount had it written in red ink on her lower back and my sweaty hands diluted it into clumsy fingerprints, and so on. Each time my body recognized the note it jerked me back to wakefulness and then it took me a long while before I got back into another version of the same dilemma. I persevered anyway. Damned if I wasn't to catch myself at least a handful of restful moments. Eventually my resistance petered out. Exhausted I rolled out of bed, sat on my knees on the bedroom floor for almost twenty minutes gathering strength to get up. Even then my head went woozy as I stood up. I

149

scratched a flicker of an itch on my right buttock and stumbled into the shower. The cold water shrunk my manhood yet opened my eyes wide. It ran in clear roots attached to the gaping plughole. Perhaps it was pouring itself upwards, from the plughole up to the showerhead, in through those tiny little holes, and down the pipes in the wall. If the note had been made of water that is the way it would have behaved, or the way that it behaved anyway. It defied sense. I rubbed myself raw with the towel. My toes looked frail and far away on the bathroom floor. In my bathrobe I walked up the door to see what the pile of mail could contain. This morning I had trodden right over it, a dirty footprint as evidence. I wiped the marks onto the carpet before I brought the mail to the table to have a proper look. The coffee percolator hissed for my attention. Then, back at the table with the cup: all the usual mail, bills and advertisements, except for one handwritten letter. Who the hell writes letters nowadays? As much as it surprised me, it excited me. I lifted the letter to my nose and smelt it as I looked out the window. How long was it since I had received a letter like this, a proper letter, I could not recall. I remembered writing excessively to my teenage friends; we had so much to say then, so much to talk about, even including little souvenirs from my life at the time so that they could partake in it in an extended material way. Receiving a letter then was more common, but the same excitement remained. I remembered girlfriends that had kissed lipstick onto the end of their letters by way of signatures. If it were from someone I really liked, I would fit my lips to the sticky mark, lips against distant lips. That was love. Only time separated the touching of the paper, and time marked the paper with spilt tea, blood, rips, smells, and burn marks. It was as if time had collapsed in that flimsy fragile filament. I was holding today's letter in my hand and went over each little detail etched upon it. It even had a proper stamp; a blue flower, and although the place from where it had been sent was illegible the date was still there. It was from somewhere local anyway. There was nothing exotic about it other than that it was a letter in a time of emails. Just as I was about to tear into it I stopped myself. Perhaps I should honor the dispatch with a knife opening, or tear it open at the shorter side very gently. I inserted my finger into the little gap of the flap and with little tugs felt the paper resist my flesh to no avail. When I was done it looked like a little animal had been at it, all gnarled and jagged it suggested a coloured content. With my index and middle fingers pressed together I fished up the communication. It laid, a folded blue green square, exposed in my palm. I opened it up and felt my heart squirm a little. Someone had made a little pastel and ink drawing on it especially. The pigments came off on my fingers. I inspected it and smelt it. Suddenly I dropped it on the table thinking of the Unabomber and mythical poisonings, but my curiosity won out, and soon I was holding the letter in my hands again. Although the colours in the artwork were pleasing the image depicted was perhaps less so. It seemed to resemble a face turned away at an angle, which allowed for it to be interpreted as perhaps any face at all. To me, it was clear who it meant to depict and it hollowed me out. There he was again, the man that refused to leave my life although he never really even was a part of it. The folds in the paper sliced the face up in four equal squares. To me it suggested crossroads for some reason. I turned the paper over and held my breath whilst staring at lettering suspiciously similar to the writing on the note that I had just traveled half way across the country to have deciphered, the one that I had just shed. All I could do was laugh. Laugh at the utter madness of it all.

"When are you going back to northern Africa?"
Luca smiled at me, took his time responding, and drank some beer in the meantime.
"Are you trying to get rid off me?"
I ignored his attempts at humoring me.

"Just, I've been thinking, that perhaps what I'd like to do now is go back, and thought maybe that I could help you out or something, earning my keep that way. I mean I do not have enough money to just go gallivanting off into the sunset, leave my job and all, but I could take a career break, or something like that."

I think I genuinely shocked Luca. He almost choked on his drink and started spluttering and coughing like mad. Unable to stop himself he ran off to the bathroom to get rid off what ever was caught in his gullet. When he came back he was composed again but still reeling from my sudden brainstorm.

"You're a nutter, that's what you are."

"I'm serious Luca."

"I know you are, that's what's scares me."

I was completely shot down. Frustration began crawling around in my abdomen, trickling upwards through the pipes with a squeaky tearing sound which reverberated in my bones. I could hardly sit still. I was feeling desperate.

"I'm sure that there is something that I could do to earn my keep."

My hands were helplessly shaking themselves at him; marionette threads were in charge of them. Luca looked at me hard.

"It's not that that I am thinking of, it's the bloody fact of the photos and all the stuff that you still, over a year later, are affected by, that still cause havoc in your life, things that you have no idea of how dangerous or crazy they might be. Fuck, you could get killed, worst came to worst, just like the cat."

"What cat?"

I was confused.

"The cat, the fucking cat, any cat!"

Luca's voice was going into falsetto.

"Curiosity for fucks sake!"

Sudden inspiration spiraled on, the plan had been dormant to the point of not being before, but now it cracked and was

152

hatching, at least in my head: yes, that was what I was going to do, go back there. I would not talk to anyone, but would go back under completely different circumstances, not tell anyone about it, just go, just to see if there was anything else to it. Just go. That was my simple and perfect plan. Luca could be playing a big part in my scheming but it would take a lot of convincing and cajoling. He'd made that clear enough. Somehow though, I trusted that he would come around, in the end. Later when he called me I smelt victory, but I was celebrating a little too early. He was holding out, not even mentioning my master plan. Indeed he was going on as if we'd never spoken about anything like that. I avoided going into it as well, noting that he would need a little more time. Nevertheless, a couple of weeks later I came back to it.

"I checked out the possibilities of a career break with work and it seems it won't be much of an ordeal at all."

I threw this into a lull in the conversation and Luca seemed to freeze momentarily. Then he continued on as if I had not said anything, or as if he had not heard me. I repeated myself. Now he turned to me agitated.

"Stop going on about that. It's not going to happen."

"Luca."

"It's not going to happen."

He was shaking his head at me with his eyes all wide and admonishing. It was amazing how the pupils stayed focused whilst the head moved from side to side. We then sat in silence for a while grumpily watching our beers go flat.

"You're not my wife." I spat out.

"You're not mine either!"

Luca returned my comment as quick as it had dropped out of my mouth. The bartender felt it hard to suppress a laugh but as both Luca and I locked our crazed eyes on him he cleared his throat, coughed and pretended that something at the other end of the bar demanded his attention straight away. We returned to punctured beer watch. Each dead bubble burst removing the plumpness and life out of the body. It was slow, and inevitable.

The desperate squeals of seagulls slid through the air above the bench upon which I was reclining. My eyes were on the river that glittered and braided itself below. The horizon was like a musical note gone dead. It was and it wasn't at the same time. I followed it with my finger, drawing another invisible demarcation between me, and its portent: the line before the line, the end before the end. My hand sank back to my knee. I looked at my defeated hand and then returned back to the river. There was something in me, which gathered strength from watching the layers and layers of water-bodies bed themselves in seaweed. This time next year, where would I be? Would all that which had taken over my life now be gone and done then? Who could say? I raised the water bottle to my lips and drank in the contents in loud long gulps, then I got up and shook my arms and legs a little before I returned into the trot that had took me to the bench. I found a speed, which let my body rest in its rhythmic movements, lulled as the river by its constant pushing itself around. Half an hour later I was standing bent over my knees sweating and gasping for air outside of my house. Sweat found furrows in my skin and ran into my eyes. The salt stung, I tried to wipe it away with the back of my hand onto my leg. I felt lightheaded and so remained in this position until my body had recovered slightly. As I stood up I was greeted by the ambiguous smile of a possible neighbor. I grinned back equally disinterested and our wordless interaction passed without further ado. That was the neighbor from just below, I thought. Did he not use to have a wife and kids? I could not recall having seen them at all since a good while back now. Yes definitely. His wife had been a young looking Asian woman with a penchant for shawls. The two kids had been terribly well behaved and practically soundless. Odd that. The way that you could have kids brought up like that in today's world, which was so full of noise and aggravation. It was almost an aberration, that cacophony could breed such silence and even temperament. I leaned on the wall with a leg cocked against it whilst watching the traffic waft by sporadically in angry loud buzzes. After a few long strides up the stairs and I did my stretches in the hallway. As I was standing there I could hear noise from my apartment, a drilling sort of sound. Immediately my mind showed me a picture of my flat turned upside-down, just like in the thrillers, and in the middle of the mess a crazed man, hair standing on end, in blue overalls with a drill raised threateningly pointing at my heart. The door showed no signs of having been tampered with and remained locked just as I had left it. Warily I unlocked it and peered in. It all seemed intact. No sign of the man in blue overalls. However, the sound of the drill continued clearly. I pulled out my umbrella from behind the shoe rack and raised it in front of me as I moved down the hall towards the noise. As I reached the living room the open window to the street was found guilty. I went up to close it and huffed at my stupidity whilst watching overalled men working around a manhole on the sidewalk. One of the guys somehow sensed my watch and turned up and then grabbed his cock in a menacing gesture. I popped my head in quickly, taken aback by having been found out, and rattled the window shut with embarrassment. I do not know why.

I was packing my bag slowly so that I would not forget anything. After all I would be gone for some time. I would need to be careful in this task, which I usually neglected. Some items went into my suitcases only to be removed as soon as they had been placed. How many socks does a man need in a country that's warm all the time? Not many, nor would I need many warm jackets, that was for sure. My swimming trunks and goggles fell into one of the suitcases, a towel, some shorts, t-shirts, underpants, and jeans. Once I felt I had packed what I needed only one of the suitcases was actually full. I closed it. Now for the other stuff that I might need or miss. Like books, I would have to bring books. It would be hard to get a hold of such things whilst there, except for leftover tourist trash in the local secondhand bookshops. Nobody ever left real stuff behind, just that which could be discarded. I went over my bookshelves with a fine-toothed comb. Tome after tome found its way into the suitcase. Soon I had too much and was sitting on my bed doing a second more discerned sorting. In the end I had some items, which would demand re-reading and some, which were so full of ideas that it would keep me going no matter how long I would stay away. Any light stuff I might need or have the urge for was like drugs, I could get it anywhere, nothing to worry about or miss. Then I sat there staring out the window, watching the rain, watching the wind, wondering how long before, or if, I would sit here again. Naturally my savings would not let me go forever, and with today's ill wind whining through the hollow halls of the financial districts my tumbleweed escape could come to mean that I would have nothing to return to in the end anyhow. This apartment building might be repossessed and my home turned upside down by new tenants. One never knew. The hooligans were already running the country; everything was to their will and whim. With brick after brick of the natural world's defenses torn down daily, nothing of this might mean anything in the long run either. I felt I was escaping, but not away, but towards, the climax. I had never been the type to scaremonger, or listen there to, yet here I was with a head crowded with real apocalypse fantasies. I closed my eyes. Lisa's face dropped down like a water curtain in the warm dark nest of my skull. Lisa was my paranoid friend when we were just seventeen. She was scared shitless of the way that the world was turning. She was almost afraid of breathing for fear of her breath leading to a knock-on effect in the world. Every step she took was painfully aware. One could not remain so conscious and not lose. I remembered the day that my father had took me aside and told me about Lisa's "leaving us". That was the way that he had referred to her suicide. Anger had burst a sour bubble in the twists and turns of my stomach.

"She fucking killed herself."

I screamed at my dad.

"She didn't fucking leave."

My dad's deflated face landed in his held out shaking hands. She who had seen life as sacrilegious, had removed her own to give way for others that might have an easier time with the gift, those that did not take it too seriously, those who were cold enough to make use of it. It was hardly like, as Herbert Spencer had suggested, that life fed upon the fittest, but rather the other way around. Like a snake eating itself. Like a devoted Jain nun life swept away Lisa's footprints, careful so as not to damage any life forms that might live in her shadow. Thus, disentangled she could walk forever. And our noose just got tighter and tighter as we faced our own excrement, unable to do anything but eat that too.

The plane was dissolving in its own heat and fuel waves. It looked like it was going to melt rather than run and lift its rattling heavy metal body off the slippery tarmac. The sun spread itself in pulsating efforts across the floors in the terminal and eventually blinded me. I felt for my backpack that sat on the floor, searched for my sunglasses, retrieved them and relaxed a little as they cocooned my poor eyes. It was the constant buzz and the blinding light that caused panic in me, just like at the dentist's. It might have had something to do with flying as well. I was not as good at it as I had been when I was younger. Luca dropped a couple of drinks on the table next to me.

"This ought to take care of any panic."

I knocked one back and felt the immediate effect of it warm my insides, loosen any demarcations between me and my body.

"Thanks."

It was good to be here, at the start of a new adventure, rather than at the tail end of one that I had had no control over. Ok, so I was aware of that I was in someway following the old, tying up loose ends, yet in another way, because I had fought for this myself, this was all mine, it had nothing to do with anyone else, unless I chose to make it so. I had had no further contact with Ciara since prior to making the decision and so I hoped that no one but Luca, Luca's boss, and me knew about my sitting here waiting for northern Africa to bring itself to my soles. I swallowed the second drink greedily and suggested to Luca; as I now had the taste for it that we'd go to the bar for a couple more, as we still had time. He approved of the plan. Nothing that alcohol could not fix, at least not in the short-term, he philosophized, and steered towards the dimmed lights and heavy smell. Luca joked about the fact that we had hardly ever spent time together without alcohol being involved. I asked him if AA knew he was trying to recruit me. He slapped me on the back and ordered another round. It struck me that although Luca initially had been dead set against this adventure; he was now taking it in his stride. We had never really discussed the reasons why, just how. He had eventually called me back and informed me of that he had arranged it with his agent that he would go back, and that he would bring an assistant along. He told me that I would receive a very meager wage for the job but that perhaps we would be able to come up with something that could complement it. There was a deadline to the assignment, but Luca said that we could talk about that later. No need to get gloomy about something that might never come. I was just so happy that things had fallen into place for once and did not push it. It did not matter how long it was for anyway. Who knew what could happen. We organized ourselves separately, and here we were, on our way.

A heavy heat coated us as we walked down the rickety stairs of the airplane. I was feeling slightly queasy from the flight and the alcohol consumed, and the heat did not exactly help. A woman in a white scarf greeted us with a lipsticked grin pointing us in the direction of the arrivals hall. Once inside I immediately sought out the bathroom but unable to throw up I ended up standing splashing cold water over my face until the internal spasms abated. I leaned on the sink and stared into my own face dumbfounded. Only now did it dawn on me, here in the cool of the Algiers airport's toilets, what an absolute fool I was having come here. I slapped the idiotic and useless realization out of my face trying to suppress the sour bubbles that popped up in the back of my throat. This was not the time for doubt and misgivings. After having organized my by now cold sticky clothes on my body I shaped up and pulled back my shoulders before I walked out the door. Luca was sitting in the shade reading a newspaper. As I came out he let it fall onto his lap and made a sign with his head indicating that we had to get going. Outside we jumped into a taxi and Luca in a very relaxed manner guided the driver towards the hotel. Algiers pulsated by outside the window and I lowered it to get some air. The same sort of drowning yellow ruled here as in Morocco. The dry palm fronds rubbed themselves together creating an eerie orchestra along with the rushes of impatient traffic. In my head the words "sticks and stones may break your bones" rumbled back and forth without a connection to anything as far as I could think. The words fell out of my mouth quietly. I watched and thought: the world did not seem exotic to me anymore. Anywhere I went I more or less knew what to expect. However, there was something else, outside of the visual that constantly changed wherever I went. Even at home, something much less specific, something almost electric, I guessed, stained the fabric. I hesitated but yes probably something psychic. Far out man. I thought of the archetype humans of Jung, of the prohibition of depictions of people in strains of Islamic thought on art, and tried to assemble a map in my head of the archetypes of humans that circulated through my life. There was also myself as my own archetype that circulated through other people's lives. Say Luca, for example, did I fulfill a niche in his life? Did I resemble someone else that he had been close to previously? How were we connected? If chance was the only tie, then he could be anyone. If I did an experiment with this, say if I broke up the friendship now, then very likely someone else just like him would enter my life to take over from where he had left off; to fulfill his destiny in my life, and mine in his. That was the way that it worked, I supposed. I had no definite proof, but as a tool to review this theory I had designated an old wooden cigar box for the images of such people in my life. I had spent over a week locating photos of these people in my life and had cut them out as intact as possible. For the people that I had no photographs of I had; with paper, crayons and a laminator, created little paper dolls resembling those image-lacking-ones to the best of my ability. I could not wait to get into the hotel room now so that I would be able to lay them out on the floor whilst the thinking was fresh in my head. The webs, I had to get a grip on the webs, and then this story would come apart, or come together. It would explain why I was traveling like this now, in this taxi in Algiers with a man that had seemingly little in common with me. A cloud of dust rose swiftly in front of us, and in a second the particles had entered through my open window, the taxi driver began screaming hysterically and Luca violently leaned over me desperately trying to quickly close the window. The air in the car whirled red and impenetrable. I closed my eyes. As we stepped out of the taxi the driver glared at me whilst he shook his clothes and picked dust out of his ears. Don't think he was too happy with me. Luca paid him and as soon as our bags had been angrily hauled out of the booth onto the steps of the hotel the driver was gone, leaving us in a cloud similar to that which I had allowed into the car earlier. Luca coughed and held his hands over his face whilst I closed my eyes hard and held my nose and stopped breathing for a minute. When the dust was around our knees our eyes met and we burst out laughing. I grabbed my bags and walked up the stairs and in through the revolving door. A disheveled reflection glimmered at me in the door's glass panels. Luca followed suit, spinning his face into the hotel. Once inside a couple of bellboys fought us for our bags and due to us becoming involved in the process of getting rooms and keys they won out. They stood straight-backed next to us brimming with victory ready for the next move. We crowded into the elevator. The metal box rose noisily and painfully though the shaft. I was staring at the ceiling whilst the others were staring at their feet doing anything to avoid looking at each other and there by acknowledging the proximity. We got off on the fifth floor. Luca and I had been given rooms right next to each other and walked in to explore each cement cavity. Simultaneously we discovered our balconies and stood studying the sea with approval and relief. The bellboys hung back shuffling but did not leave until we had shelled out some change for their effort. Thereafter the rooms went quite. I went to have a siesta whilst Luca remained in a chair on the balcony reading. As night presented itself by offering a new hue I heard Luca call from the balcony for me to get a move on, that he needed to get some food and did I want to come along. I grunted at him, got up, let cool water wake me, and dressed freshly for the eve. As on a holiday I seemed to have more stamina even though I lacked food and sleep, only this was not a holiday as such. I thought of what I would have to do and realized that I had not prepared myself at all for this. Through it all I had forgotten all about my cigar box.

A day could go by so quickly I would have no check on how it broke into evening. One moment I was sitting at the edge of my bed listening to the calls to prayer lost in thoughts about the dream that I'd just left, the next I was finishing off my supper still feeling hungry. This fast forwarding of time scared me so much so that I decided to account for everything that was happening by whispering it to my self whenever a discrete moment arose to do so.

"I am looking at the railing that fences me in from a fall down into the empty streets below, the fencing that I hold on to so as not to be blown out into the sea, that flirts and flickers just an arm length away, is very flimsy. The time is exactly, well it is dawn, according to my dead watch that keeps a firm if sweat slippery grip on my left arm. I can feel goop in the corners of my eyes and I lift my right hand index finger up to remove it. I flick it over the balcony. I can taste the nightcap deep in the cavities of my mouth and watch a large solitary black bird scoop a bit of ocean up before rising towards sunrise with its fleeting offering. As if on order the call to prayer flutters out into the air and into the hollows of my chest and abdomen, it reverberates and rests there until a new prayer rides in on a stronger wave and replaces the previous dying one. I fill my lungs with air. I feel the air fill up my mouth before it streams into my pipes and then down into what feels like my stomach but must be my lungs."

Luca stepped out on to the lip of the building.

"Mumbling to yourself again?"

I grinned at him sheepishly.

"Something like that."

"Let's go down for breakfast. We have a long day in front of us."

Long day?

In a studio in the middle of town I get my first crash course in photography. This is the shutter speed, this is how you load the camera, and this is how you rewind the film. Make sure that you never let any light into the camera body where the film snugly rests or you will have ruined the whole thing. This is

162

how lighting works. Distance. Aperture. 100. 200. 400. Reflectors. Shades. Composition. I was drinking it all in as best as I could. I would never remember this in the morning.

"Perhaps best that you practice yourself with the cameras for a little while. Look here. Here!"

Luca was aware of how my attention slipped. I gathered my concentration on him again.

"I have these old cameras here for you to practice on, and this book. Remember, once we get going I do not want any shit from you. You are getting paid for the job after all."

Then he went out and I heard him joking with the girl that had organized the space for us. I stood dumbfounded in front of the equipment. Picked up one of the manual cameras mumbling to myself trying to recall Luca's directions. Stupidity was mine. Here I was, as I had demanded. Where would all this bring me? I felt as if I had made my life into this big joke, a joke on me, a joke that everybody else could enjoy in their normal, run-of-the-mill jobs and lives. How the hell did I end up here, doing this! Life was hardly as complicated as I was making it. What was I doing? Stalking my own past in a completely different place from where I had actually been. Did I think that all of Northern Africa would be concentrated on me! That it was all the same? Silly me. Why the hell would anyone want to do the things that I seemed to think that they had done, to me! I pinched my arm until I could feel the skin coming off and tears built up in my tear ducts. Why had Luca not stopped me? My hands were still moving the dials on the camera but I could not see much now. Wiping the tears on my shirtsleeve I tried to remain focused on my task rather than self-pity. I turned the dials and looked in the book as I did so, but still could not make out exactly how it was supposed to work. I only had myself to blame. I had demanded to get out here and here I was. I had come up with reasons to be here. After all I had nothing to lose. Sure, I had nothing. I sat down on a rickety chair in the corner of the room and tried to read. I would make the best I could out of this. This is what I would do. This was an adventure. I would learn what I could and do the best job that I could as Luca's assistant. Perhaps this was my true calling. My destiny. God, was I queer or what? The drama! But I was right, nobody would argue with me, it was best to try to work this rather than return home a failure. Reading each line in the book aloud to myself the details began slipping in one by one. A couple of hours must have gone by before Luca returned. He smiled and waved a couple of tickets at me.

"We'll do a little outing for a couple of days, for you to get a feel for it."

I must have looked like I had not been listening as he repeated what he'd just said, and added:

"Then you can come back to practice anything that you need before the real stuff starts."

He started gathering the cameras and the rest of the paraphernalia into a purpose built army green bag. He handed it to me.

"Come on, that is enough for today. I'll buy you a beer."

The next day my flesh and bones were bouncing in what seemed like a southerly direction. Enthralled by the landscape and stray beings, after hours of journeying I began to form word rhythms in my mouth. Like bubbles I let the chants out when no one was listening or looking, out into the landscape, like prayer, like incantations or blessings. I was not sure what I was really doing this for, and the words only sometimes made sense, but that did not stop me from creating them, a long string of them. Sometimes the same word would keep me captured, its nuances going against my gum, or sliding around too easily, it repeated on me. I looked over at Luca's stone sleeping face every now and again, but he seemed to be just that, sleeping, most of the time. Either that or he was contemplating the world's woes in a very dispassionate way. His lips parted every now and again, rearranging themselves on their pillow, slipping a little air out and taking a little extra in. Otherwise he was stock-still. There was a lady, sitting just in front of him, who was unable to sit still, and each time she moved her headscarf would twist and so she was over and over reshuffling her hair and scarf. Meticulously her hands, with each finger doing its fair share of work, moved across her head. Not a hair out of place, or in disgrace. I think she noticed me watching her routine, and now and then she would turn around with a very dour mien, putting me in my place. However, the gesture was the same each time. She never really got any more upset about it than she had been to start with. We were finding our own rituals in our new close quarter habitat. Every time the bus would do a pit stop there would be a rush for the toilets but Luca would nonchalantly circle the bus with his smoke, and I pretended that he was putting a spell on the vehicle for safety purposes. I could even see the smoke gently cling to the sweating metal before it absorbed it completely. It made me feel safer. Once, he did not stir, so I nudged him awake to make certain he got his nicotine fix and we got our wispy charm. You could never be too safe. Eventually our destination arrived at our reclining bodies. The world stopped outside the windows. "This is us."

It was Luca's turn to rattle my body into action, and it did not take much for me to move. It was high time to get a cold beer into my body, and maybe even a decent meal. As I stepped out into the passageway the woman that had been fidgeting in the seat in front of Luca also stood up. Again I got a killer look, which made me immediately obey. It was She, I joked, to myself, Rider Haggard's "She." I think She heard my thoughts, for once again, even though I really had stepped off her territory, she made her unhappiness towards me known. I smiled back at her, and she positively hissed. Luca, winked at me as I stepped out.

"I think she had a soft spot for you. A little more charm and she would have been all yours mate."

"You got me all wrong. I like earlobes, see."

"What are you on about?"

"I cannot date women without earlobes."

Luca's face contracted to a "what?"

"With her scarf on I hardly think that you got a glimpse of her ears!"

"No, but I could tell by the way that she listened to things, and the way that the scarf fit to her head, the close proximity of her eyes."

"You are joking me."

There was no joke, just confusion. Exhausted I replied.

"Yeah, just joking."

Before we had time to enter the place where we were to rest our weary souls for the evening we were caught up in a crowd that drifted with agony through the streets. I saw Luca's head bop up here and there in front of me and tried not to lose sight of him at the same time as I made attempts at hollering at him anytime he appeared, trying to find out whether or not he knew what was happening. He was unable to hear me through the din, but every now and again he seemed to be aware of that I was still there, floating with the mob, and so he waved a sign for me to go with the flow, as if I had another choice. I felt hands move over my pockets but could not ascertain where they came from or to whom they belonged. As I had nothing to covet on me; other than that which was in my bag but I had that secured above my head, I let the hands wander as they pleased whilst watching the bag intently. At points I felt as if I could have lifted my feet off the ground and still would have been carried forward, but I did not feel confident enough to experiment. The crowd dispersed as we arrived at the river. Soon we were all standing in a long line along the flowing waters staring. Finally I spotted Luca and wound my way to his side, excusing myself for dislodging people slightly with each step.

166

"What's going on?"

I was still very uncertain of why we were standing here, what all the commotion had been about. To me the world was alright. With his hand outstretched Luca led my eyes to a strange object that sucked itself to the surface of the frivolous water. I strained and strained but the object remained a mystery, then all of a sudden an arm seemed to raise itself up slightly only to be falling back into the boiling mirror. Little by little I noticed more objects that half emerged. The body of a black pig rolled around, perhaps a desperate attempt at swimming or just dead weight dancing to the tune of the motion. The difference between life and death was hard to tell from my standpoint.

"What's happened?"

I screamed at Luca, but as I turned to where he had been standing I noticed that he was now crouched closer to the water a little further down the bank with his camera tightly set to his eye. He let the shutter do his blinking for him: a mechanical dream machine, devouring images then dropping a curtain of nihilistic dark, gaping again, taking another moment from the world, or into it. Turning back to the catastrophe I froze as I watched an increasing number of human and animal bodies come careering down it as if they were late for some appointment with a huge drain at the edge of the horizon. The river seemed to fill with a deadly cargo and all we did, all we were, were spectators. Not one person did attempt to reach the desolate river passengers. There were no attempts at in the least hampering the progress of the travelers. No, we were all ossified, that is until this woman started shouting louder than anyone had previously been able to. I am not sure what she was shouting but she made a piercing noise which set a few of the men into motion. Soon ropes started to be thrown into the water. They snaked for a moment and then sunk. The throwers were aiming for the bodies, perhaps hoping that if anyone were still alive they would grab a hold, to let us take them away from the course that they were on. The ropes came back as slack as they had been thrown. The river bubbling, churning, frothing brown plant materials releasing here and there all manner of debris, and then as a trophy of catastrophe, a child's bloated corpse. The women wailed, the children screeched, the men heaved, the ropes splashed, the river snorted and spat. My ears were ringing. Luca was remembering, but unable to breath.

The village was in an uproar. The air seemed encrusted with anxiety, and if I looked real hard I could see the walls of each house swathed in a similar vapor, sweating it. We had gathered in a courtyard listening to a local politician or leader; every soul solemn in its task of listening and remembering what needed to be done and just how. The man in charge was unnecessarily loud as he delivered his solutions. Behind the houses the long pregnant howl of the river remained constant. It still poured forth in the eyes of the people that had been to watch it. I could see it in each one that turned their faces towards me. The manner in which we looked at each other was new to me. I looked at each stranger with a deep sense of love and belonging. I could reach out and touch them if I wanted to. I could touch strangers as if they were my family or my dear ones, they would allow it. Nobody would turn away at a moment like this. Nobody would be offended. I stepped back and felt something stop my progress abruptly. I fell backwards but managed to catch my fall with a quick turn of my upper body. A cold wet muzzle hit my cheek, as my head hurtled towards the dry rough ground, which made my body retract in its movement but without much point. With a thud my bones hollowly connected with the dirt. I lay still and watched the puddle of blood that I had landed in and the cow's head that sat in the midst of the dark red pond, a fountain feature, but not a spitting fish, a urinating boy or a woman with an ever-flowing vessel under her arm, not this time. If the blood had not been there I would have sworn that the creature wasn't dead, but rather that it was rising from the depths of our world, coming to join us. Its eyes were still moist and protruding, pleading with me to come to its rescue. Its eyes were no different from all the eyes that I had been looking into just before I took the wrong step. Neither were the eyes of the dog that now had taken advantage of the moment and stood licking up the blood, curling it gently up on its rough tongue, depositing the gel like substance at the roof of his mouth. He smiled at me. His eyes were full of the same love, same sameness. His tongue reached out again but this time he aimed it for my face instead. I did not flinch. He cleaned and cleaned. I felt his tongue in the corners of my mouth. I closed my eyes and felt the clammy muscled dog body part move over my eyelids without exerting an uncomfortable pressure, slipping between my lashed slits. I imagined myself as a newborn pup.

Propped up against a porous ochre wall my eyes find themselves and take charge. I feel the back of my sticky shirt rub the wall as I move a little and bits of loose plaster fall into the space between my trousers and my skin. The room is dark with only a square of soft light drawn on the cool tiled floor. Luca is sitting on his haunches in front of me with a bottle of water at the ready. His left foot is in the light box. He pushes a stray lock of his hair out of his sight and holds the bottle up a little higher, not sure if it is within my field of vision. I shake my head at him. I do want it, the water, but have no strength to complete the motions necessary.
"You ok?"
This time I nod.
"Good. Good."
Luca turns his attention to someone at the door, says something unintelligible and then returns to make sure that I have recovered.
"I'll be back in ten. Just rest here ok. I'll be back."
With that he stands up and returns to whatever preoccupies

him outside. I let my eyelids fall back down and they do so so quickly that I picture them actually making a big booming noise, like a door shut with force, with ire. Then behind the little optical foreskins I sink into water, deep, dense, dark and chilly. I keep my nose above the surface. I don't want to die.

Somewhere in twisting time I am picked up by Luca and led back to the place where we are to sleep that night. Luca leaves me again though, once he has put me to bed and asked a young boy in a New York Yankees baseball cap to keep an eye on me. Every now and again I can feel the concentration that the young man is issuing as he looks after me. I believe that I see his little hand pull the sheet up for me, and then hear him whisper something to console to me, whilst I drift back and forth in and out of consciousness, blissful and scared to death, and not sure of what is what. Then in the semi dark I wake to a clarity that remains. I say to myself I knew something like this would happen. I should not have insisted on this trip, on this. This will be the death of me. Then I start laughing at myself, my petty and repeated concerns, in the midst of a natural disaster. I am ridiculous again. It is this focus on oneself that prevents one from fully taking part. I sit up and look around for the boy but he is nowhere to be seen. The sparse type of furnishing of the room suggests to me that we are in somebody's private house. The boy probably part of the family. A cough ascends from my lungs and as soon as I make a sound the boy gently appears. Only half of the boy is seen at the door before he runs for help. It must have been ok whilst I was not moving and talking. Now, he just does not know what to do with me. Probably he has run to fetch an adult. But I am wrong again. The next minute he appears with an apologetic mien, he enters the room with a bowl of food. His concentration complete, making sure that the bowl is delivered with all food still in it.
"Thank you."

The bowl changes hands. He looks at me shyly and blinks. Then he stands there for a few seconds just looking at me, before the behavior is checked and he rushes on out. Looking at his wake momentarily I wake to the heat of the bowl and set it down on my lap, couscous with what appears to be lamb and plenty of greens. Smells great. I heave the spoon into my gaping mouth. Starved. When did I eat last? What time is it? Where is Luca? And what is happening out there? I am such a hero. Slip, and slip under. In no time the bowl is emptied and the heat from it gone. I set it down on the floor and lean back in the bed. What else can I do? I lift the sheet and look over my body but cannot see any direct marks from my fall, or any obvious reason for me to be bedridden in the first place. With the help of diverse muscles my feet swoop over the side of the bed and gradually reach for the floor. The chill of the floor is initially reacted to as if it emits heat: my knees pull up reflexively. I try again, this time knowing what I am getting myself into. There is a careful knock on the door and I turn around. An old toothless woman all dressed in black comes in repeating words at me whilst waving her hands around, stirring the air, and approaching me hesitantly. I get up and roll my shoulders a little, confused at her torrent, yet unable to react to her in a manner that will stop the commotion, which she is lost in. The young boy stands in the doorway watching us. It is not on purpose that I do not respond to her. It is just that I feel completely astray. The boy equally reactionless seems to confirm my behaviour as normal as he considers my being from across the room. By now though the woman's proximity has become almost uncomfortable, and every now and again I can smell her and sense the top of her head below me as she circumambulates me. I inch backwards towards the bed, but she moves along with me. The boy takes a step back and utters a little sound perhaps urging her to layoff but she does not hear him from within the bubble from which she is operating. Eventually I fall back on the bed and the drastic change in my

171

size seems to surprise silence into her. She still looks at me as if I am an uncertain creature encountered in dark woods. I look back at the boy but he is no longer making a shadow of himself in the light of the open door. He is not even in the room. He must have gone. Maybe he has gone to collect Luca to save me from the crazed woman. I hope this is it. All of a sudden she stirs, turns on her heel and abandons me to the hole of her disappearing cacophony. The world has gone eerily still. A little breeze creeps awkwardly in over the floor and the dust bunnies dance like uncertain rotund ballerinas over it. I get up, stick my feet in my sandals and move towards the door. Outside is an empty courtyard that I cross with trepidation. I stare at a rusted old bicycle that leans against the trunk of a dark tree as if it is an enormous spider, or something; it feels so out of place. Each step of mine releases a padded echo from the crumbly walls. I can feel the air filter between my sole and my leather shoe each time I lift a leg to move on. I feel turtle'ish in my progress. Then the boy shows in a new doorway, the one that leads from the courtyard out into the outside world.

"Janus" I whisper to myself.

The boy nods at me with an imprint of a smile not seen but sensed, like a ghost. I do not return the greeting but my hand reaches out for the boy. He offers his shoulder for me to grab onto, as if he realizes that I need his guidance. He turns and my hand finds a comfortable seat around his skinny little right shoulder. I feel the bones of his shoulder shift and dance in my palm and under my fingers, and it makes me think of piano keys. We walk out like that, welded to each other. The sun still thick in the air and lying everywhere pulsating and panting, even in the shadows. People pass by in a frenzy, not taking any heed of us. We move slowly in comparison. My legs do not seem to carry me properly, no matter how I try to shake them or stare at them. I feel as if I have aged forty years in a manner of hours, like a president. I get bumped by a young woman in a hurry, and braze myself against a wall, almost bounce of it, but the boy immediately steadies me by stopping.

"Luca".

The boy is encouraging me by referring to the one stable point in my life at the moment. I look into the light brown eyes of the boy as I want more from him, another word perhaps, but he only repeats Luca's name and gesticulates with his head in a manner which seems to suggest that Luca is where we are heading. I compose myself and we move on, snaking through the melee. Eventually we ended up where Luca was. He did not see the boy or me but was busy helping pull a jeep out of the cascade. The men pulled one way, the river the other. How they had secured the rope around the car I had no idea. Surely nobody had been so foolish as to go out in those waters for the sake of a stupid car. As my eyes hovered on Luca I noticed that he was thoroughly drenched and I hoped that it was from labour, rather than the river. The boy and I just stood there, a pair of useless spectators. I am sure that even the sun was annoyed by our presence as it tried to move around us as if we were not there. Once the jeep was on fairly solid ground Luca slapped one of the heavers on the back and raised his eyes to us. Perhaps he had been aware of us all the time. He sauntered up.

"What a day."

I looked at him and then at the jeep. Luca by way of an answer to my look said,

"See that man in the red t-shirt. It's his only possession in the world. Not even sure if it will work now, but he might be able to sell it for parts or something. His family is over there." By the sand bank further up a woman and five kids stood in a row, paralyzed by the scene. No relief was evident by the rescue of the vehicle.

"Can I do anything?"

The moment I uttered the words I knew that they were as useless as my watch. Luca ignored my question.

The light of the candle swayed. The voice on the radio: tinned and one-dimensional. "Flooding levels in southern Algeria have reached an all-time high. Torrential rains have created havoc in the country. Over six hundred people have been made homeless and over three hundred people reported dead at this moment. Hundreds more still missing and feared dead."

I looked at my bare feet at the end of the bed, moved my toes. I tried to suppress a cough that was working itself out of my lungs but unable to, I had to let it rattle my chest in choked gulps. I had slept some more, but now I was wide-awake, and hungry to boot. Trying to imagine our escape route from here I got hung up on pictures of the day that still circled around in my skull. There was no way out, and anyway Luca did not want to leave. There was so much to do he said. I guessed it was a photo opportunity for him as well, but I had seen less and less of the camera as the days went on. He seemed to find a comfort in being of assistance, so much so that the job he was here to do took second place. I had not expected this of him. I guess I imagined him as one of those unscrupulous war reporters who'd walk over corpses to get a good shot. I was wrong. It was something else that drove Luca to do the things he did so well. I watched him sleep close to death with exhaustion across the room oblivious to the radio or the candle. His hair was sticking to his head and a dark shadow enveloped most of his lower face and neck. His mouth was firmly shut. There was nothing that his sleep would utter. His absolute stillness scared me and I went up to check that he was breathing. He was. I tiptoed back to my bed and turned off the radio and blew out the candle. I would try to get some more sleep. Tomorrow I might be able to actually do something myself, and tomorrow was to be here very soon given the amount of light that trickled in underneath the door.

Soon, the door was wide open and Luca's shadow hung fragrantly over me. I blinked at him and moved up and out of bed as fast as my still slumbering body would allow.

"We'll go down to the river to see what needs to be done. I'll wait for you out here. Ok." His shadow was gone and in its stead was a direct radiant morning. The t-shirt I threw on was a little cold and damp, calling for me to get that sunshine onto my skin. Holding the doorframe firmly with both hands the white light forced my eyes shut whilst I waited for my body to assimilate. Once ready I went over to where Luca was sitting and partook in the food that had been set out.

"You'll need a good breakfast for the work today, and more so, don't you think, because of the way you felt yesterday."

Luca was talking to me between bites, but was doing so more for the sake of it, rather than for having something to actually say. Ignoring him I concentrated on the food. The coffee was thick and did the trick. I felt life stride into my head and limbs. Perhaps Luca was nervous? No, surely he was a man of the world, a man that never could be surprised or shocked. I watched his face for a second, and his focus was intense although not here. His forehead lined in deep grooves, eyes narrowed, he kept rubbing his finger together. He was making plans I surmised. I stood up and let him know that I was ready. He did not wait around in reacting to my signal, but was almost up before I had made the move. The morning seemed less chaotic than the previous one, but as we got out on the banks it was obvious that the tragedy continued. Women were crying and praying in groups by the river, watching the waters sideways with trepidation and anger. The river paid them no mind, but just ate and spat the space with a ferocious sound of its appetite. We walked along waiting for some heroic deed to become called for. Luca did stop now and then to take a shot, but it seemed mostly for show. He did not ask any assistance from me. After a good whiles walk we did come into the presence of someone in need. This time it was an old woman

175

wrapped in a blue shawl that called us over. She sat on an upturned red plastic bottle container. Her dry straight grey hair at points hung disheveled out of the shawl, but she was not concerned. In a pinched voice she toothlessly rambled on to Luca who did not seem to get all the details that she offered him although he tried his hardest. After a while he stood up and spoke to me.

"Her son has disappeared. I asked if he might have been in the areas that were flooded, but she just keeps repeating the same thing although in different ways. I am not even sure she has lost her son here, or at birth. Not sure if she is really here."

Luca looked out over the river again.

"I think I will hear this rush of water in my ears for the rest of my life."

The woman went quiet and watched the two of us with disgust. We were useless to her.

The good deeds of that day seemed to be limited to having coaxed the old woman away from the side of river and back into the village. However, once there, we found out that she belonged to a house just on the outskirts and so we proceeded towards her home keeping to the rhythm of her painstakingly slow walk. The house we came upon was more than derelict. Once we had organized for fresh water and food for her we did the best we could to put plasters on the big gaping wounds of the home. We cleaned up the yard, put things in piles and repaired the most glaring troubles the best we could. I was still tired from the day before but contrary to what I would have expected my strength returned in little gusts as we worked. We washed her sheets, her curtains, her clothes and whole bedroom in hope of ever so faintly making a difference for her. By the time evening fell the place looked new, even if the underlying problems were still there. I don't think that she knew anything about anything that we had done, and she probably did not care either. Her world was the same. The way that the building had fallen apart suggested that the son that she had referred to either never had existed or at least never came to visit her. She might as well have lived at the edge of the world, and at the end of it. As we left her she sat humming to herself wrapped in the blue shawl underneath a pomegranate tree deeply burdened with fruit. We waved at her. She did not wave back.

The next day the sun rose and made booming flapping sounds. I ran out of bed, my body taut with excitement and strength. Out in the courtyard I recognized the noise as a helicopter and ran alongside some kids towards the bursting and bruised waters. The helicopter hovered, a silver insect, over a flat area, whipping water and what was left of the dust in fury, the thin metal wings slicing the air methodically. I could see the concentration on the pilot's face as he set the round swinging body down on stable ground. Out hopped an energetic woman with long black hair dressed in a white shirt and black slacks. She ran bent over towards the kids and me but as she got closer she straightened up and stopped for a moment to tidy herself a little. Then she took her time and walked gracefully and purposefully up. A self-assured smile, eyes glinting, she greeted the gaping group. I must have looked the village fool standing there with my wrinkly clothes and hair on end in the midst of a group of snotty, driveling brats. She gave me a surprised look that confirmed my sense of self, and then she spoke to me slowly. She was from the main television channel and she wanted to report on the disaster, did I know where she could begin? Who was the chief of the village? As she was talking I noticed a young man that had followed in the woman's footsteps so well that he had more or less been invisible until now. He stood like a shadow behind her with a pad of paper in one hand and a pen at the ready in the other. I shook my head and came to, then, I even began acting my age. Sure, let me take you into the village. I am here with a photographer named Luca and perhaps we could be of some assistance. I could tell that she was relieved that I was not as idiotic as I had come across to start with. She trusted my guiding her into the village and the boys all washed up like foam behind us. I could sense her looking me over every now and again, surprised by my appearance at a place like this no doubt. As we walked through the doorway into our courtyard the kids peeled off. I offered her a chair and got a drink of tea for her. I looked for Luca but he was not around, so I went back to the table where she sat and sat down myself. I began explaining our story in the village so far, and she was taking notes with a strong and nimble hand. She was quite striking: her dark brown eyes had long curled lashes, elegantly drawn eyebrows and were then delicately framed by a short straight fringe. A scatter of freckles over each of her prominent cheekbones made her beautiful features more friendly than sterile. In the naked space between her shirt and her neck a small round globule of porphyry was visible, seemingly suspended in thin air, it vibrated in the hollow where the collarbones meet. She caught me looking at it and moved a little in her seat before letting her fingers grip the thin invisible chain that was holding it and turning it a little to give me a sign to stop staring. I got it. In my head I said sorry, and then continued on with the story. Too soon Luca came back. He stopped in the doorway a little confused by the appearance of a city woman at our table, but soon recovered and advanced confidently. She seemed relieved that Luca had arrived. Perhaps I had been coming on too strong. I think that I had lost all my sense of appropriateness over the years. Luca shook her hand and she offered her name.

"Rada."

"Luca. Welcome. I don't think we've met before."

"No, but I have heard about you. You know the guys at the news desk at.."

She quickly pulled out her card and handed it to him.

"Ah, yes of course."

I started to feel like I wasn't there. Luca looked so dapper and heroic with his broad shoulders and two-day stubble. His white shirt seemed unreal in its cleanliness and so did his blue jeans. If a woman had a choice between the two of us I do not think that there would be a contest. I did not feel half as romantic as Luca presented. I mean even his job carried an air of romance with it, and he knew it and used it when it came to women. I watched them talk for a while and felt distinctly jealous. I wanted to be her point of interest. Her breasts rose and sucked at her shirt, and something stirred in my pants, which surprised me slightly as it set off a thought about how long since I had felt that.

"What do you think? Good idea huh!"

Luca's voice intruded on my train of thought. He must have realized that I had been elsewhere.

"Going up in the helicopter this afternoon, to get a proper look at the situation."

I nodded.

"That would be great. Thanks."

She finished up her tea and stood up.

"Let's meet by the helicopter, say around three?"

We agreed. She walked off to talk to people in the village, and this was when I noticed the young man again. He had been skulking by the doorway and now fell into a trot behind Rada's purposeful march. Luca laughed at my inability to act, slapped my back.

"Don't waste your time dreaming, mate. She's not into men."

I pulled at the strap; it got caught, I let go of it; it snapped back into its lair. Once again I grabbed the buckle, but this time I gently tugged at it. Again it got caught. I swore loudly. The young man, that had turned out to be Rada's assistant, asked me nervously and quietly if I would like some help. I snapped a no-thank-you back at him. He was an annoying thing, so demure and insipid. The seatbelt finally relented and I secured it around my waist with a sniffle. I glanced over at the man. A

179

wallflower, that's what he was, the epitome of a wallflower, if I'd ever seen one. There he was crunched over his thin long hands that rearranged letters on a page of a pad of paper. No doubt he was only pretending to be busy so that nobody would notice him. There were six of us in the helicopter in all. In the pilot seat was the man that I had seen when they landed. Next to him sat Rada, who constantly was leaning back, making sure that we all were ok before the glass bubble in which we were seated was about to sink into the ether. Besides Luca, the young man, and me there was a forty-something bearded cameraman who kept pursing his lips and scrunching his eyes, seemingly deeply concentrated on his camera. The steel lasso sucked us up, and I held my breath looking at the ground that let go of us so easily. The rock, where I, as of late, had stood daily overlooking the water, shrank rapidly to a pebble. My head swam with the loss of the usual perspective. I felt as if we were moving in circles into the rotating blades, rather than the other way around. My eyes were jumping in their sockets. I bit my teeth and shut my eyes momentarily. Then having regained my senses I leaned close to the window and drank in what I could of the disaster. Beneath us hovered an earth full of water and waste, it vibrated and the colours sprung new hues. I put my head to the cold window it bounced slightly with the spasms of the engine. Rada turned her attention on me and screamed.

"What do you think? It is gorgeous at the same time isn't it?"

All I could do was to nod at her. How could a woman like that be into women? Naturally I knew that there were some lesbians that were not as ugly as sin, but I never would have guessed that such a fine looking woman, as Rada, would be gay. Never. She turned to the pilot and hollered something, then we all leaned right and my head swung away from the window, a heavy bud on its fragile stalk bending to gravitation. For a while I was hypnotized by the noise and the fleeing world, then the pilot dipped us and a tiny little island came into view. The closer we sank the more details of the island became visible. On the island we could see two panic-stricken chestnut barb horses with wide red nostrils, dark black eyes, dance back and forth around each other with their heads held high. We could almost see the foam rise from their terror filled bodies. One half of a tiny stone house stood securely on the island; doors and windows shut to the world, whereas the other half was submerged in a gravy looking mud, thinking about taking the plunge. A bright yellow bucket stood still outside the door of the house, unaffected by the wind and the rage, filled to the brim with brown brackish water. Three barren trees bent and bashed themselves against the walls of the house, whipping the dance to continue unabated. Rada slipped the seatbelt off her taut body and crept over to us in the back. She pulled a long rope from a compartment in the floor, checked each centimeter of it, and then pulled out two other contraptions out of the floor, which again she went over in detail. The cameraman who initially had been filming the horses had by now handed the camera to Luca who sat watching Rada and the cameraman with his eyes wide and confused in the disharmony. The cameraman and Rada worked fast and dedicatedly towards the same goal. Rada fastened a harness around her butt and tugged at a string of buckles and straps tightening what needed to be tightened. Then before I had realized just what was going to happen she had hopped out at the edge of the helicopter's side, her hair practically standing right up off her head, and begun lowering herself towards the infernal little space below, every inch of which was covered in deep hoof holes. I think we were all holding our breaths. Rada swung and dangled precariously halfway between the opposite of an oasis, and an airborne glass bubble. Her legs kept reaching out, but she was nowhere near a footing. The horses seemed speeded up to a higher frequency of frenzy with this furious spider hovering just at the corners of their eyes. They could not blink our existence away, which sent further spirals of fear through their bloodstreams, and their

181

horse voices emitted hoarse sounds of dread. Once Rada had put her feet down in the mud she sunk down to her ankles. She bent down and scoured the ground for bits of trampled soggy vegetation, anything to lure the horse attention despite the mayhem. Then there she was standing very still with her hands held out towards the dancing pair; a sign of peace; the cameraman leaning and filming dangerously over the edge of the helicopter, not missing a second. Next, another miracle, Rada made contact and then one of the panicked animals, soothed only fragilely by her being, let her slip a harness across its liquid flanks and stomach. She stepped back as far as she could from the caught animal and we began rising slowly. The animal lost its grip on the mud and then went limp like a rag. The fear must have been total. Meanwhile the animal still on the island danced an even more intense dance of solitude, its mane flowing upwards towards its companion in flight. Now Rada was hanging in the air again, a bit higher up than the limp horse and on the other side of the helicopter. As we got over stable land again the vehicle lowered itself and its cargo. Rada landed first and snapped herself free from the rope running towards the melted animal. The long legs of the horse buckled slightly before it realized what had happened and what it now needed to do. Rada took advantage of the stupefied moment and unhooked the horse in one fell swoop. Even after it had been set securely free down on our earth again it did not move, but stood still looking at Rada who was walking backwards not taking her eyes of the horse. Then the horse with its head lowered, in a sign resembling horse like gratitude, started walking on shaky legs towards Rada. She stopped and let the animal come to her. Then for a moment the horse rested its big head against her stomach, its eyes closed. Rada just stood there with her arms by her side limp as the horse had been just minutes before. The horse lifted its head to her face, and then Rada came alive again. She raised her hands and put each of them over the horse's eyes and pressed her nose to the horse's muzzle, breathing in ever particle of the animal as time stopped. Later they unraveled; she patted the horse on its muscled neck and walked quickly towards the waiting ropes. She hooked herself up again and we swung back through the thick air for the second animal.

Once night fell the whole group felt elated by the rescues. However, the cameraman seemed to have got into a huff with Rada. In snatches of angry words Luca caught the point. He told me that the cameraman felt that Rada had neglected her duties whilst saving the horses off the island, as there had been plenty of people out there; that they subsequently had brought to safety, but who could have been saved earlier if it wasn't for her girlie whim. Both Luca and I partly had to agree, but at the same time we had to recognize that we had come away with a goldmine of pictures, film, as well as other more destructible and fleeting images. Rada ignored the man's sulk and anger, and did not even bother responding to his accusations. She disappeared to clean up in a makeshift hotel that had been arranged for them by one local family moving in with their relatives for the night. I was leaning back in a rickety chair in our courtyard watching a celebration of sorts being arranged by the local women. The smell of food cooking began to fill the dawning darkness around us.

Lost in a deep discussion with an elderly woman of the village Rada looked bursting with vitality where she sat at the rough table. The woman, who was on Rada's right, seemed completely smitten with her, whilst the young man, who's name it turned out was Peter, sat on Rada's left in a despondent mood, stealing glances towards the women when not staring at his plate where a pile of raisins had been pushed carefully to the side. Peter did not seem to be drinking at all. I watched him and imagined that he might be a religious type. Luca and the cameraman had hit it off and sat guffawing at one end of the table. Looking around like this I started to feel an odd and uncomfortable kinship with Peter. There we were, neither of us talking to anyone, just observing life in the others, like two misfits. Perhaps I should give him half a chance. At least I might be able to get a little more information about Rada from him if nothing else. I whistled at him and he raised his uninteresting face. I signaled for him with a quick side movement of my head and a wink, he looked at me dumbly as he took a while to realize that I was referring to him. Indeed, I felt like a most fascinating character in comparison, it could do wonders for my self-esteem to hang out with him for a while. He pushed his chair out but kept looking longingly at Rada as he detached himself and drifted over to me. I pulled my chair away from the table and twirled an empty chair around for his cold little ass to slither onto. He smiled apologetically as he sat uneasily at the chair's lip.

"How are you?"

He just awkwardly nodded as a response.

"You want a drink?"

He shook his head.

"You mute?"

Well, a comment like that was bound to make or break this stalemate, but again there was no rubbing him up the wrong way. Maybe he was a bit simple? Or a boy genius? Surely he would not have got a job with vibrant Rada if he weren't able to do the job he was set to do. Rada did not seem the sort to allow for incompetence. I got him a drink even though he had declined. He took the drink in his hands but did not raise it to his lips, instead he just cradled the glass, wrapping his fingers around it protectively whilst using it as an anchor for his eyes.

"So how long have you been working with Rada?"

A rustle of his clothes gave way to a timid thin voice.

"A year now."

"And how do you find it, you enjoy it?"

He nodded keeping a close eye on the yellow liquid that moved

184

to his own movements. Ok, I would not get anywhere with closed questions. They worked as the easy way out for him. I needed something broader, something that he could not cringe out of.

"What do you do for her?"

I gesticulated towards Rada with my head.

"Assist."

Ah, that was it! How infuriating.

"Like what?"

"Well…"

I had a sense that the longest sentence of the evening would now limp across his lips.

"Well, I, transcribe, and, do other, things, she asks, of, me."

He sucked his words back halfway before committing to uttering them, thus emitting a string of half words and half meanings. I stared at Peter in bewilderment. How the hell did a boy like that end up doing such a fascinating job? Perhaps it complemented Rada's exuberance in some way?

"Do you only work in Algeria or do you go anywhere else?"

"Well, we, some, times, work, else, where around."

I was losing hope and my eyes started to wander around the table in search for anything at all that could help me from wanting to slap this thing next to me. His mannerism enraged me. I should not have encouraged him to come over, now I felt stuck with him. Rada looked over at us and grinned politely at my attempts with Peter, before throwing herself back into the conversation with the woman. Maybe she found me chivalrous, or, this confirmed me as the idiot that she had encountered on the banks of the river as she first arrived. No, most likely I did not even register on her radar.

"She's quite amazing isn't she."

I offered this to Peter, hoping that his admiration for Rada would wake a conversation if not a confession in the least.

"She is, a very, talented, woman."

My sigh rolled up from my guts and got longer as it reached my lips. All that stagnant air I was holding on to in wait for Peter to talk blew out into in the mellow evening.

"So she's gay huh?"

Peter looked at me more dumbly than usual as I let my lips rise involuntarily to a semblance of amusement.

"That's, none, of your, business."

Finally: an emotive subject.

"What's wrong with that? It's just a fact as far as I was aware."

He straightened up a bit.

"It's, still', nothing, to do, with, you."

He was put out by my question, but that was better than nothing.

"Alright, alright, but you can't blame a guy for being interested. Not everyday you run into a woman like her."

Was that sufficiently soft for him to allow me in to a conversation? Peter remained shut. Next thing, out of desperation, I decided to try to treat him with his own silence. I sat there, close enough for him to know that I was still engaged somehow, but without a word. There was a perfect stillness to start with but then Peter began moving uncomfortably in his seat, even at points nudging me with a spasm, expecting me to take the cue. I ignored him and only looked up sometimes to reconnect by looking him in the eye with a benevolent facial expression locked onto each of my facial muscles. Then Peter broke.

"Where, are, you, going, next?"

I felt like getting up and doing a dance of victory. Peter had asked me a question! Ok, I had not given him much room for anything else, but anyway, he had mustered the required energies to ask a question. Not bad. However, as I could have milked this moment something shifted in the dynamics of the gathering. A group of new people began popping in through the doorway as if released by the night. They weren't from the village, and had a definite air of international life about them. I thought that I even heard familiar languages in the background somewhere. Rada stood up as soon as they entered and many of them flocked to her sharing kisses and hugs. From a relatively sober situation the night now shifted up a couple of gears. I forgot all about Peter as I got up to have a look at whom and what this was all about. I looked over to Luca who had become embroiled in a conversation with a nice looking woman in what seemed her early thirties. Her long neck was given extra attention by her blonde hair being casually arranged in a ponytail. I moved forwards towards them trying to get a better look at the woman. As soon as Luca spotted me he grabbed me by the arm and introduced me to her. It turned out that she was part of this loose group of people that in different capacities was either working in the wider area with NGOs or news organisations. She gave me a long look, which to me suggested that she might have liked what she saw. I was relieved to be talking to someone that actually spoke back, and such attractive company to boot. Luca stood by our side for a little while, throwing in a word here and there with a big drunken grin on his face, but then got distracted by two guys that walked in looking around a bit awkwardly. Luca excused himself and walked over to them. From over Lise's shoulder I could see Luca fondly embrace each of the men as long lost pals. Lise's voice was rather high but the manner in which she slowly pronounced things, the way that she dragged the words out, made her way of expressing herself seem sensual, thoughtful and erudite. She was working with a Danish NGO that sought to address educational issues in Northern Africa. She had been with this NGO only for a few months, and this was the first time she was sent to Algeria. At length she explained the ins and outs of her work. It seemed she was a bit of a disaster manager in that she would have a special focus on towns or regions that fell under the spell of calamity. She would try to ensure that the schools, their staff and equipment were affected as little as possible. Lise's blue eyes were full of warmth and care as she talked about her job, and she would often put her hands on her stomach as an emphasis for her points which would allow for me to momentarily give attention to her ample chest. She obviously really cared for what she was doing. In an attempt to build up my interesting points I mentioned the work that we had done during the day whilst avoiding my actual status on this trip. I talked of the fabulous island with the horses, and the rescue of them, without referring directly to Rada. Lise was fascinated. I deliberately gave her jumbled information as to who had done what, so as not to blunder into the exactitudes of the events. Realising that both Luca and I had hijacked poor Lise since her arrival, I excused my bad behavior and asked if she would like a drink. She agreed and I bid her to follow me. As we walked over to the drinks, Rada appeared behind the table offering to pour us both a drink of choice. In my head a small torrent of swearwords swept up. I hoped that she would not ruin my chances of impressing this woman by blurting out any truths about today. Rada looked hopelessly attractive where she stood. Her hair positively shone, and her eyes were slightly hooded by the relaxing effects of an exhausted body. I looked over at Lise to see if she was getting smitten, to see if there was a way that I could distract her from Rada, and although she was not fully caught up yet I could sense that Rada was making a big impression. That's when Peter walked up to me whispering in my ear that Luca wanted me to come over.

"In a minute. Tell him I'll be there in a minute."

I patted Peter on the back and pushed him gently on his way. Rada perked up.

"What's that? You ok?"

She was too cute.

"No nothing."

I turned back towards Lise hoping that Rada would get the hint and leave us alone. No matter how much I would like to get to know Rada, there was more of a point with Lise. At least I had more of a chance of getting somewhere.

"Here are your drinks."

Rada forced the focus back towards herself. I snapped my drink up from where she had sat it on the table and waited for Lise to be handed hers, but Rada held onto it until she had come around the front of the table and then handed the drink into Lise's hand directly. As she was moving around the table Rada managed to instigate a conversation with Lise by asking her where she was working. Naturally, Rada knew someone that worked in the same organization and so managed to hook Lise's interest. I knew my chance was gone as soon as Lise began asking questions of Rada. Where did she work? What was she doing here? Had she been part of today's rescue mission of the horses? Rada looked at me briefly, smiled knowingly and winked. With my right foot I kicked the ground as hard as I could without making a spectacle of myself. I excused myself and slunk back towards Luca. Damn her. Simultaneously the cameraman came out with a television in his arms and the young boy of the house dragged a bunch of leads and extensions in behind him. Everyone quieted down and soon the news jingle pierced the air. The grainy footage revealed the rescue mission of people to start with, but ended with the more majestic sequence of the horse rescue, which made Rada look like a warrior goddess. Everyone around the courtyard started applauding as soon as it was over and all attention was on Rada. By now Lise naturally had been thoroughly converted. There was no mistaking her focus. I swore under my breath. Luca noticed, and patted me on the back.

"Never mind."

I had no idea why he had not gone for her himself. Perhaps he thought that I was in more need of human contact than he? Luca motioned for me to come with him and soon I was swallowed up by boisterous male company, a glass brimful of whiskey stuck in my paw, grinning idiotically at the blurry faces that zoomed in and out of sharpness.

It was a rough extended cough that led me to discover where I was. My back ached badly and my eyes were so dry that opening them was torture. What came into them as the lids scratched their way over the eyeballs was an early morning doused in fog. My hands grappled with the stony ground that had served as my bedding and inch-by-inch my body was suffering to raise itself into a less slumped over position. I swore and panted as I exercised my muscles. My tongue was a blackened brick in a hollow burnt out oven. No wonder I had coughed. Then another bout of the cough reached my ears and I realized that it was not actually I that had rent the morn with that noise but some other poor soul that in a drunken stupor had stooped where their energies failed them, not far from me: another badly displayed mannequin sprawled in a suggestive manner against the tree in the courtyard. I did not recognize the man, but his state was an indication of that he most likely was part of the over-indulgers' group, and hence probably should have been recognized by me. I felt yellow dust clogging my nostrils and began to feel a slight jaundice at the back of my throat as well. My body spasmed at the thought and I spat as thoroughly as I could. A small brown spot spread carefully on the ground next to me. I watched it dry with my head lolling on my shoulders. Inelegantly I balanced my body into different positions in an attempt to get up. Once standing, I leant on the wall for a while before going to the well. The empty one-dimensional sound of the bucket hitting the water stopped my winding motions in surprise. Then the squeaking of the overflowing dancing bucket kept me entertained and smarting until it hung there enticing in front of me. I had to really think, before the maneuver now needed was clarified in my head. Someone clapped his or her hands behind me and I lost all composure. The bucket hurdled back into the well, the rope slipping razor blades through my dry hands. Then I just stood there with my burning hands, my eyes shut, and the slack rope a leftover garland decorating my sculpture of pure pain and dismay. A disgustingly merry female laughter seared through the fog in the courtyard. Surely it wasn't that funny. But I must have cut a pathetic excuse for manhood in the state I was and perhaps it was that which called for such glee. I did not turn around or open my eyes.

"Bravo, bravo."

More hands clapping and more laughter ensued. I tried to shut my ears by pushing the insides of my head against the sound tunnels with a stretchy motion of my jaws. It did not work. I tried to close my eyes from the inside as well as the outside but the darkness remained tepid.

"Sorry, perhaps I should not be teasing you so. We have all suffered similar states at times."

Rada's voice was accompanied by a giggle, from Lise, I supposed. As I turned around I slid my eyes open to offer a semblance of composure, which probably wasn't even called for. I had nothing to prove. I had already lost.

"Hope you had a good night."

As I said this I realized that the words worked to embarrass me more than them. I, covered in dust, having made a fool of myself, wrinkly clothes, barely able to stand, hair standing on end, reeking of alcohol, obviously had not had a good night. It could have been different if Rada had not been here.

"Thank you for asking. Yes, we did indeed. How about it, do you want to come down to get something to eat with us in the square? You look like you could do with a bit of food to get back in shape."

To sit and eat with them in my state would make me a glutton for punishment. Of course I needed food badly, but not that badly. I thanked them for their concern but made up an excuse of having things to do this morning. They went off without any further requests for my company. I fished for water again. This time undisturbed the bucket found its cold metal arm caught in my hand and without getting my shoes wet I secured it on the ground before leaning over it in the manner of a praying man

191

scooping its contents into my two shaky palms and lowering my face to its cool quickening to let it escape into fleshy fissures. It was unbelievable how water could taste so sweet. Rada and gang would leave our village today and with that the entourage that had gathered would disperse. I was waiting for the self-sufficient life of: Luca and me, to return. We were better off left on our own. I stood up, set the bucket down and went in search of the man. The angles of walls and light filtered made the world askew and I had an odd time trying to walk straight. Luca had managed to find his bedroom and was sprawled out naked on his stomach. He emitted gurgling noises that most likely would have been snores had he been on his back. I watched his lean figure for a moment before I flicked some water at his face. He did not react. I flicked some more but he just grunted and turned the other way. There was no way that I was going to get him up now. I went out, filled his pitcher full of water and returned it to his bedside reach. Once back in my room I changed my plan as I sat on the edge of my bed. I let my body fall back and returned to sleep. By the time I got up in the late afternoon, my stomach now rumbling loudly, I could hear a faint sound of distancing vehicles. I walked back to Luca's room but found only an empty space. The pitcher stood empty next to his bed and the sheets lay crumpled up in a design suggesting that he had wound them tightly around his body throughout his labored sleep. I turned to leave and came face to face with him.
"They've gone now."
"That was quick."
"No, just you sleeping late. Did you have anything to eat yet?"
"Just woke."
"The landlady has some food in the kitchen, just ask her."
"Sounds good. Where are you off to? Did you see them off?"
"Yeah, the whole lot of them gone now. Feels like the village has been cleared out, after all the noise and bustle of yesterday. Took some photos of the great escape, and now think I will

retire for the eve, or at least till dinner time later. Got a book of one of the guys that seems pretty good. "

He paused looking at me with that faraway look of a hangover.

"Tomorrow though, think we should start thinking about moving on. Perhaps we should go back to Algiers and then move on from there."

I was surprised at his suggestion. I felt as if we had got somewhere. That we could move on from here, but what he was suggesting, it seemed to me, was that we would go backwards and then begin again. Of course I realized that he would need to check in with the relevant people back in the city, maybe to be able to get an idea of where it might be most lucrative to go next, but at the same time, if that was it, he could have sussed something out from the gang that had just been here. Surely they would have known the next hot spot. We had come upon this one by chance it seemed. It had not meant to be as major as it turned out.

"You look disappointed."

"Just, I thought, that we had really begun the travels."

"We have."

"Yeah but going back?"

Luca looked at me like I had gone mad.

"It's all the same. We need to go back. I need to hand some stuff in and talk to one of my contacts to really get the best out of the trip. Without that sort of information we would be traveling blindly, which would be fine if this was a holiday. It is not. This is work, for both of us, and if we do not get the money in, then the trip is over. Simple."

I sulked. I don't know why. I must have annoyed Luca. He walked off obviously annoyed, his soles pounding the ground. I turned on my heel, walked to the river and sat there on my haunches staring angrily at the stones that I was hurling into the water. After a while the anger abated and I thought myself a fool. Why the hell was I arguing with Luca? This was a woman's whim. Why the hell would I have to travel on from here? Why could I not think of going back to Algiers? I must have lost the plot. I sought Luca out and after a bit of softening him up he relented and began speaking to me again. I admitted to having been an idiot and blamed it on last night's defeat and today's hangover. He let me wallow in my apologies a bit longer than I would have liked, but then that is what you get for arguing with your employer. By the time we woke the next morning life was back on track.

Justice had had nothing to do with it, the way that the weather had worn the landscape and the people, and not just worn, but rubbed out, flushed out, much of life in both. Luca was still incensed by the act of God, and helpless in his rage he was unable to let sleep in, his whole body rigid against everything. It was a wonder he managed to keep his food down. However, me, I was astonished at the tenacity of people. Life got on with it. The man with the donkey went to collect firewood with his young son, thin wisps of smoke rose elegantly suggesting women bent over boiling pots, prayers were said, and dogs chased each other through laneways raising veils of dust. If one ignored the by now toned down thunder of the river right behind the centre of the village, life seemed to have been only marginally effected by the devastation. People needed even less than they had assumed before. Where was my life in all this? Why had I taken part in this disaster? I had all the luxuries that these people at points only dared dream of, yet here I was, benefiting and enjoying my visit to their meager reality, finding it sufficient, and perhaps more real than my own. I snapped to it. What the hell was I on about? We needed to get out of here. The river was soon to return to its usual path, and then, the bus would come. We would get on the bus, and be out of here, for good. Until then I would sip my beer, have my dinners and do what I could to restore that which needed restoring. Luca came over to the table where I was sitting. I think he was irritated over that the plan that he'd hatched had been delayed by the fact that the bus company had not returned to regular services out of our area yet. He lit a cigarette and took quick drags one after the other until it was gone and got ground under his angry foot. He plonked himself down in a chair, then got up, got himself a beer and stood leaning on the wall next to me guzzling as irately as he had smoked. I thought I heard him whispering to himself, and turned to him.

"What?" His eyes wide open and head pushed forward to me whilst his bottle almost lost a little of its contents as it followed his wildly gesturing hand.

"Nothing," I said, and blew the air out of my nose. There was no point in asking him anything about how we would get out of here in the state that he was in. We were at the mercy of the bus company now. In retrospect we should have asked Rada and gang for a lift, but it was easy to be smart after the fact. They might not even have been able to offer us one. Later I tried to get some information from the man who was in charge of the bus timetable but I had little luck in gleaning anything. Our languages clashed and he was not willing to compromise in any way. He just threw his hands in the air and walked off, as if I was annoying him, as if my quest was petty and ill considered.

The day the bus arrived I was not at all prepared. I had almost got to a stage where I had forgotten about it. The day the bus arrived the river had become meek and mild, brushing gently past its banks like a cat expecting to be fed. Purring and ploughing watery folds presented themselves deceitfully as a coherent, peaceful and useful body. The bus driver, if not better informed, might even have suspected us of lying about the devastation we had lived through. Mind you, he did not seem to be that bothered either way. Luca hurried me, saying that we needed to get back to town. As if I had not got his point a long time ago. At least a couple of weeks had gone by now, and we had initially only meant to have stayed a couple of days. Luca said that he needed to get to a doctor as he had suffered from some strange ailment, which had developed since the flood. His ears were ringing constantly; it was, he said, like underwater screeching, it was driving him mad. He thought that it might have been the sound of the raging waters that remained, that would not drain. Later he was to find out that he had developed tinnitus, and he was forced to listen to a CD, with the sound of crickets at night, just to get to sleep. Luca said that he was certain that the river had forced itself on him, that it would never stop reminding him of this trip, these tragedies.

We stepped off the bus at a corner from our hotel, right at a fruit and vegetable stand, which was guarded by a very grumpy old woman. Her face twisted into folds that folded into other folds thus hiding any glimmer of joy from the world. *This little light of mine, I'm gonna let it shine. This little light of mine...* entered my head and echoed there whilst a smile nudged my lips open. The last little jump off the step became a serious athletic move as our bodies had been hibernating for an absurd amount of hours by then. I stretched and watched as the bus rattled away with every screw holding it together praying for it to remain whole, to not dissolve into metal flakes and bits, at least not before it got to its end station where some mechanic could see to that the bits would hold for yet another journey into the beyond. I looked around for Luca, saw him enter a store, and followed him. He was picking toiletries off a shelf and I joined him adding similar articles to a basket of my own. We had got so used to each other by now, traveling this closely together, that little verbal communication was needed. We grunted at each other every now and again with full awareness of what that would mean. The man serving us at the till looked suspiciously familiar and I grunted at Luca to see if he thought so as well, but he grunted back in the negative. It was not until that night when I was lying in my bed watching a very clear blue moonlit night outside my window that it returned to me.

196

That face. Half asleep I realized that the man had reminded me of Musa. A shiver went through my body and I rolled over on my back. The ceiling echoed the blue theme of the night by way of the charged globule that hung like a shaky white hole in the sky just outside. My naked body contracted briefly as I felt something land on my stomach. Shivers trekked across my skin in waves. My pupils searched themselves downwards in their sockets but without making a major move I was unable to get a full picture. However, I had seen a winged creature and thought it to be a huge moth. I closed my eyes and felt it move its dusty pasty body with little sucking sounds across the world of my belly. I felt my dick move under the sheet and held in a gasp of stupidity at the reaction of my flesh. I must have fallen asleep like that, with the moth on my stomach, and with a stir of ridiculous arousal, for the next thing I found were the remains of a wet dream clinging to the sheets and my nether regions, and a new day dawning briskly peppered with traffic. I got up, irritated by my lack of control.

The coffee cup weighed my hand down, as Luca got lost in a conversation on Gas Lightning. Every time I was about to gather the metal lip to mine he launched into some new fantastic issue around this topic which made me unable to fulfill my task, as I had to respond. Finally I decided to ignore his enthusiasm and took a couple of seconds out to drink whilst it was still hot. However I did have to nod a little as I performed my wish and need.
"Do you believe it?"
"It sounds outlandish." I said, after having finally swallowed.
"It does, doesn't it? I mean who would believe that those sorts of things happen! How far do people go in their efforts to lie and or conceal things, to drive each other mad? That is the question."
I was interested, and the issue seemed to ring true in my own former life as well. But now here in Algiers, that life, those

problems seemed a lifetime away. Sure it was because of this that we were here in many ways. We seemed to have had escaped it, and although Luca somehow was linked to it, this comforted me in a manner, just because it confirmed that I was not crazy, that I could have a life which was not weighed down by suspicious happenings. Luca stopped talking for a little while, lost in his own rumble of thoughts. Outside the window a scuffle of steel and flesh bodies wrestled the dust in thinly disguised sunshine.

"You know, a true story, I was told when back home last year. There was this woman from Bangladesh right, and she had come to London as the arranged wife of this London based Bangladeshi man. She was lucky in the sense of that her mother and father were quite wealthy and so lived in the same city as her for major parts of the year. Anyway, her life rolled on and to everybody's delight she gave birth to a son. However, no one really knew what was going on behind the scenes. See her husband, right, was siphoning the welfare system in a very sinister manner. He had asked her to pretend to be mentally unstable so that he could collect her disability welfare money. Then, little by little, he managed to get her to actually take the medications that she had been given by the psychiatrist; seemingly suggesting that she would be more believable to the services. So she did. The more she took, the more her body responded by actually developing problems similar to the ones that she was pretending to have. Her husband then sought a divorce and full-custody of their son due to her deteriorating mental health. He placed her in fulltime care of the social services. This is the point where her parents were informed. They could not understand how a perfectly healthy woman in her mid-twenties suddenly developed these symptoms, not having suffered any signs of this earlier on, or indeed without a hereditary background. Her father in particular got involved, and realized what had happened. Thereafter he desperately tried to juggle the courts, her welfare and his business back home in Bangladesh. Most of the time when talking to social workers the father would break down asking how all this can have been allowed to continue without anyone querying it, or figuring it out."

His story triggered one of my own.

"It's like that woman journalist, you know, in the US; although she had self-diagnosed mental health problems, who went into different mental health services to write about them, and the lack of understanding that even the so-called professionals have of what is referred to as mental health. It is scary how much they pretend to know and how little they actually understand of it. I mean what would happen to you if you found yourself without mooring mentally and socially. They would take full advantage of your vulnerabilities, that's for sure. Especially, if there is no one there to question it, or say no."

Luca nodded.

"It is frightening."

Silence returned to our table for a little while, then Luca carefully began.

"It's like that stuff you talked about, back home I mean."

I did not encourage him by responding. I did not really want to tempt fate and talk about it although of course it had entered my head as well.

"Your honeymoon and all that…"

He looked up at me to see why I was not allowing him to discuss freely what was on his mind, but the sensitive soul did realize that maybe I was not ready so he did not pursue the issue any further. I was grateful.

"Let me pay for this ok."

I tossed a few coins on the table and the chairs scraped noisily across the floor as we rose to go. We had not got further than around the corner when I crashed right into a broad shouldered man who, this time, really truly turned out to be Musa. The first thought that fizzed through my head was: we should not have mentioned anything.

"Musa!"

"Sorry, so sorry."

"Musa, it's me."

He looked up and a big grin rippled his features.

"Well, well, well, what do you know."

He looked genuinely pleasantly surprised. I introduced Luca and Musa without elaborating on how I knew either of them. They shook hands and then Musa turned to me.

"What are you doing here in Algiers?"

"I was just about to ask you the same question."

Oh, how to make all this natural, and how not to think that having talked about the past we had dug it up into reality somehow?

"We're here on a job."

"Well, so am I."

Awkward silence crept around in our mouths. Nobody wanted to share details it seemed. Luca broke the spell suggesting that we would meet for dinner later to have a proper chat. Relieved we all agreed on a place and time and then we separated onto our different paths.

"How bloody typical." I said angrily.

Luca, trying to be helpful, clarified the situation.

"We do not actually have to go meet him. If we don't, then that will be it. Am almost a hundred percent sure of that we would not run into him again. Algiers is too big of a town."

I did not respond, but Luca continued.

"We could even change our hotel to another part of town."

After a brief interlude he went on again.

"And we're off from here very soon."

A bike rider passed us by a little too close for comfort. Luca swore at the man and then followed him with an angry stare as the man swayed on down along the road. Eventually, as the man on the bike had got too far away to sense his burning stare, Luca let his eyes off the biker and turned his focus back on me.

"Think about it."

The sheet over my feet felt like sandpaper and finally I had to do a half sit-up to lift it off before it drove me demented. I had thought that this was the only thing that separated me from my siesta, I was wrong. My toes now ground against each other and my head was crammed with a tumultuous carnival. Dwarves dressed as bank directors dragged their walking sticks against the bark of my brain, emitting a sound similar to that which comes from a kid's bicycle wheel when dressed with a plastic playing card. It was snap, crackle and painful screeches that burst in bubbles in my ears. A hollow-boned shock of birds lifted off the balcony railing, perhaps scared off by my groans, before I had even known that they were there. Mermaids crawled over glass to get to a small basin filled with filthy sewer water covered by an oily film, and dingoes ate mangos in the shade watching the spectacle, watching for babies, whilst blind vultures sat in the eucalyptus trees picking each other's teeth. Do birds have teeth? Can they go blind? I pulled the sheet over my head hoping to silence my thoughts by immersing them in a dull world, but the shadows that played upon my makeshift tent caught my eye and then my thoughts flailed after them. Musa was a ringmaster with a severe looking cow-prod in his gloved hand, and my past was running in rings around him. Shoes covered in sawdust. That was why we had run into him now. He was at the centre of all my morbid regrets that were slowly thawing into unshaped memories. Just as I was gaining trust in at least one human being, Musa showed up to let me know that there is no one, not a single soul, that you can trust, or share trust with. And although Musa had been a positive and fairly safe haven then, now he was just a part of a bad past, a past that I had hoped would remain such. I had all but forgotten about it, and even though I had insisted on traveling to this part of the world it had mostly had to do with a shedding of that skin by really rubbing up against it, at least as close as I could come to it, without really putting myself in danger from it. Luca was right though, I did not have to throw myself in

201

front of that destructive mystery train. There were many different options for me that I could make use of. I snapped the sheet down off my chest and lay there, with my hands on my chest, for just a split second before I stretched and emerged.

I had to wait for Luca almost half an hour and was just about to leave the lobby for a walk when he sauntered down. I joked with him about the housewifely duties that I had taken on and he laughed. He handed in his key and as we walked out we began to chat about the last of the preparations for leaving Algiers again. Not today, and not tomorrow, but the day after, early in the morning. This time though we were hauling a lot of stuff and so had rented a jeep. We were to pick it up tomorrow and it was my job to ensure that it was packed and ready for the trip. I cherished the opportunity to take my mind of anything else by submerging myself in a duty and already was packing the car in my mind. Luca noticed my distraction but thought that perhaps I had gone off in the wrong mental direction.
"You alright?"
"Sure. Just thinking of the stuff that we'll need."
"Good."
He had the sense of not allowing that which he had feared enter the discussion. I reigned in a stray sentence that in my head ran off in the direction of Musa; because it was expected somehow, by looking up into the sky at the birds that flitted past. Then my sight swooped down from the sky, ran along the buildings, and hit the street with steely determination. I felt every speck of sand under my sandal. This was my choice. I would not go and see Musa tonight. If he was here to find me; to extend the ill that had begun in that space of my life, then he would, and then I would be sure of that he was as involved as anyone else. If he did not return or try to contact me again, then, I would feel more secure of that what had happened in Morocco would stay in Morocco. Buried in Morocco. I looked over at Luca who just was about to enter a shop. I followed him putting my hand in

the print of his on the open door that leisurely moved towards to me. A wall of air-conditioned cold hit me but I melted through, into its belly. There we stood in front of the counter. I watched Luca watching the stuff behind the counter whilst the shopkeeper had one eye on us and one on the busy street outside his cool cocoon. Luca negotiated with the shopkeeper who packed a bag full, which then sat on the counter until Luca had parted with the paper bills in his wallet. A clock ticked loudly from the room behind a bead curtain. A bus honked repeatedly at a half parked car just outside the shop. Half the human contents of the car disengaged, the door slammed shut. A fist rose at the impatient bus driver who responded with a prolonged beep, which tracked the car as it released itself from the tarmac artery it had clogged. All three of us were watching the skirmish, but as it dispersed we woke up and moved on.

The last bag had just been fitted into the jeep. I slammed the back door shut and searched for the key in my pocket. I locked the car but remained with it all the same. It would not be safe leaving all our belongings, and especially all the borrowed belongings, in the street even if the car was locked. So I leaned on the car surveying my surroundings in wait for Luca again. I tried to will my shoulders down and took deep breaths as invisibly as possible. Musa had never showed up. There had been no strange phone calls or appearances, but it was not until now that I began to let my body forcefully relax. Although my action, or rather non-action, in this case, had been calculated to figure out the angles of surprises, I had not been left with the type of peace that I had anticipated. No, now I began to change the reasons. Now the reason for him not to have contacted me was calculated. Indeed he might not himself even have showed up that night for the set meeting. He had only wanted to show his face, as that would be sufficient to start my paranoia again. It had been bait, which I could not have avoided in any single way. I was screwed any which way. I changed my position in which I was leaning on the car and smarted at the heat that shot through my leg, the split second after that I recoiled, and then bit by bit lowered a clothed part of my leg onto the metal hoping that my flesh could tolerate the temperature that way. As I concentrated on my task Luca appeared. He nodded at me and pulled at the door-handle of the car whilst I put two and two together fishing for the keys again. The smell of Luca lingered in the air around me and it confused me. Had he changed his cologne? There was something new about the way that he smelt. I asked him but he ignored me.

"Come on. Let's get going. There is nothing else to be done."

Luca got into the passenger seat thus offering the rein to me. I baulked at the task, had not even considered the possibility. It seemed that I had lost almost all power to act as a separate being since arriving here. I felt constantly at Luca's beckon call, but more than so I felt that I needed his guidance in the sense of that I was a novice and a foreigner. He was my superior and my taskmaster. In the car we both hurried to lower the windows before the heat got hold of our capacities. Luca looked over at me and gestured with his chin moving forward: the action that now was required. I checked the gears and turned the ignition. The car belched, and I inhaled the petrol and at the same moment took in that new smell of Luca's, which stopped me right in my tracks again.

"Have you changed your cologne?"

Luca's nose wrinkled and his eyebrows lowered as he gave me a look suggesting that I was an imbecile concerned with idiotic quests.

"No."

He had answered just to placate me. He had no interest in my interest in his new odor. I put the car in first and leant around checking that the coast was clear as I switched on the indicator. We moved out into the narrow streets, weaving through the mesh at a very irritating speed to the fellow vehicle dwellers. I could not hear myself think for all the honking that hung around the car in the same manner as Luca's smell did. I did not think of the driving but was thoroughly caught up in speeding through my chest of memories looking for the connection here. I felt romantic in a tragic sort of way and tears rose in my throat. I swallowed hard and shook my head. Luca gave me another one of those concerned and irritated looks of his.

"Alright, alright."

I picked up a bit of speed and asked for his aid in pointing out at least the direction that we might want to be heading in. As our car loosened into the movement of the madness I began to enjoy the task and leaned back in my seat a bit. Once we had picked up the main road out of town I felt myself relaxing a little more and eventually I swam without a hitch. Luca lit a cigarette and tilted back in his seat. The car shot off into the distance. In my rearview mirror the city stood confused in a halo of sun with its arms out in our direction pleading for us to return before it was too late.

In a deserted spot, following a small creek off the road that we had traveled for a good few hours, we stopped to eat and rest. After we had finished eating Luca lay down under a tree whilst I sat leaning on one of the tires slowly sipping a bottle of water. During our drive we had hardly spoken. I had been lost in a maze, tracing the contours of the preoccupying odor, without getting anywhere closer to its effect on me. Luca had been tired, grumbling at anything that would come close to communication. He tilted his hat over his eyes and put his faith in me, wholly. I did what I could and after a while lost all need to fear that I knew not what I was doing. I just drove. At points I even got off the track inside of my own head as to the smell, but as a new cloud wafted over me my mind started running in circles again. Thankfully this did not transfer into my driving, although it had been more or less impossible, in that alternative routes soon became less frequent. As I leaned on the tire I watched Luca's contentment with a bit of annoyance. It felt like I had done something wrong, and Luca did not even want to let me know what it was. I turned my head and watched the creek, the flitter of birds and insects, and the lethargic movements of the tree branches, deciding that I was being stupid and that I needed to get some rest myself most likely. I closed my eyes and felt a weight of sand move into my veins. Soon in a haze I saw a hand reach out to touch me where I stood on a street corner in a busy city. I turned to follow the hand up the arm, up towards the face that the body carried and was taken aback, but joyous too, by the arrival of Fidel in my life again. He had been gone a long time and as we were friends we both fell into laughter at our luck to meet up like this. I closed my eyes and leaned in for an embrace and as we stood there with our arms around each other I felt him shift; in a snake-like manner he squirmed and wriggled. He seemed coated in a slippery mucous and was moving out of his clothes. As he stirred I pressed him closer and closer to me until eventually I was standing there hugging a shirt, a jacket and a pair of pants. I looked down at an empty pair of loafers, looked down the street, but he was nowhere to be seen. My eyelids shut and I was left with the smell of the clothes as the sounds of the city faded. Luca's hand shook my shoulder and I awoke with a jerk. Luca's face leaned over me and was showing concern.

"You must have been dreaming. You were making painful sounds."

There was the smell that I had cradled.

"We got to get going again."

"I'll drive now if you don't mind."

I got up a bit groggy. Luca's new smell was Fidel's. I kept looking at Luca amazed at his audacity to not acknowledge the major importance of this dream, this moment.

"Stop staring at me. You're giving me the willies."

There was almost a sucking sound as I averted my eyes towards the spill of the road in front of us.

The goat steadied itself against the car window, its two hoofs precariously balanced on the slick paint, as it bleated with a look of both anguish and anger. We were in its way, but we were also capable of anything. It opened its mouth again, its tongue red and rough behind a row of yellow ragged teeth, to let out an assertive bleat but Luca laid his hand on the horn and beat it to the punch. The goat scrambled off in a sudden movement of dust-bursts and hair, its poor goat heart almost shattered. I turned to Luca.

"Why the fuck did you do that?"

"Just a goat, man. Chill."

My fists clenched together uncomfortably, but as Luca moved the car with a gentle even pressure on the gas pedal, I let them fall apart on my thighs. There they lay in careful segments, like two peeled oranges. Don't know why I got so touchy about the goat. A slow light rain tested the air. I stuck a hand out the window and let it try to get wet with difficulty. The rain was so weightless it was impossible for it to attach to anything; like pure souls, not weighed down by the sticky matter of karma. Luca leaned forward, leaning his torso on the steering wheel, looking intensively at the slow moving houses around us.

"We gotta find the house. I'm bursting."

We were now in the town that we had set our sights on. The road from Algiers had led mainly here. The goat had been our welcoming committee. Perhaps that was the reason for my anger with Luca. That, and then the fact that he still refused to say anything about the new smell; that, and the fact that he just seemed off in general over the last couple of days.

"Ask this guy here."

I pointed towards a young man leaning on a well whilst watching a young girl working on filling a plastic container. Luca stopped, retrieved the directions for where we were heading, but for some strange reason, instead of finding somewhere to pee at the same time he just got back in the car. Five minutes later the car jerked to a halt as Luca fumbled with the seatbelt in a desperate effort to unhinge himself before his bladder would do so. My shorts were sticking to the seat and I leaned back so that my arse lifted off the seat and then turned my body in the direction of the door. I had found that this was the least painful way to exit the car without half of one's skin remaining on the seat. Luca had already entered the house in a flurry. I stood outside the car, stretching my body in each and every way. I felt it slowly wake. Luca came back out, said that he had found the house locked and that he had had to relieve himself in a bucket in the corner of the courtyard.

"Hope that bucket is not for our drinking water."

I joked. He grinned back at me. That was the first positive vibe I'd got out of him in a long while. Perhaps it was going to be ok. Luca took out his mobile and dialed for the connection that was supposed to meet us here. We sat idly waiting with the car doors ajar listening to some local music that the only radio station offered up. Wafts of fresh air stirred the heat every now and again, and each time this happened one of us uttered some words that lazily glided away, otherwise silence ruled comfortably. I started thinking of my cigar box of characters again and would have loved to have brought it out then and there but given that it most likely was packed away at the bottom of one of my trunks I relinquished the idea with a slow analytical movement of my hand over the dashboard collecting the dust that had gathered there. Nevertheless, internally I brought each character up in front of me by ignoring the light that still filtered through my stretched eyelids. It was a like an animation, or like a drawing game that I would have played when I was small. The figures moved around each other with jerky actions. Their little paper mouths spouted many colored letters of different sizes and cases. The words gathered in funnel like shapes and stayed there seeming to either pour out or into each pair of lips; forever or until the moment when I shook away my concentration on this. The jangle of a rickety bicycle got loud enough for me to turn my head. A young boy, perhaps twelve years of age, in a large yellow t-shirt peered into the car with an inquisitive smile on his face whilst balancing with his chest against his far too large bike's handlebars.

"I have keys."

Then the boy dangled the keys in through the car window to make sure that he had made himself understood. Luca shook himself out of his stupor and unglued himself from the seat.

"Thanks. Great."

In no time we were out of the sun inside the dark cool rooms that now would be our base. I ran back and forth from the light to the dark with our belongings, carrying in a little heat into the rooms each time, depositing it there like sticky smears on their chilled dimness. I took pleasure in the physical work, and stretched a little extra in each movement to get the full benefit. Once the bags were all inside I crashed into my bed and slept, deservedly it felt, until night began to encroach. When I woke, a different, less defined, gloom rested on the furniture, walls and doors. I lay watching my new nest satisfied with the sense of it. This was going to be alright. My thoughts fluttered through the glinting slit in the door down the hall into Luca's room where his exposed throat pulsated, tiny little hard black hairs bristling and moving: that smell again, and I groaned as the sentiment rose into my skull. I got up and stuck my whole spring of a body into as cold water as I could get. I massaged my scalp and seemed to feel the attachment of each hair. I watched the water jump off each projection of my flesh, and then dance in a plethora of bubbles down the drain along with bits of me. For a while I stood with the towel wrapped around me tightly just staring at the mirror without actually looking. There was an eerie quiet to the night. The white t-shirt stuck to my torso where I had not dried myself properly. The deodorant was cold against my armpits. I slapped my face in the mirror after having shaved, as if I needed to rearrange my thoughts, but my eyes remained pained and ever so slightly tearful. Only I could recognize that though, I thought. I looked out into the hallway but it lay as still and quiet as everything else around us. A slight rustle from the palm trees infiltrated the ruling silence. No birds. A deep sigh from inside my stomach joined the air as I again raised my eyes to meet mine. I could be anyone. Even as my mirror image touched his face my thoughts circled the idea that I had nothing to do with it. There was no connection. I could turn my back to it and it would be left there, in that shadow land where images walk away, alone.

I went for a walk. My distraction was broken by an unexpected pained squeak, a whine, and then the muffled sound of paws beating sand in a hurry. A quick turn and I faced a fearful galloping black dog who as he or she spotted me bared its teeth in a malicious grin, completed a speedy dive to the left into the undergrowth and was gone, tracing its footsteps as they were laid down, as fast as its legs would carry it. My heart pounded at the same pace and a taste of blood appeared on my tongue. I swished the taste around biting my teeth together. I had been walking westward for over an hour and a half but the further I walked the less it seemed appropriate for me to be out here on my own. Naturally this did not stop me. I might as well keep on walking. I had nothing else to do. I had asked Luca what he hoped to catch here, but he had been as vague as I imagined that the assignment in general was. No matter. I explored the stretching nothingness that surrounded us. Soon I discovered that even this nothingness was full of action. A good twenty minutes were spent staring at a beetle that tried its best to crawl up a sand hill, slipping and toiling endlessly and for no reason other than to move forward. Another twenty minutes, or more, I stayed with a small bird of prey before it dove to scoop up a tiny little mouse. I saw the mouse wriggle for as long as it was visible. What a magnificent death: the world swirling underneath, life slipping away to meet itself. The other night I had learnt of the Towers of Silence in Zoroastrianism, where dead human bodies were laid out naked on stone slabs placed in a circle inside an open roofed tower of sorts. Laying there, in wait for the winged carnivores that spiraled down towards the circle, dropping a downy feather here and there, the feathers gyrating towards the naked like darts, and then when the beaks got close enough for one to see the thin little nose membranes rise and fall, the human body torn into strips, carried in vice like grips of talons, through bird shaped perforations of the sky. Or at some point hanging in trees between the same rubbery steel talons, draped over robust upper branches in high high trees whilst the beak shreds and shreds, swallows. I found myself staring at an empty point in space, blue as blue can be. I thought myself hearing a flute playing a mournful tune but knew that it was only in my head. Then the black dog burst up out of the brush, it stopped stock still, staring right at me and leaning its head to the left listening to the noise that I might make next. My lips pursed and I made a kissy sound without moving a muscle. The dog's head leaned to the right, eyes wide. Slowly I moved down on my haunches. The dog backed up a little raised its face and smelt the air. You can never be too careful. I made another noise and the black nose moved forwards towards me but the body remained still and on alert. The dust and dirt on my shoe looked perfectly distributed and although the initial thought was to wipe it off I caught myself and refrained from the impulse. Looking up, the dog had now sat down without taking its eyes off me, but once I looked at it, it leaned to the right and bit at something itchy on the back leg, concentrating deeply. I got up, threw another sound at the dog, but it ignored me, so I turned on my heel and begun my travels back. Lost in thought every now and again I would recognize the patter of paws behind me but I did not turn around. Once I stood at the entrance to our compound I did check around me and sure enough there it was peering around the corner at me. I stood for a while to see if it would come closer now, but it didn't. I walked in and shouted out for Luca. The place remained silent and dead. In my room Luca had left me a note saying that he had gone for a short excursion. He would be back towards nightfall. What a useless assistant I was, disappearing like that, but then again he had not said a word to me about what was to happen next. I grabbed the book off my bed and went back into the courtyard to find the way up to the roof. Thought I make myself comfortable up there, reading till dozing. That would travel the day. I was a bit hungry but could not be bothered fixing something up. Grabbed a beer instead, that would kill the gnawing in my stomach, at least for a while. Soon I was installed and nodded off before even a page had passed through my fingers.

A drop or two hit my face and I don't know what it might have metamorphosed into in my dreaming world but when I woke whatever it was had evaporated. I was left with emotional debris strewn through my body like islands desperately separated from each other, unhinged, and as in entropy, never to come together again, never to explain themselves. I was staring up into a spotted night sky. A bat threw itself recklessly across the waxing moon. I felt as if I should do something. It had got cold and a shiver ran across my spine raising each tiny little hair up to attention on the way. I went by Luca's room but could see no sign of him being back yet. I returned to my room and found my watch. It was after nine. Maybe he had got caught out, wherever he had been, surely he would be back tomorrow. I roused my energies with great force to go get something to eat. After eating I found myself full of unnecessary energy, I tried to walk it off and was soon confronted by the edge of the village. What the hell! I kept walking out into utter dark.

Morning tripped on the blocks of night that littered the horizon, sent forth bright, sensitive, lukewarm mercury between dark sides of stones jagged in cold. My feet stopped in a pool of warmth that gradually grew in both size and heat. Tiredness had not reached my body yet. I did not know how this could possibly be. I had not stopped to rest until this very moment. I did not think that I was lost. I had been careful in attempting a circular direction and, if I had calculated correctly, should not be more than maybe a half hour or so away. I trusted my sense of direction completely. I hoped. The night had been an entranced journey where each step calculated the outline of the next. I had only perceived the barest sketch of my action, it was as if a luminous skin laid before me, each touch of the ground filled the skin, each lift from it, emptied it.

Leaning over the boiling pot I watched as the eggs nervously gathered over spiraling bubble-nails, there they quivered loudly before falling off, and then they moved back to get impaled again. The steam rose, gathered on my face and then dropped back into the pot, into the chaos. Eggs, the only thing that I could think of that would satisfy my by now desperate hunger. I had arrived back; my sense of direction had not failed me, had looked for Luca, but he was nowhere to be found. Sadness welled over me, emptied my stomach, and the eggs were the only thing that seemed real. First I had checked the eggs in cold water. Luca had taught me that eggs could be tested as to freshness by submerging them in water. If an egg were off, then gas would have started to build up within its thin walls, making it buoyant, just like any soul. One of the eggs had taken flight but the rest had remained more or less earthbound, waiting for my stomach acids to break them down to size. What if Luca had died? What if he was broken down to size by something impossibly large? Something beyond all the madness that had enveloped me since we first met. It was not until we arrived here in Algeria that things seemed to have moved on a bit, from all that previous stuff, that is, after we had lost Musa in the city. Outside of the city I almost felt as if nobody knew me, as if nobody was after me. As if my troubles were far behind. Here I was locked in a more 'civilized' life, a life where nobody really

could track my faint traces in the sand. It was the best thing I could have done. I had begun to recognize the smaller things in nature again, the colors and textures of leaves, the smell of animals, the early ever so slight change in the weather that heralded a major upheaval. This was the way that things were supposed to be. I had started recognizing things in myself, the way that I grew mentally and physically, my boundaries and how to push them. All that sort of stuff that you only get to when life forces itself upon you and you stop having a choice of distractions. If Luca were dead, if he was gone, all this would end. I would be forced to return back to my own country, back to my old life, long before I had planned to do so, long before I really should; unless I came up with some alternative plan? Without Luca, that would be more or less impossible. I removed the pot from the heat. The eggs swiftly calmed their dance. I got out a spoon and balanced them delicately whilst submerging them one by one in cold water. Each shell cracked, each soft warm body of an egg gliding in my palm onto a patterned turquoise plate where it slid to a halt. Someone should have painted that still life. Luca should have taken a photo, a Polaroid that I could stick into my back jean pocket forgetting about it until a moment when Luca would no longer be around, something to remember him by. I felt the heat of the eggs escape me. Hardly a wisp of steam emerged anymore. I was leaning over the plate with my hands placed on either side of it. There was a knock on the door. I stopped breathing.
"Yes."
Another knock, this time, a bit more insistent. I must not have made a noise although I thought I had.
"Yes."
This time I called out as loud as I could and a voice responded. It wasn't Luca's voice.
"Telephone call."
It was the voice of a young boy. I went to the door and found the same boy that had given us the keys on the other side of it. I

looked at him; it must have been in a manner, which seemed quite exhausted, because he began to apologize profusely for disturbing me whilst trying to convey to me that there was an important call from Luca. He did say from Luca. However, when I lifted up the cold receiver it was not Luca's voice that came to me. It was *for* Luca; someone from the office in Algiers, someone that wanted him to get back to them as soon as possible, as Luca had promised. I agreed to let him know, took the name and the number, but clarified that I did not know where he had gone. I said that I had expected him back yesterday but had not heard anything from him since yesterday morning. The man on the phone sounded as if I was supplying him with far too personal and unimportant information as he sighed and then again demanded for Luca to contact him as soon as possible. I sucked on an insult before composing myself and assuring the man of that I would relay the information to Luca, if I would ever see him again.

"What you suggesting?"

The man stumbled in Frenglish but still managed to convey his displeasure with me keeping him on the phone.

"Nothing, just letting you know that I am worried about him. He was supposed to have been back last night."

"So, he probably met woman, something to keep him. Sure he back soon."

There was a pause and then the man continued.

"If you want...... call me if he does not come back. Ok."

He had offered me a resentful peace offering. If I shut up and stopped acting like a girl, he would allay my fears with a hope of support. That was all I could have expected of the man. I sighed this time, and then let him go before he decided to hang up on me anyway. I went back to my room and stared at the complex pattern on the plate behind the eggs, and then followed the slow disappearance of the white wet bodies resting unawares on its skin; my body, anaconda.

Two days, two nights, no sign. Luca's mobile phone lay on the bed in his room. I did not know how it was possible for Luca to have forgotten the damn thing when he went out. He practically lived with that object sewn to his hand. Now it was blinking away in the tumultuous sea of unslept sheets. Earlier I had thrown a pillow over its wailings, and so every now and again it was making muffled noises, making the pillow tremble ever so slightly. It was still alive. It struck me that perhaps Luca would have called his own mobile in an effort to communicate with me, knowing that my own mobile was probably turned off and fairly far down in a bag in my room. My hand dug in under the pillow and found the little metal object. Just as I held it, it rang. By sheer surprise I dropped it back onto the bed but bent down to retrieve it and to look through the little window to see if a name that I would recognize had appeared. Only an N was displayed. I pushed the pick up button and grumbled a hello.
"Luca. It's me."
Me? That me sounded very familiar but I was unable to place it immediately. I grumbled a little further to encourage more information to be gleaned, but the person grew suspicious.
"Luca?"
Then silence. In desperation I hung up. I stood staring at the dark window of the phone. Was that what Luca would have done under those circumstances? I decided to forget about it but began to look through his call history, and messages instead. Perhaps I would be able to find out at least where he had gone? Although I had no car, maybe I could borrow a motorbike or bike or something. If I had been a suspicious type of man I would probably had found quite a lot of the information on Luca's phone strange and a reason for frustration. I decided not to react to anything but that which was obvious, that which I really could read. The first thing, of the category that I had chosen, that I came across was from a man called Neil. Neil suggested that Luca should visit the lakes on the way over to him. This message had been sent three days ago. I looked to see

216

if Luca had responded to Neil, but found that Luca's sent message folder had been cleared. I pressed the button to call Neil. The phone rang out and then clicked over to an automated messaging service. My voice, caught in my head, spun, quivered and reeled as it responded to the silence that wanted to eat it. Surely Neil would call me back as soon as he got the message. The rest of the messages went back a bit too long and none of them seemed to have anything to do with the future as I scanned them. I looked through Luca's address book, but found nothing that stood out. I stared at the N for a while, but then decided that it was none of my business. Whoever it had been they obviously did not know that Luca was missing and so would be of little help. I kept the information stored in my head in case for some reason this whole situation would have to be referred to the police at some point. This felt like a possibility now. I stuck the mobile in my pocket and left the room in darkness, shutting the door tightly after myself. Not long after this I felt the phone tremble to build up its voice. I stopped, took it out of my pocket and answered it.

"Yes?"

"Hi, this is Neil. Did you just call me?"

"Yes, sorry, this is Luca's assistant. I am looking for Luca."

"But, you have his phone, is he not there with you?"

"No, see I thought he might be with you. He left his phone behind when he left a couple of days ago. He was supposed to have been back that same evening but has not shown or contacted me since. I thought that you might know where he might be? He never said where he was going."

Neil went quiet and we swayed together in the calm for a little while.

"He was supposed to have come over for a little while, but when he never showed I assumed that he had got side tracked with some assignment or other."

More echoes of breath.

"Have you checked the hospital?"

What an idiot I am!

"Where would he go if he was brought in to a hospital?"

"He might be brought in to a local clinic, and then possibly transferred to the capital, but then I assume that they would have called you if there was something. Maybe."

Neil's maybe had been added on as new thoughts invaded: what if Luca was so ill that he was unable to communicate, so that they did not know who he was? No, they probably would have traced the rental car. But what if it had burnt, beyond recognition? What if he had burnt? The same thoughts went through my own head, even if not in the same order.

"Where was he going?"

"He was coming here to me. I live in a small village just beyond the lakes. I had suggested to him that he would view the lakes on the way. Something you have to see."

I ignored his virtual tourism, had to keep this on track.

"What road would he have taken? Do you have a car? Could you trace your way back here?"

Neil sounded guilty.

"I'm a doctor."

I shook my head.

"What better person to go looking for a man that might be hurt!"

Obvious logic.

"No, I mean, I have responsibilities here in the village. People depend on me being here. I need to be here."

"Surely you could take a little time off, just to see if Luca is alright? Nobody would mind."

"It's not that simple."

"What could be simpler!?"

This guy was taking the piss. It was as if he did not care, as if he had no intention of going to look for Luca. As if he was going to let Luca lie there in a pool of his own blood, dying, just because the doctor was afraid of taking a few hours off. I was

218

ready to hang up on this selfish fucker. I think he could hear my anger venting through my nostrils.

"Yeah, alright, of course. I'll drive over. Let me just jump in the shower and grab something to eat."

He obviously had his priorities right. I swallowed hard.

"Give me a ring when you are on your way if you don't mind. How long do you think it will take to get to us?"

I cleared my throat.

"I mean, here?"

"Should take a couple of hours, or so."

The little metal brick lay like a ten-ton truck in my wide palm. It felt as if it was burning me. I sat idly staring at it whilst trying to get my body and brain into a state of action. I should have asked Neil to contact the hospital and such before he left, or maybe it would be better to do so afterwards, at least then we would know if there was a reason for such enquiries. Lacking in aim the only thing that I could think of doing was to go back to the roof. This is where three or so hours later I discovered a new car noise from just outside the house. I leaned over and saw a jeep, similar to the one that we had rented, pull up. Assuming this must be Neil I started down the stairs as fast I could, still a bit dozy from either sleep or sleeplike ruminations, I could not tell which. The man that greeted me on my doorstep did not remotely look like a doctor. He was short, balding and pudgy. Not exactly the idea of a doctor that would have flaunted itself in front of my mind's eye. I think that perhaps he recognized my lack of trust in his character because the first thing that he did was excuse himself, for being late, for having treated me badly on the phone, for having been rude and so forth. Again this confirmed my distrust. A doctor would never admit to being wrong. Somewhere amidst my reactions lay other reactions, such as, where did I get these stereotypes? I had never even known a doctor before. I suppressed these secondary reactions as best as I could. One had to let gut reactions rule. A twinge rose up my spine though, as I thought

219

my secondary reactions a lot more reasonable. But, I convinced myself, the reason for my gut to have first dibs on what would happen was not because of reason, but precisely the opposite. Those reactions came to because there was something there that did not make sense, not yet at least. I screwed my eyes into 'the doctor' and he smiled nervously in response. To him I was probably some nutcase he'd been forced into close proximity with. He must have been used to just that. He dealt with it as carefully and quickly as possible. I did not return his smile, but moved out of the way for him to enter my temporary home. I wanted to hear what the outcome of his journey and enquiries were. However, he didn't look burdened with information, and this was not very promising. I brought him a beer whether or not he wanted one; bid him with my hands full of beer bottles to sit down on one of the light-blue plastic chairs in the dimly lit room. He plopped down seemingly exhausted and accepted the cold bottle of beer with a satisfied nod. He drank for a long while, the bottle almost empty by the time he removed his fleshy lips from its cold neck to a dim sound of release. I watched him throughout the whole process. Any movement he made I was ready to decipher. Finally, he was ready to talk.

"There was no evidence of an accident on the way. Some bus had gone into a ditch a few miles from here, but I stopped and had a chat with a guy that sold fruit not far from the accident and he claimed that the bus driver simply had been drunk. There had been no other vehicle involved. Anyways, the accident had only happened a couple of hours ago. It would have been unlikely for Luca to be so close to here at that time anyway. I mean if he was on his way to us."

"Could he have taken some alternative route? Did you contact the hospitals?"

Neil took the questions in his stride, used to people panicking and full of distress.

"There is not really any other route to take to our place. That is if he did not really go out of his way for some other reason. I mean, of course, he could have gone somewhere completely different to start with. I asked one of the nurses at the station to check the hospitals as I drove over here. I'll call her now to see if she has heard anything. If you excuse me…."

He held up his mobile phone and I grimaced at him, hinting at something above us with my finger.

"You probably get better reception on the roof."

I got up and led him into the courtyard and then up to the roof. I sat down on a chair as he hovered by the stairs concentrating on finding the number in his address book. I heard the beeps the mobile made as it located the nurse in some village way away. Neil chatted quickly and demandingly, an incision here, a stitch there, a little seepage blotted with cotton precisely perched at the end of a metal claw. Voila. Nothing. There was nothing that the nurse could tell us now, nothing that was different from before. Luca was not anywhere it seemed. He was neither hurt nor found. Neil looked at me exasperated. I was not impressed with his inability to produce results. I shouted at him.

"What am I going to do! What the fuck am I going to do?"

Neil still looked useless. He got on my nerves with his fake interest and insincere acts of contrition. His arms straight and still by his side, his neck and head pushed into his shoulders, and his lips tightly compressed in a painful half-arsed sorry-smile which lent the whole lower part of his face the semblance of a constipated hand-puppet.

"Just get out of here!"

I was pointing towards the stairs. Neil pleaded with me.

"Look there is not much more that we can do at this point, but I promise you I will keep trying. There's probably a perfectly good reason for all this. Luca probably just met someone he knew, or discovered something he needed to shoot right then and there. He'll probably call you soon. There's always a reason."

His platitudes angered me as much as his appearance. I rushed at him and he backed away holding his small little neat hands in front of him as if they would shield him from my anger and frustration. I shoved him hard and he broke one of the plastic chairs in his fall.

"Please. Please!"

That was all he mustered as he lay in the plastic debris staring up at me towering over him with clenched fists.

"You useless piece of shit."

I think I must have frothed at the mouth as I saw a good spray sprinkle his features. A bubble on the tip of his nose suddenly focused me, it quivered with the rest of his body. I stopped my manic attack instantly. What was I doing!

"Sorry. I don't know what came over me. I am stressed out. This thing is really getting to me. I don't know what to do anymore."

I reached out my hand to pull Neil back on his feet. He stared at me, then at my outstretched hand, and after a careful deliberation considered it a possible move by hesitantly raising his hand to mine. I wobbled under his weight and the struggle, but he did get back on his feet. From relief his face shifted to out and out annoyance. How could I be so rude! I must be crazy. He should get out of here. I could see the thoughts sear through his brain by the twitches that riddled his face. He pulled at his clothes as if to pull himself back home, back to normality, then he turned on his heel and fled down the stairs. I decided against pursuing him but then his sudden dash triggered something in me, some animal impulse, and I got pulled into his bolting. He looked truly frightened as I caught up with him. He was by now inside of his car and was desperately trying to wind the window up that little bit extra whilst turning the key in the ignition with the other. He seemed not to be able to get an actual grip on the damn key and split seconds gathered in piles. I was not banging on the windows as perhaps could be expected but rather just stood there staring in at his fear and loss of control. Perhaps this scared him more;

my sudden immobility and calm. The car abruptly jumped into action and he looked surprised as if he had had nothing to do with it. He glanced at me one last time and then gunned the vehicle right out of my life. I fell to my knees in the dust cloud, cradling the absolute barrenness he left behind.

Another couple of days and nights passed in a mockingly lit blur. I was locked up in my room in the half-dark trying to not be there. I had the sheet over me and my stomach was growling aggressively in an attempt to get me up and out. I paid it no heed. I focused on the pain, allowing it to steer me down to pass the point, which I hoped would have no return. There was no return. I had nothing in my life to which I longed other than here, with the pain, alone under the sheet. I orbited this realization endlessly, coldly. The sweat on my body layered itself until my cells were as clogged up as they possibly could be. I was getting no air. I was suffocating my body and my mind. Allowing nothing to stir or develop. Each thought cut short to be brought back into the snail's body that had become mine. I swear I was producing a greenish oozing slime through eyes, nose and penis. There was no light at the end of the tunnel but a gluey foul smelling seepage. I was quivering inside of this cocoon of snot-like existence.

Then on the third day I rose, or rose might not be the exact word, more like slithered into an upright position. There, standing there, naked on the floor, the sheet wrung around my legs and a pulse of a draft somewhere on my body, I felt as if born again. I imagined the slime that cradled a newborn baby, the faeces, the sweat, piss, bile, mucous and womb water, the clogged nostrils and gooey eyes. I imagined such hopeful things for such a hopeless situation. Mostly I listened to the silent shriek that trickled through my nerves, nerves that themselves were standing on end but doing little but rippling unaffected to what they contained. Instead of going straight into the shower I searched a painful way up to the roof and stood there with my eyelids guarding my eyes completely and my face raised to the blinding. I felt myself go rotten first and then, soon, stale. I had no idea if anyone else could see me, if I was being watched. I thought that it was likely, as even the elderly people in the village probably thought of me as the village idiot by now. Then when I could not stand the sun no more, before I fainted by the pure pressure that the light was putting on my putrid body, I searched my way down into the improvised shower and reached it right on time. I had to sit crunched together on the floor for a good while whilst I peed and the water knocked holes in my back before I could muster the energy needed to stand and actually properly shift my hands over the rest of my body.

I was packing my bag, but not in the way that I had packed it for my journey to North Africa. This time I was packing as if it was only a temporary and informal process, which I had to suffer. I had to sit on my bag to get the mess it contained shut away. I managed. As I looked up I realized that the box of paper people had been left out and I remained on the floor leaning on the bed pulling them out. There was Ciara, Luca and Musa. I held the three of them in my hand and then placed them carefully next to each other on the floor. Luca was smiling and leaning on something. I seemed to recall he had been joking about his fantastic ability to move walls, right at the time that the aperture gaped at him. Luca, the creature that most often pointed apertures at others, now, he himself was only that flat image that he had created through that small hole, over and over again, of others. I remembered that he absolutely adored old photographs that one could buy in flea markets and such, and that we had had a discussion on the morality concerning buying these objects and the weight that they carried. Luca insisted that the images took on new lives, new journeys, once they had passed out of the hands that knew them, whereas I argued that they were pointless and dead. Once nobody remembered you, you were lost: a drop returning to the ocean. There they were Luca, Musa and Ciara, on their way to become drops returned into at least my ocean. Even Luca it was hard to remember now, what he talked like, what he really looked like. These visual aids did jog my head, but then my thoughts went elsewhere, making things up that as soon as I thought them I began to rationalize and question. Had it really been like that? The figure of Ciara was especially unclear. I could not for the life of me remember where the photo had been taken. Perhaps I had not taken it anyway? Perhaps the photographer here on the floor next to her had been the one to fasten her semblance to paper? I looked at her as if at an image in a magazine, but had a difficult time really looking at her with that same detached boredom. She was somewhere in between. Musa on the other hand, was more recent and hence more there. I thought that I could recall his smell. His photo was definitely one that I had taken, some night out, some place where lots of drinks and loud music had been served. He was turning with his shoulder to the camera, that blinding great smile of his. I was probably more likely to run into him again, rather than any of the others. I picked them up, placed them on top of each other so that they could only see a blank cookie cutout approaching and then smothering. The three of them were returned to the container on top of a crude drawing of mine of Fidel. I shut the lid and shoved the box into my backpack. I was more or less ready.

Twenty minutes before the bus was supposed to arrive I stood at the centre of the village with my two suitcases and a backpack already dripping with sweat. I had requested of the young boy that had given us the keys that he would wait a week and then pack up the rest of the stuff should Luca not show. The boy was to send the stuff to a hotel in Algiers in Luca's name. I had left him a bunch of dollar notes that he seemed more than content with. I found some shade and sat down on one of the suitcases with my hands resting on my thighs. At least I had enough to get somewhere half civilized. From there I would have to figure out my next move. One could hear the bus from miles away and I had stood up in anticipation but sat down again when I realized that it had been a preemptive move. Then of course the bus rolled in. It panted horribly and came to a dirty confused stop not far from my feet. The doors were already open; an effective primitive way of air-conditioning, so all I had to do was to walk right in. The driver looked angrily at me as I spoke to him in halting French. I don't know if his anger was related to my disastrous language, the question I asked of him, or my sheer presence. He sighed and rose from the seat to help this 'old lady' with his suitcases. He was not a happy man. He managed to stow my bags with further aggressive gestures and then screamed at me to get on the bus. At least I thought that is what he screamed. I had no idea, but got myself onto that crammed and sweaty vehicle. People stared no more than usual, half unconscious from the heat and the monotony no doubt, as I dug my way to an empty seat. The seat received me with a pull into its sticky gut. It held me like that more or less against my will until we reached a small town towards the southern tip of the country.

Again I found myself in a strange cold room, which functioned as a womb of sorts for my travails. What else could I do? What the hell was I doing? I had managed to organize a smallish loan via Algiers and now here I was with little to my name yet with some type of illegible purpose written on my brain. I pretended that I had purpose. This was the way that I would continue. Continue where? Well that was something else. Southern Algeria seemed as good a start as any. At points I pondered the reasons for me having ended up back in Northern Africa again, after all that had happened around my marital times, but the pondering did not last long as the suppression of reason set in.

From now on I would live solely as life functioned: temporarily. It sounded perhaps a bit Buddhist of me, but I assure you it had nothing to do with such esoteric thoughts. I was thoroughly practical in my reasoning, purely practical. I had nowhere else to go, and it seemed that down here, and perhaps even further down, I would be able to hustle a livelihood that would allow me to live for longer than anywhere else, especially on such meager funds as I had to my name. I had decided that I would not spend anything unless it was absolutely necessary, and hoped that I would find some kind of employment to see me through.

The coke bottle seemed heavy in the little boy's hand as he reached it out to me. This was exactly one of those luxuries that I should not splash out on, but then it was the first day of the rest of my life, and why not celebrate? The slippery coolness of the bottle soothed my hand and as I raised its mouth to mine I leant back a little, shut my eyes and let the content fizzle into me in just a few long gulps. As I removed the bottle from my lips, I put my head back down and opened my eyes. That was that. I handed the boy some coins and then handed him back the bottle. The bottle quickly got stored in the empty bottle crate; it jingled its emptiness with its empty friends. I found myself staring at the crate as if it meant something and then the boy shooed me aside for his next parched customer. I stayed around though, looking for someone that could have some mercy on me. All the passersby stared me down, but seemingly did not want to have anything to do with me, their stares very standoffish. I looked at my watch and a fly landed on it simultaneously, obscuring the little hand. I blew at it quite hard but it remained resolutely in place. I wiped the face of the clock towards my thigh and that must have done the trick because as the arm returned there it was: quarter to four. I straightened up and tried to get with it. Now, for a place to stay, I took my body off towards what looked like a carpet shop. The store was very quiet and nobody came to greet me. I let my hands pet the carpets in an effort to suggest interest should anyone be watching me, but nobody cared. My flip-flops looked worn at the edges, I let my eyes rest on them for a little while, perhaps I should buy new ones? No, again, these were the luxuries that I would need to do without. From now on I was a tramp, homeless, a vagabond, and my way of thinking would have to seriously change. A man coughed at the back of the store, and I coughed back to respond as politely. I saw the top of his head as he moved for the first time since I had come in, and then he appeared fully limbed but with a patch over his right eye. I took a step back. This man was a dead ringer for Musa. His left eye was only half open; he must have been sleeping back there, and his mouth still slightly ajar. He grunted at me. The few words that I had within me to respond in an orderly fashion dried up. It had something to do with his Musa-ness I think. He wasn't Musa. I thought I knew that, and his absolute disinterest in me should have confirmed that, if nothing else. However, I did not trust my rationality. It had not got me anywhere in particular before. I fumbled with the language but the man pretended that he had no idea of what I was trying to put forth. I tried again, enunciating meticulously I thought, and this time I hit the target. We managed to seesaw like this into a territory where he was to contact someone that was going to take me to someone that might know someone that I could live and work with. He motioned to a stool at the back of the shop and I dutifully took a seat whilst he busied himself with a boy at the entry to the shop. I kept staring at him out of the corner of my eye. He did not speak like Musa at least. This was comforting. He approached me again and this time had miracled up a tray with tea. He served it, handed the cup to me and then proceeded with the same ritual for himself. He sat down on a stool near to me and we both rustled in the silence that was left looking stalwartly at the floor. The arrival of another boy at the opening of the shop brought our vacuum to an end. They busied themselves in hushed words and then the Musa man waved at me and sent me off with the boy. I followed obediently. I felt a sense of déjà vu. The walls of the houses, as well as the heavy sky, seemed to be registering our movements with dull sweeping hollow sounds that spent died in our short shadows; a little sigh from which a small wisp of dust evaporated. We walked out of town.

Horizontal, finally. From a mattress on a floor I lay back watching the flies endlessly circle a broken bulb that defiantly hung onto the blackened ceiling. My new momentary home had turned out to be an orange farm quite a bit out of town. We must have walked a fair few hours, until we began to smell citrus fruits in the air and then eventually saw groves everywhere. This was it, but just to get to the main house we must have walked at least an hour after first having encountered the groves. The place was huge. Once at the hub of it all, the boy arranged with different people that milled about to hold onto the right line of information that eventually led us to their leader. The owner was a thin but big-framed man in his sixties with a fairly severe looking moustache. He had the widest of shoulders, like a scarecrow I remember thinking and then that name stuck. The scarecrow hollered at another important looking fellow who did not hesitate to take the long rigid strides that were needed to get to our side. A brusque conversation took place and a third man, this one really skinny but with a welcoming smile on his little face, arrived at our side.
"This is Aswan."
Aswan shook my hand and did not stop that friendly smile. He seemed genuinely happy to see me.
"I'll take care of you now." His English slightly hesitant but there nonetheless. Another comfort to take.
Aswan led me to a room with a mattress and encouraged me to take a rest before he would return later on to bring me food and

all the information that I would need for the days that were to follow. He told me to really enjoy this short spell of rest, as there would be a lack of moments like this as soon as work started. Hence, there I was, horizontal finally, but my thoughts chased the flies around the bulb with panic at what had led me here, and what was leading me on, further out into the desiccated landscapes. Further away from any chances to settle, any chances to create a semblance of a life, which I could have led. The flies were effervescent shit rising to the top of my limited space, swirling around up there until the heat cast them off, to then be trampled under bare feet that brought my overwrought dehydrated body to the bathroom.

She was nonchalantly leaning her back on the fence with the shattered glitter of the setting sun scratching cooling holes in her image. I gave a look, the first one a sudden unexpected discovery, the second a deliberate double-take due to having found something pleasing, even if perforated, amongst all this heat and dust. I let my look linger but as she shot a look back, mine slipped to her feet. Then I thought what the hell and let my eyes skate a slow explorative journey that eventually led to her face. Her thin body a knife-edge, or mountain ridge. You could cut yourself. Looking at her I forgot about the pain of the work but also all else that had preoccupied me since a few days back. I felt thankful. Then I realized that perhaps the look that she was now returning did not offer the same sort of benevolent thoughts. No, she looked thoroughly pissed off. I looked away, then back. I raised a hand slowly, hoping that it would be interpreted as a peaceful gesture. A quizzical grimace of hers led into a bemused smile. I had dodged the daggers. I just kept on with the work.

Days later as I was leaning over some baskets full of piercingly ripe fruit I felt the sensation of a new kind of surveillance. It wasn't my boss. There she was, again reclining on something, this time a wall, studying me with that same knowing smile locked onto her lips. This time I tried a small nod of my head to acknowledge and disarm her. She did not nod back. I busied myself with the work at hand, trying to ignore her as well. As I finally dared to look back in her direction she was gone. I looked around, but there was no sign of her. I called out to the guy next to me, hoping that I would be able to make myself understood. "Did you see that woman, the one that was just there by the wall?" The guy looked at me with a roll of his head in the same direction as I was motioning, but then he looked blankly back at me. The guy obviously had not understood. I searched for another person that might have had the opportunity to see her, but everyone seemed engrossed and overwhelmed by the work. No point in asking anyone. However, later that night I met up with Aswan, the only person that I really could have a discussion with in this god-forsaken place. Did Aswan know who that woman could be? Had he seen her? Aswan smiled at me. Of course he knew. There weren't that many women around this place, had I not noticed? No, I hadn't noticed. In fact, if she had not been placed in my way in the manner she had that day, I would be none the wiser. Aswan sighed desperately at my ignorance. How could one man be so blind? Yet, this was his friend, in a place were you really did not have friends, you did not really have time for them, and also the work force rarely stayed the same more than a few months. Aswan patted me on my back. It's alright. No point in thinking anymore about her anyway, she was the boss' daughter. Not exactly an option for me, or anyone else for that matter, although there were stories of the ones that had ignored the obvious and had begun a woebegone romancing, in vain, but not just that, in plain foolishness, a dance that was no longer than a step long, then who knows where they ended up. They sure did not work anymore. Not here anyway. I smiled at Aswan. Ok, that made sense. No worries, I had no such intentions, was just curious as I'd seen her around and she had

231

seemed so dismissive, yet attentive.

"Kill cat" Aswan grinned at me.

"Yeah, it sure killed the cat", I laughed back at my friend, "but I'm no pussy". We both burst into merriment, and went over to get our dinner.

I stood up abruptly as I felt a hand on my ass. Turning around I was greeted by a close up of her face, the daughter. She didn't say anything, but then again she did not need to as her hand moved to my dick. I looked around dismayed at what could happen through no fault of my own. Nobody around. She probably had made sure of the same thing. Mind you, she might not care either way, the way that she was behaving.

"Do you like it?" She spoke English quite easily and her hand moved up and down over my crotch.

"You shouldn't." I took her hand off me.

"You don't like it?" Her tone accusative. Shit, now she would be angry with that, which could cause just as much trouble.

"You're very... beautiful". I didn't have to lie. "But maybe this is a bit too fast." Stall her, think. "I've heard your father doesn't take too lightly to men that are interested in you." She laughed.

"Are you afraid?"

"Well...I'm not stupid."

"A man like you, my father might not mind."

"That's a bit of a chance to take, at least for me. Not that I wouldn't want to. Who wouldn't want to?" There, flatter her; that ought to do it.

She seemed to take my hesitations in, took a step back and looked around again.

"I like you."

"You don't know me."

"I don't have to know you."

"No, but. Well, I guess that depends upon what you are after, and I guess that you've made that abundantly clear anyway. But, your father would surely be less inclined to accept such a

232

booty call?" She looked at me seemingly asking for me to clarify myself.

"A normal courtship would surely be more appropriate rather than jumping straight into bed? No?"

Now she smiled.

"I see what you mean."

I was glad that she did; yet I had no bloody idea of what it all meant. Then she walked off, as if our conversation had finally made her come to her senses. I was not sure that that was what I ultimately had wanted, but things run their course, and after all I had no reason to fret about my behavior.

Days went by, and perhaps her attraction to me had rubbed off. Increasingly my thoughts began to move around her. I saw us clinging to each other in all sorts of places. I imagined the shape of the hollow of her foot, the curve of her breasts, the small of her back and the smell of her neck, her curled toes and trembling parted lips, as soon as a moment of quiet set in. It was a way of entertaining myself, like that guy in a real proper Belgian coma who after twenty-three years was discovered to have been awake and aware throughout his whole ordeal. When asked what he had occupied his time with whilst in the coma, he answered that he had meditated and *dreamt himself away*. I had almost started to cry when I read that. Then I had started to think of cryogenics and then the argument about the possibility of reaching nirvana whilst in a living body. Here I was, doing the same, *dreaming myself away*, but at least and in some way I had a choice of sorts. I guess I could have left at any point. Left this god forsaken stifling heat, this emptiness, this opposite of expected living, at least from the places where I had spent much time of my life. But then I had nowhere to go, no one to see, nowhere to return to now. *Nowhere to run to baby, nowhere to hide from you*. What was that song....? Not anymore. Home had moved away, to a time, which no longer existed. Home became only a translation of an abstract. This was all that I had to contend with now, all that I could expect. And so my dreams involved themselves with the possibles of life as is. Hence here she was, forming herself around me and then into my fantasies. In a way, given that the women that had had this effect on me as of late were very few, if not non-entities, this was sort of comforting; a proper heterosexual attraction that could lead to a lay. Perhaps I wasn't as fucked up as I imagined. I laughed at myself. My thought processes were so inane, and I was absolutely sure of my fuckedupness.

She kept on arriving at my desire, both in person and in my mind. At opportune moments she got real close, pushing her breasts into me, resting her head on my shoulder, whispering promises. I kept a close eye on our surroundings hoping that nothing would go wrong. I really needed this. I needed this bubble. And indeed nothing seemed to impede the progress of our little romance. Not even Aswan asked me about it. It was as if we were living separately from everyone else, undisturbed by reality and its petty concerns. It did not take too long before we found the moments and places to consummate our desires. We weren't exactly discreet but we were not reckless either. My days lightened, things began to seem possible again.

Her collar bones were hollow tunnels beneath me, beneath a layer of soft skin, piercing lines of pencil lead imprinted on my own chest, she was so terribly thin. Yet I lay there letting my heavy head wear her down, making her body press further into the mattress. How could a body get this emaciated? No, no no, she wasn't starved, it was just that she was young, her lack of shape based on that I assumed. I'd never been with anyone so young before, not at my age at least. Ok so she was in her early twenties but to me that was almost the same as being with an eighteen year old. She was barely formed, and neither was her body, nor her thoughts. She: words in the sand that beckoned the tide. My thoughts meandered; *to breath return eternal*, and the

234

ocean's breath drum rolled into my head. I rolled and turned over on my stomach, stuck my right hand under my face preparing to fall into sleep, leaving her there, by my side: rest and unrest next to her. I could feel her lean over on her side to watch me fall. Perhaps she was annoyed with the fact that I dared to leave her alone in the dark. She turned on her back and sighed heavily. I could hear her try to breathe in the evening with long peace attempting draughts. She must be able smell me all over herself. Suddenly I realised that something was changing, something hardly perceptible was changing. We had gone on like this for almost a month now, staggering sleepwalker-style through a furtive passion. We could sense the condensation of this sort of love dissipating, leaving our bodies revealed, the vapours sinking spent ringlets to our feet.

My foot was sucked into a muddy cavity. As I pulled it out it made a noise, which in turn pushed gruff breath from my mouth and nose, I guess, almost a laugh. I looked out down the grove. People were scurrying in uncoordinated ways across and around. I moved out lightly. Now a few more days than usual had passed without either one of us making an effort to stealthily meet up. There was no particular reason for it, but just the way that things were working out. I guessed that we were both just letting the whole thing slip. It had served its purpose, and so had we. Throughout we had never really tried to get close in any other way than sexually. We had just been two bodies and we had let the bodies do what they do whilst our minds remained wherever they had been prior to the encounters.

After sometime she returned to mean nothing to me. Considering my initial, staggered, preoccupation it was a bit tragic how quickly those fires could hiss to damp and go. It had never really been meant to be, that is what I told myself. It saddened me slightly, that sense of the fleetingness of passion, but I was not one to hold on to sentimentalities. Not really. Yet, without the slightest awareness of contradiction, my nights began to get populated with Fidel and Luca again. The two men came back in full colour. Ghosts waltzing around each other through a clatter of old fashioned flashbulbs burning out. Until then, when she had been around me in a physical sense, they kept away, held at sway by the more urgent and immediate preoccupations of the flesh. Now, that the flesh had returned to toil alone, they took their chance. Increasingly they colonized more of my time. I was out spraying the pesticide, and in the noxious rainbows it cast off I could see Luca and Fidel like tiny holograms making a world of their own by my feet, the sour smell rising, as they frolicked under my surveillance. Sometimes they would tease a laugh out of me, but the realization that I was staring at the ground laughing to myself immediately made me lift my head to scan the surrounding area for anyone that might have spied my rising insanity. Most of the time I got away with it. There was too much noise or too many people that were fully enslaved to their tasks.

The rustle of palm trees had transformed ever since I had lost Luca. From a previous impression of utter calm, a soothing motherly hush to sleep, they now moved me in the same way that a bunch of rats would that scurried through a large pile of autumn leaves. I felt myself sitting in the middle of the pile tied and gagged with my bloodshot eyes wider than wide and nostrils flaring awaiting the first touch constantly, swearing that it already had happened until a new sensation made my body recoil and my sight disappear.

As I arrived into my room towards the early evenings I was looking forward to getting my bucket out to have a quick wash before dinner would be served. My days had once more become as evident as pearls on a string, one followed the other, looking very much exactly the same as the one before, but then again it was probably a more fitting description to think of some kind of shit strung onto a blade of grass. Anyways, they followed each other and I followed them with the habits that the place and living in general called upon me. This evening though I was disturbed by a variation. A brown envelope had been placed on my bed. I advanced as if a hazard had been introduced in my cramped space. I moved around it, as far away from it as possible, rather than moving to remove it. Nobody knew I was here, nobody that would need to send me a letter. Picking it up with my left hand I could discern that it seemed to have been dispatched from Algiers. I ripped the side of the envelope leaving a jagged edge through which my middle and index fingered pinched the slip of paper embedded in the slit. Unfolding the four creases that had bedded the words they became clear as day on the yellowing paper.

For life will never tell itself, it will always pretend to be somebody else.

The scrawl was pedantic, lacking emotion and mistakes. I turned the paper over a few times but the words remained the same, and nothing else was distinguishable as a mark of recognition. I flung the empty envelope onto the bed again, pretending that it had not had an impact on me, and then placed the note with care under the candleholder by my bedside. I picked up the bucket and went out to proceed with my ablutions. As the water's dark wisps sought my sweat and dirt and took it in turns to the night soil beneath my square feet, my thoughts whirled uncontrollably, bursting the banks of my wormholed brain. Luca pulsed in explosive flashes through every bone and hollow. Was he truly alive? Alive, and why? The more balanced scenario would be that he had passed, away, not in anyway implicated in the dark mass that my past formed, clogging up disbelief a little further, if that now was possible. For my hiding in the heart of life, in plain sight, had a reason, even if I, as such, could not reach it, and Luca alive in this mess was a contradiction to all of that which I tried to make sense of. As I calmed down with the cold water I shook myself and argued that my assumption that this note was from Luca was in the first place absolutely unfounded. I had never really paid any attention to Luca's handwriting. Also, that this note was from someone meaning me well was not something that I could take for granted. After all, if someone wanted to warn me of something surely they would have done it straightforwardly. What's the use of warning someone with a riddle, unless, that is, you were afraid of that the thing would somehow lead back to you, and that this would land you yourself in hot water. But then again, why would anyone ever land in hot water from contacting me? I could cause no harm. I stepped out of the low walls that surrounded the bathing area. The moon cut the darkness and drank and drank at the endlessness with a coy smile. Stars danced and flirted around the white hole all the way to the contradicting recesses.

Days traveled their distances, reaching their homes just in time for nights to take over. Nights relayed perfectly in the same faultless pulse. One could depend upon this. However, in the farm work I found another dependency that worked. The routine was ceaseless, it was rhythmic, and I boogied willingly to the sounds of repetition. This even I understood and could follow. I began to realize that as long as I could keep the beat I would be ok. The aberration of the brown envelope in this tack, tack, tack, tack, tack tack tack, tack, tack, tack, tack, tack tack tack, was sinking to distances. I still treasured the words, but solely as another rhythm in my head, like a poetic revelation, the surge of the froth due the abyss. The smoke of the burnt letter hovered somewhere over the barrenness that it had created, but then went down with it sometime when I was not paying attention.

Then, another letter arrived, perhaps more shockingly naked and new than the previous one. The same handwriting snaked across the brown envelope. This one seemed to have been posted only a week ago according to the black ink that smeared the stamp. Nevertheless, when I opened the letter, and this time it was an actual letter, the date marked at the top of the page was from prior to me even arriving in Algeria. Sure one could put any date on a letter. It does not mean a thing. Well, what whoever was trying to mean with this dating was beyond me anyway. It was a game, and a sick one at that, to try to belittle me. I, who had not a thing in this world.

Dearest Leo,

There are things I want to tell you, before you come, things that might keep you from actually going through with this whole thing.

I have not been entirely honest with you. I have tried, but there have been things in the way, in the way of my honesty and not just the sort of things that you usually keep from your friends or lovers, those deepest and most horrid of confessions, but in this case it is someone else that has come in between me and the full friendship which I have offered you.

Do you remember how we met, well, all that seems like a great coincidence to me, and I'm sure that it is somehow, even if it also seems like there is no other way that it could have gone. I appreciated your friendship enormously, and by and by you have become a very dear mate. Yet, not long after we had returned home, or rather after we had met again at home, I was approached by a man in the bar who seemed to think that our friendship had been a set up, that somebody else was in charge of it. How the hell that could have been I'm not sure and to me it seems that it was a ridiculous statement. Only you and I could have steered our paths in the way that we did, yet the words out of this man have played havoc with my sense of reality ever since. I do not recall the exact words, or the information that he used to confirm his theory, but there was something there, which obviously took hold somehow. Ever since I have felt like we somehow have betrayed each other. I know it sounds crazy, it does to me too, yet it won't let me go.

So I've made a big deal of this, and still I can't really put my finger on anything, and it won't stop me from going on as we planned, but I just wanted to let you know this because I won't feel right unless I do. I know that with all the strange stuff that was going on with your ex at the time of our meeting this perhaps fits into that miasma, and that maybe I was reading the situation in the chaos that was, and hence the translation and the taste of it is as it is. Nevertheless, and finally, the man's name, as he told me at least, was Fidel. After he had said what he had come to say he excused himself, went off to the loo, and then I never saw him again. Read from this what you will, but remember I remain

Your friend,
Luca

My jaws were so clenched that I had a hard time breathing. I must have bit the inside of my cheek as I began to taste blood. I knew not what to do with this information. Although I seemed to believe in the fact that this was written by Luca, doubts still entered into my mind around the author or perhaps whoever it was that might have coerced Luca to the act. Nevertheless, this had also brought me to the realization that no matter what it did not depend upon Fidel as such, because he was solely a figment of life. My life.

"Leo".

The shock of a voice in the midst of my dwellings caused a rain of hairs to stand at the back of my neck. My shoulders went up in a protective manner and I shook. The voice did not continue, but I could hear the person breathing in the doorway. I let my shoulders come down and turned around a little bewildered. Aswan was staring at me seemingly waiting for me to calm down and respond.

"Aswan.."

"Just here to see if you want to come for a beer."

"Yes, give me five. I'll come over to yours."

"Alright."

Aswan was gone. A restless shadow remained where he had been. I tucked the letter under my pillow and stood up to unfurl my body and thoughts, stretching as far as I could reach I watched my dry hands and fingers reach for the ceiling and tried to imagine that I was untouched by all this, for now.

My hand gripped the beer bottle a bit too tightly; my knuckles were whitening with the pressure. Aswan looked over, down at my hand and then at my face. I followed his instructions, shook my head and watched as my fingers got their colour back. Things were alright. I gulped at the liquid without really tasting anything. Round and round in my mess of a brain the thoughts seem to congregate around the idea of escape. I need to get out of here. I need to get on. When my grip on the bottle came into focus again I noticed my anemia returning. Consciously one by one the fingers let go. The din that accompanied the combination of about twenty people outside in the small courtyard was unbearable if you let it in, but I had no problems keeping it at bay thanks to a stonewall of panic.

The bag has been easy enough to pack. There was not much in this world which I felt I would need to carry or keep. There were useful things, but some I did not own and the ones that I did went easily into the side pocket of the raggedy backpack. The car that took me away was shaking across rivers of sand, balloons of particles blooming behind it in celebration of any action taken in such a quiet heat sunk place. I was squashed into a corner next to a woman with a toddler on her lap. The baby was as listless as its mother. The shaking and the heat seemed to have lulled them both into the state they were in.

241

They had no idea of my existence. Neither had I of theirs. My head began sagging towards the window but as it hit it ricochet back into a simile of an alert position. I was almost ready.

"Trust me."
The man's hands were held out with the palms facing the impetuous sun. My eyes swam in the lightness of the skin so brazenly exposed. My head held contradictions in its grip and I avoided an answer to assure that I had not made myself commit to anything. This was the third time in the second week of my travel that a person almost demanded of me to submit to some plan, which was supposedly for my own protection. I was in a place where I stood out like a sore thumb and although I had next to nothing to my name the reasons for robbing me, or indeed doing me any harm still remained I presumed. However, over and over I was told the opposite by these more and more frequent sentinels of truth. I had shook off the previous two, but this one, for some reason, perhaps the mere fact that he was the third, made me pay a slight begrudging attention. Throwing an arm out to the right a couple of times saying "please" brought an upward movement to my head as my eyes closed. Go on then, was what I meant. The glee that sprang forth in his previously nearly dead eyes was worrying, but I could leave at anytime. Just because I had agreed now did not mean that I would have to go through with the whole thing, whatever the whole thing might be. He wanted to bring me to a safe place. All he did was to bring me to a place which had had another foreigner stay at some point in the past, a place which had an impropriator who spoke a good few words of my own language which meant the first longer conversation I had had in a while, but it was still a very limited interaction. I missed Aswan. I had left him a letter explaining my departure as best as I could without giving anything essential away, anything that could confirm the madness that was my life, my reasoning. Who would believe me, who would believe that someone

would go to the lengths that they had to drive me mad, just out of sheer malice, or maybe joy. Surely this must cause somebody joy, whether it was Fidel or whoever, one had to get something out of all this. Somebody had to. Something good. Anyway here I was, and this man, Ahmed, hurried off a few hoarse sentences in the direction of my guide and then we were left to ourselves. Ahmed explained that the "guide" had been trying to ensure that I got somewhere safe, but at the same time my "guide" had hoped that I would be able to spare some cash as a reward. Ahmed had immediately gathered, smart man that he was, that I had nothing on me, but he, just like my "guide" wondered if I needed help to get to a place where I could secure a wire of money or something. I explained that I had no one to wire me any money, and even if I had had someone that could perform the task, there was no place which held money of mine since at least a year back. I had no money other than the few coins that were left from my previous work place.

"Where was that?" Ahmed enquired.

"Oh, just some plantation north of here."

Ahmed pushed for more information, even gave me a drink, but as he got nowhere he eventually asked me straight out if I knew where I was going next. I shook my head.

"Do you have anyone looking for paid employment here, even if just for food?"

I knew that my question most likely was a stupid one, but still I asked. I did not know where else our conversation could have gone.

"I'll ask around."

He left me sitting in the shade with the empty glass in my hand. I was thinking to myself that I was not even sure that I wanted another job, but at same time, there was little that I could do other than that. How the hell would I eat tonight if I did not get more work, the coins I had left would just barely allow for food, they would never allow for me to leave other than tucked up in the benevolence of someone kind's truck. I waited.

243

Dozed. Waited. Ahmed returned with the onset of evening, but he had little hope to offer me. He had done his utmost. He offered me a space to sleep after a share in his family's evening meal, which I had no choice but to accept. Rolled up on some blankets in the corner of a room I ran to sleep without rest. At least now this would be a few hours of not thinking, if I only could find sleep somewhere in this begging dark.

Next day, I moved on. There could be some work perhaps in the next village, or the next one, or the next. I had got some sustenance into my system and carried water for the journey. Ahmed had given me a contact in the village after the next, and I hoped that I would have strength enough to make that journey in a day. If not, something had to work itself out. There was no other way. There was no other choice. I felt my body walk and lent my soul to the rhythm as best as I could. I lost myself in the zone.

The next village lay still but vibrating in the midday. It was almost too hot to move. No one had any idea of what to do with me, but I managed to find some shade to rest in and some water to fill up my flask with, but then I was back on the road, in the most horrible of limbo. Hunger began gnawing on my nerves as the sun worked its maddening intensity on my skin and brain. Each hair on my body was pulled to the point of being slowly and painfully removed and my eyes burnt with lack of moisture. All I could think of was the ocean, or an endless cold shower. Ice floes. I marched on, each step enormous in my head. No one else around. Evening finally came and although the dark was welcome it was also disconcerting in that I was unsure of how much further it would be. The water was gone. A fruit had been found on the way; thanks be to whoever the gods of that road were, and that had been all that my stomach had had to work on since very early in the morning. Then, at the edge of despair, there it seemed to flicker, the light of the village of Ahmed's friend, if, he was there. I had to sit down for a little whilst locking the village in my mind and eye. It would be ok, somehow. I felt as if someone was lovingly caressing my dick and as I could not see anyone around I decided to continue with the same. A great relief rained to settle in a funny looking shape in the cooling dust. I sat looking at it for a little while; how life was so fragile and so meaningless, yet a deft hand could produce relief with a few strokes, but then it all in a flash could become less than it promised again. I felt like I imagined a person addicted to drugs would feel, just wait, just around the next corner, just with the next fix, just soon, just nearly now, then everything would be ok; just another person, just another village, just another goal. I stood up and shook off the stupidity.

The fag end burnt an orange hole in the night and offered the fragile fringe of another stranger. I too a stranger; haloed by a light, with the body of the moon behind me drawing out a milky substance from the night, leaving me an outline on its pregnant lactose dreams. Thought I wanted a cigarette, badly, but probably I was mostly hungry. The man I had encountered did not know many facial expressions. He remained ossified by the dark but as he still emitted a strong smell of working sweat in regular puffs of air I knew that he was breathing, and possibly thinking about what to do with me. After too long of a time of me listening to him breath, smoke and think, he finally grunted and led me, I hoped, further into the village: I, ever a willing follower of an inchoate adventure. He found me a corner with a bit of hay on the ground and then signed for me to stay put. I remained in the same pose, almost holding my breath until I could hear steps approaching across the ground. There he was again. He handed me a blanket and a bit of bread. He turned on his heel to return into the ever mass of dark but then had second thoughts and returned nudging my arm offering a cigarette. I thanked him and put the cigarette to my lips. He lit it and nodded, never a smile. I heard him leave again as I stood with the cigarette hanging from my lips staring at the moon being chased off into the night by dark clouds as the smoke circled my head. I felt as if I was under water and that the moon up there was indeed way above the surface of the sea. I thought of the smoke as air bubbles racing giddily towards the thin veil of freedom. Where was I going?

The squawk of a busy bland looking curious hen woke me with a start. She was staring at me in bewilderment unable to make another noise as she watched my eyeballs move in their sockets. For a second the thought of her attacking my vulnerable head filled me with dread but then as I moved an arm up out of my cocoon she herself shook loose from her rigid observation pose and screeched loudly as she maneuvered her fat rump in the opposite direction whilst still having her beady eyes trained as much as possible in my direction. I could but laugh. I sat up and looked around. This was any courtyard. This was any day. The breadcrumbs that stuck to my clothes seem to suggest that I had tried going to sleep simultaneously as eating. I did not remember a thing after watching the moon bopping heavily across the surface of my own private sea. The purpose of my travels returned to me in fragments. Ahmed's possible contact must be somewhere around here. I stood and brushed the crumbs and the hay off my wrinkled appearance. That's a start. The man was found, we haggled over the possibility of work, and he relented eventually perhaps realizing that I was not going to leave until he had done so. At least if he managed to get me to do something it might give me enough sustenance to continue out of his way, out of his village. I jubilated inside against a dark backdrop. A few shiny shreds danced on the charcoal base. I let myself focus on the glitter.

My arms and hands were trembling with the labour. I was shifting huge stones from one end of a field to the other with the help of a makeshift wheelbarrow. I was the only fool working under a sweltering sun. A couple of children hung out in the shadow of a scrawny tree laughing quietly whilst lazily observing me from under heavy eyelids and intermittent blows to each others legs and arms. I thought that at any moment they might fall asleep mid laughter unable to keep command of their mirth as well as their languid violence, then I lost myself in my chores and they faded from my consciousness. Once I thought of them again they were no longer there. Another young boy came carefully towards me with his tongue pressed into a fine whitening point between his teeth and a cup of coffee on a tiny little round tray which he precariously kept as still as possible whilst a dangerous cup of coffee hovered in its midst. He was traversing an obstacle course, each step a probability of a plunge from grace and goodwill. But he made it. I took the cup off him, smiled and patted him on the top of his head, his hair coarse against my dirty, coarse hands. Released from his tight rope prison he squirmed with pent up energy, sprung loose, and soon gamboled off in the direction of other children's voices. I stared at his disappearance until the pause in which I was held brought me back to the cup. The bitter taste of the coffee trickled warmly over my tongue and my brain responded in an almost immediate alertness. For a short while the stones seem to respond better to the strength my arms exerted on them, but then the heaviness returned to both stones and body, the world returned to its lair of gravity.

At the end of the day's labour I was fed, and given that the work had been so hard the man decently communicated to me that he would let me rest for the night but also assured me that he had no further work. I understood. I would be on my way in the morning. The night fell by, not a dream, not a breath hardly passed it seemed before morning rouse me with difficulty and the aid of one the children, of the day before, shaking one of my hands in his two with tiny jerks. When he was sure that I was truly awake he let go of my hand with a fright and threw his body out of my sight. I ached all over. I rolled onto my side and groaned. There was a cup of coffee, some fruit and bread by my bedside that I carefully sat up for. After this breakfast I stiffly gathered my bones and belongings and got on my way. I left without saying anything more to the family figuring that anything that needed to have been said had been so the previous eve. Anyway our communications were very limited due to language barriers.

The road, the bare bone of a road, lay splintered before my feet and the sun. I coughed, stretched and made the initial moves, which soon propagated into continuous motion. As soon as the body warmed to the movements it let go of the worst of its piercing pains and allowed for me to get into a traveling mode. I kept thinking of the texture of orange flesh on my tongue, not to freshen and salivate purposely, but for some reason this thought was on a loop in my head. It was more about texture than hydration but it worked well for both sensations and allowed me to freely travel without being bogged down by negative thoughts, which might impede my progress. I had less of a direction now than I had ever had before, yet something dragged me forward. I felt as if my past was falling like fragmented pictures behind me and as if the future in its constituent parts gathered and in slow motion rose before me, but I understood little of it. The patterns were unclear but lured me on the same. When I was little I had tried to control my dreams by making them up as I was about to fall asleep. I wanted certain scenarios, certain people to take part and so on. I was force-feeding my unconscious but it rarely would have any of it. I ended up with the dreams that were, not the dreams that I wanted. The discrepancy niggled at me but it was not like the actual dreams I dreamt were lacking in anyway, they just weren't the ones that I had set up. Now that I had no dreams, now that the future was a haze in front of me, now, I had no will to control it anymore. I never had control. I had resigned myself. I would have to let life do what it had to do with me. All I could do was to keep on keeping on, hoping that maybe some kind of clarity and gentleness would reach me. I hoped, but had no knowledge.

At some point in this journey of mine nature took over, life took on softer and softer tones, greening steadily yet imperceptibly, making it impossible to say exactly when the natural succession would be the sea, or some body of water, but making it equally impossible to be without this conclusion. So I traveled to green. Eventually. I rested. Eventually. I fed myself by default and watched a country of watery gasps. Days and nights fell by the breathing spluttering beast before me. People passed, communicated, and passed again in ever widening circles making up this maelstrom that was my life, the past, present and the future all sucked up into the same pinprick, the idea of me.

I had waded far into the waters. The depths seemed to be pulling away from me. My legs pushed the heavy water ahead. My feet not so much tested the bottom as claimed it. I looked back for a moment, half turned, but although the beach was by now very far away it seemed illogical for me to go for a swim without being able to immerse my whole self. I swerved on my heel again and waded on. Stunned I found that the waters had suddenly grown. I was where I was supposed to be. I closed my eyes and bent my knees submerging into a shallow deep, enjoying the suction in the water, the scuttling of water animals around my superimposed body in their world. A hologram: that is what I was. I opened my eyes with salty difficulty. I expected the sea would wash away from me, like any passing fantasy or fancy. I blinked and my eyes watered painfully, trying to dispel the forceful body of the sea from its globes. I looked above me and found my body reel with the reality of the surface desperately having moved at least ten meters above me. Panic gripped my stomach, and a scream rose like a shuttle through my fleshy threads, but my mouth guarded me well, although filling up with bile and alarm. All I would need to do was to keep calm, breathe slowly, and rise. Like Jesus, I smiled at myself. See, even a smile entered me in a situation like this. I bent my knees and pushed off from the bottom, whilst my arms lay on the ready by my side to paddle the body quickly to safety. My feet barely left the sand. A school of assorted fish pushed by, twisting my body around them. I bent my knees and pushed off again. Again I had no buoyancy of any kind. I was riveted. There must be an undertow, a slipstream, which cemented me. I tried a labored move sideways. My change of position was slow. I gave the push another shot but all that happened was that my mouth opened ever so slightly with the exertion and slipped some of that growing scream and bile, which then octopus-wise formed a temporary yellow cloud in front of my face. Finally I pushed off again and this time I did rise. My arms began to drive the bottom away from me, but as I rose the waters turned a reddish hue and the surface seemed to have disappeared. My wasted body sealed in this red watery cocoon felt heavy again, a thick red swirl caught me and twisted me as other human and otherwise materials seemed to reach out for me. I saw Fidel smile hidden by a swaying clump of seaweed that he held onto to stay put, his tie waving or dancing in similar currents. I did not wave at him. I opened my mouth to finally speak. Brightness entered this vessel.